VINEYARD MAGIC

VINEYARD MAGIC

Jean Stone

Cover design by Phil Aucella
Cover photograph by Paul B. Willis

ISBN: 0692599622
ISBN 13: 9780692599624
Library of Congress Control Number: 2015920953
Acorn House Publishing Group, Edgartown , MA

VINEYARD MAGIC

1

"Did you hear about Libby and Walter?" Emmie Malloy pitched forward on her chair, the fringe of her silver-threaded scarf dipping into her chilled cantaloupe soup. Devon might have mentioned the *accidente d'ensemble*, but she was no longer amazed when her friend made an ass of herself.

"No. What?" Candace asked coolly, as if she didn't crave gossip. In fact, everyone in Manhattan knew that Candace Cartwright was the primary go-to girl for the juiciest dish about weddings, divorces, and charity balls, about which au pair was pregnant and which college had accepted/rejected whose child. She even knew which facilities were best for stowing aged parents, though it was rumored her own mother had once lived a hush-hush life somewhere in the western part of the state and, like Candace's father, had been dead for eons.

Emmie's breath raced; her blue eyes shot off sparks of alarm; her complexion erupted with delicate blotches the same shade as the soup. "They've lost it all: the co-op, the trust fund, the house in Belize. Plus, I expect, the place on Martha's Vineyard, though it was in Walter's family, so no one seems to know for sure about that."

"No."

"Yes." Emmie nodded with fervor. "Yes."

Devon examined her plate of arugula and goat cheese and wondered why she still lunched with Emmie and Candace. After all, the only things they now had in common were private-schooled

1

daughters who'd once pirouetted together at the New York Ballet Academy until other interests like horses and boys and bulimia took over. Actually, only Candace's daughter had wound up with bulimia; it had been treated at Mount Kisco and was no longer discussed.

"That will teach them to trust a relative to handle their investments," Candace asserted. "Besides, what did anyone know about that horrid little man—what was his name? Oh, I don't remember. He was from Charleston, as I recall. The *South*."

It was hard to imagine that some New Yorkers still considered *Mason-Dixon* as a line designating *them versus us*.

"Her whole family is southern," Emmie said, as if that explained it, as if she would know, given that her mother was from Lexington, Massachusetts, and her father from England. *Wales*, Emmie often corrected.

"Pity," Candace said, and returned to her Sauvignon Blanc, the sharp edges of her comment aligning with the angles of her nose and her chin. "I wonder what will happen to their seats at the center."

The *center* was, of course, Lincoln Center, where the ladies provided Philharmonic endowments that assured the best seats in the house. Their interests had swung from the ballet to the symphony once their girls had outgrown their tutus and tulle.

Devon, of course, no longer attended social-register-soirées since she and Josh had separated two years ago and her status had changed from society wife to plain old working stiff. She wondered if Libby would need a job now, and if she'd have the funds to go back to school as Devon had done in order to get some credentials then a marketing job at *JW* where they imported fabulous handbags that few could afford. The position had been essential if not for Devon's wallet then for her mental health, because though her not-quite-yet-ex still took care of her finances, she'd needed something productive to do. Being Josh Gregory's wife had kept her so busy.

"Devon?" Candace continued, "What do you think?"

"I think rather than worrying about Libby's seats at the center, it might be nicer to ask if we can help."

"Help?" Emmie whimpered, then noticed the situation with her scarf. "Oh, no," she said. "Look what I've done."

"If Libby's lost everything, I'm sure she won't want to lose her friends, too," Devon continued while Emmie began cleaning. Candace watched Emmie with one thin eyebrow cocked, an indication that she believed she could handle the grooming debacle with more satisfactory results.

"Well, that's ridiculous," Candace denounced without shifting her gaze from the melon-tipped scarf. "What can we possibly do? Take her to lunch so we can gawk?"

"We're her *friends*," Devon said. "Shouldn't we be worried about her?"

"Worry all you want," Candace replied, dabbing her linen napkin in Emmie's club soda, unable to resist hovering, mothering, smothering. "If I were Libby, I'd feel as if we were gawking. Besides, it won't resurrect Walter's assets."

Devon checked her watch and stood up. "I have to get back to the office. In the meantime, if I think of a way we can help Libby, I'll let you both know."

"That would be nice," Emmie said. "Libby's taste in decorating is so sublime." The comment seemed to make sense to her.

Devon tossed down three twenties for the wine and the salad that she'd barely touched. "See you tomorrow," she said, because that's when their daughters would march through the daisy chain and exit Miss Porter's with honors. She wondered if

Libby would attend graduation, then decided not to ask Emmie and Candace their opinions. Instead, with air kisses, Devon swept from the table and the restaurant and out onto Madison Avenue, wondering why her stomach felt so knotted up when she no longer had anything in common with Libby LaMonde, either.

⌣⟶

Libby stared out the window of the three-season porch at the lawn and the dunes and Edgartown harbor. The Vineyard sky was late-springtime-azure and the breeze was high enough for kite flying, though hardly anyone did that sort of thing anymore except once a year at a festival in Oak Bluffs. It had become one more traffic-jammed island extravaganza, like Tivoli Days, the Agricultural Fair, and vacationing presidents, not to mention the sporadic reunions of *Jaws* aficionados.

During the chaos, Libby pretended to dislike the increased clutter of people and the inability to dine anywhere without a name-dropping reservation. Secretly, however, she loved the energy the activities brought.

She drew in a tiny breath as if it might curb the ache of her impending loss.

Moving to the white wicker loveseat, she sat on a thick cushion she'd had covered in pale yellow that blended so nicely with the soft blues and lavenders of the hydrangea-colored toss pillows and the copper accent pieces on the ledge atop the white wainscoting. She supposed she should be grateful she'd recently had the house redone. Surely, it would bring in more money that way.

Then again, she knew that a nine-bedroom, ten-bath monstrosity (with private guesthouse; a short walk to the village) that was set on a sprawling, velvet green lawn that sloped down to the water and had a prime view of Chappaquiddick would not be easy to unload. Especially since it would take time to untangle the paperwork that had at least kept the house out of cousin Harold's smarmy hands.

Cousin Harold, whom she'd adored her whole life, stupid her. They hadn't spoken in months—how could she talk to him now? She barely talked to her husband these days. Though Walter hadn't come right out and said it, Libby knew he must despise her for having convinced him to trust Harold because Harold was *family*, and *families* took care of each other.

Or so she had thought.

Still, it wasn't as if Harold's actions had been Libby's fault. It wasn't as if she deserved blank stares from Walter each time she entered a room or he entered one where she was sitting in an *OhMyGod* stupor. His world, after all, was not the only world that had been crushed.

Their daughter would graduate from Miss Porter's in the morning, not that Libby could go to the ceremony. Her friends would be there: Candace, Emmie, Devon. How could she face them? How could she face anyone? It was bad enough that Alana, her darling child, might side with Walter about whose-fault-it-was-they-were-in-this-mess. At least the girl's summer trip to Europe had already been paid for and Libby would not have to face her until mid-August when Alana would be back in the States and show up at the house on the Vineyard.

If they still owned the house on the Vineyard. If they, indeed, had a house . . . anywhere.

She wondered how long someone could live there without paying the taxes or the electricity bill. It wasn't as if she could ask her parents for money because they were retired and living a high life in Scottsdale and would scold Libby for "not paying attention" to her fiscal responsibilities after all they had gone through to get her married to Walter.

Her small chest felt as if it were being stepped on by one of her dress-up stilettos. It was simply inconceivable that only last Tuesday she'd been playing civilized, pre-season tennis and ordering monogrammed soaps for the guest rooms.

But now there would be no guests from the city.

There would be no brunches, no cocktails on the terrace, no croquet played on the lawn by those who preferred to act as if they were in the Hamptons.

There would be . . . nothing.

With weary resignation, Libby removed the nine-millimeter Glock from her pocket and rested it on her lap. She regretted that the color of blood would clash with the new pastel décor on the three-season porch. And that she still hadn't decided whether she should shoot her husband or simply do away with herself.

2

Unlocking the door to her apartment, Devon stepped inside and let out an elongated sigh. She'd decided that sighing was one of the benefits of living alone: She was free to express her emotions whenever she pleased without being accused of over-reacting or of attempting to irritate someone else in the room. Someone such as Josh Gregory.

Now, she was merely annoyed with herself. Since leaving Candace and Emmie and the overpriced restaurant, Devon had lamented life's unpleasant follies. Her mental state had swiftly careened into a headache, and she'd only lasted at the office until four o'clock.

Stepping out of her heels, she moved from the foyer into the living room and lobbed her bag along with the day's mail onto the pearl-colored suede sofa. The sofa was relatively new to the room, thanks to Libby, who'd graciously redecorated the place after Josh had ungraciously left.

Devon glanced quickly around at the accents of mint julep and turquoise and at the creamy oyster, semi-gloss walls. Emmie was right. Libby had great taste.

"A new life deserves new surroundings," Libby had stated with the authority of someone who'd "been there," though at the time she certainly hadn't.

Devon wondered what kind of surroundings her friend would have now if she, indeed, had no cash or credit or real estate holdings and no doubt even less hope. She wondered if Libby would regard a phone call as gawking.

Padding across the zebrawood floor ("If you want wood, go with the exotics," Libby had instructed), she opened the small refrigerator that was discreetly tucked behind the bar. She took out a bottle of water. Living alone also meant there was no need to serve cocktails at the end of the day, which was fortunate, as alcohol no longer went down smoothly, not that it ever much had. Perhaps the small bit of wine she'd consumed at lunch was more to blame for her agitation than the company of her longtime, spoiled friends.

She returned to the sofa, plopped down, and uncapped the bottle. It occurred to her that she—the daughter of a 19th Century English Literature professor at Sarah Lawrence and a minor, but much beloved opera singer—had also been spoiled for nearly two decades, having been fortunate, at age twenty-three, to have met the dashing, young, Choate-Harvard-bloodlined Josh Gregory at a gala at the Metropolitan Opera, then marry him within a year. Yes, for almost twenty years, she had been spoiled. Until her world tumbled, as Libby's had now.

Sometimes, when Devon tried to recall those first months without Josh, she could only conjure a gray, airless blur of days spent in fleece pants and hoodies. She had wallowed, and wallowed well. It had taken a while, but she had slowly crawled back into life in her own way, on her own terms; she supposed Libby would learn to fend for herself, too. Then Devon remembered her therapist's comment: *People who are used to being on top don't always do well on the bottom.*

She sighed again, hating the reminders of how much life could suck. Then her gaze fell to the envelopes and catalogues that had landed in a near-perfect fan. The day's collection most assuredly held bills that she would forward to Josh by way of his prickish attorney, a snotty, bespectacled man who must have loved that she had not yet signed the "papers." The longer she waited, the fatter his fee. She supposed her procrastination was irresponsible, and that cavalierly tossing around her not-yet-ex-husband's money was like wasting natural resources and leaving a huge carbon footprint.

She smiled. A few years ago she'd been only aware of the term "carbon footprint" when Josh used it as politically correct banter at fundraising events or when she'd seen it printed in propaganda-ish oil company ads in *The New Yorker*. Today she actually cared about the world and its environment. Her awareness had come on that long crawl back into life as her potential had blossomed, as she met people who actually lived south of Central Park, as she worked beside people who had carved out good lives while earning much less than seven figures a year. People who knew how to live *on the bottom*. In spite of an occasional lapse into romantic fantasy of what she once thought her marriage had been, she cherished every new day. She loved being depended on to work at a job; she loved being a small part of what made the economy tick.

She was definitely, however, frittering Josh's assets. Perhaps her squander seemed more heinous now that one of her friends was in financial peril.

As Devon mused, her cell phone rang. She refused to let herself sigh again. She dug the phone from her bag: a photo of beautiful, laughing Julie filled the screen—Julie, her daughter, the only treasure from her old world that was completely essential and beloved in her new one.

"Hi, honey."

"Hey, Mom."

"'Hey?' Did they teach you that at Miss Porter's?"

"No. I learned it from you."

"Very funny. So what's up, kiddo, did you ace all your finals?" She wondered if her voice sounded as worn out as she felt.

"I don't know if I aced them, but I know they're finally over. Hey, that's funny, too. Finals. Finally over. Get it?"

Devon swigged so she wouldn't sigh. "And to think you are my only child."

Julie giggled, which triggered Devon's smile. How could it not? From the day her little pink daughter had been born, the girl had been making her mother smile. She was so sweet, so loving, so perfect, with her tangle of dark curls (Devon's curls), her bright turquoise eyes (Josh's eyes), and the light spray of freckles that had not yet faded as she headed into adulthood. She was the masterpiece of what had once seemed like a promising union.

Pulling herself from the sofa, Devon walked to the window. From her position twenty-seven floors in the air, she could see Central Park Hospital, the place where sweet Julie had entered the world.

"Are you ready for graduation?"

"Sure," Julie said, her tone turning solemn. "But Mom, I have a big problem."

Her pulse quickly pattered up to her throat. "Are you okay?"

"I'm fine. I've been busy packing. But I just found out Alana's not going with us to Europe."

Alana was Libby and Walter's daughter, one who had tutu'ed and tulle'd with Julie and the others.

"Oh," Devon said. "Well." Her pulse quieted: It was a daughter-emergency, but, thankfully, not hers.

"She has to go, Mom! We made a pact!"

Devon closed her eyes. "Honey, the four of you were in the fifth grade when you decided to take this trip. Things happen. Things change." She didn't add that Julie should know that better than the others. Julie had, after all, been the only one in her group (so far) whose parents were no longer together.

"Her Mom and Dad lost their money."

"I know."

"Her mother's at the house on the Vineyard. Alana thinks she has to go there and take care of her. She thinks she can make everything better again."

"Well, it's nice that Alana wants to be with her family, but she can't change the facts."

"I know! I told her that! I told her about how when you and Daddy broke up, I tried for the longest time to get you two back together. Remember?"

Yes, Devon winced, *she remembered.* A small, sour taste pooled in her throat. "This is different, honey." She stepped from the window, turned in a small circle, then found herself staring outside, over the treetops again. "This is about money. Your father and I . . ." Her words floated off on a gray cloud that defied explanation.

"Mr. and Mrs. LaMonde argue all the time. Alana said it's really awful."

"I'm sure it is, honey, but they'll work things out. People often do." She didn't add that if Libby's cousin had, in fact, caused the misfortune, Walter LaMonde would probably take it out on his wife. He had always acted superior in intelligence and breeding and most things.

"But, Mom," Julie went on, "Alana's trip is already paid for. So I've been thinking maybe you can help." It was almost as if

11

Julie had been at lunch in Manhattan and not in Connecticut packing four years of God-only-knew-what into several cartons to ship home and one suitcase and a carry-on for her ten-week trip. "And Bree's mom could help, too," Julie added. "And Tiffany's." Bree's mom was Emmie; Tiffany's, Candace. Sometimes Devon needed an org chart to keep the women-slash-daughters correctly connected.

It was certain, however, that Julie was hers. Julie was the one who cared about people the way Devon did, the way that sometimes got you nowhere and nothing but hurt in the end. Gulping her water as if it were, after all, an end-of-the-day, headache-provoking cocktail, Devon asked, "What makes you think we can help?"

"You could go to the Vineyard. Give Alana's mom some best girlfriend time. If Alana knows you're going, she might change her mind and come with us."

Devon paused for a heartbeat. Then for another. "Oh, honey," she said, "I don't know. It's really their private business." She wondered if she would have let go of the entrails of her marriage more quickly and with less angst if she had let her friends come to her aid. If she hadn't been so insistent on *fending for herself*.

"Please, Mom?"

She turned from the view of the hospital again. It was hard to remember that Julie was no longer an innocent baby, that she had developed a teenage girl's emotional mission to help solve her friends' problems. Devon had been only twelve when her own mother had died: after that, she had learned to stuff down her emotions. There had been no one to help her grieve, no one to help her understand life's inequities. Her father had been gentle and kind, but he'd also been silent and sad. She had vowed to herself that Julie's life would be different, that Devon would always be there to listen, to try to understand, and, above all, to respond.

"I can't speak for the others," she said quietly. "But I'll think about it. I promise." Then she said that she had to go and that she loved Julie. She clicked off and returned to the sofa.

In an attempt to recharge her spirits, she set down the water bottle and picked up the mail, just as an envelope from the prickish attorney sneered up from the pearl-colored suede.

~

The letter was formal, typed on stark, white linen paper embossed with the names Siegel, MacGregor & Bachman, as if snooty, impressionable letterhead still ruled and e-mail or texting had not yet been invented.

Dear Devon Gregory, it read.

On behalf of my client, Joshua James Gregory, I urge you to seek immediate counsel regarding Mr. Gregory's request for the formal dissolution of your marriage. Since your marital separation began, my client has been both patient and generous. Back then, as you know, you were financially dependent on Mr. Gregory. It has come to our understanding that you are now employed in a full time position.

Oh sure, Devon thought. As if her salary could do more than keep her in a modest working-girl wardrobe and pay the maintenance fee on the apartment. She hissed at the linen as if it could hiss back.

*In spite of your gainful employment, my client's current Wall Street position, coupled with his concern for your future, will enable him to continue, as perpetual alimony, the substantial support he has been affording you. This imbursement will be in effect until and unless you remarry, providing you retain counsel **within thirty days** and resolve the division of property **within ninety days** from receipt of this letter.*

The terms were in boldface, no doubt a scare tactic to jolt her into action. She'd learned the assertive type-font technique in the business writing class she'd taken last winter.

Then she stared at the words again: **within thirty days; within ninety days.** She remembered that Josh had always enjoyed counting the days that led toward milestones: when his custom Jaguar was to be delivered, when the Democrats would leave office, how long it had been since he'd quit smoking.

She supposed he could tell her the exact number of days it had been since he'd left her, not counting the earlier nights he'd spent at The Pierre because they had argued about this or that.

She decided to ignore the comment about "until and unless" she remarried. It was, after all, the last thing she would do. Ever.

Her gaze fluttered back to the paper.

My client would also like to remind you that support for your mutual child, Julie Norwood Gregory, will not be affected, as her financial care is protected through the trust fund established by Mr. Gregory's father at the time of her birth.

Although Devon's father had left her what might be considered a "tidy sum" somewhere other than in Manhattan, she had thankfully married a man whose family funds ran quite deep and would run forever. Then again, she'd once thought Walter LaMonde's family funds would also be everlasting, since the two men were cut from a similar, Upper East Side cloth.

She mused at how much one often didn't know about friends.

Visitation terms are no longer required, the letter continued, *as the child has now reached the age of eighteen.*

Julie. Eighteen. That fact still amazed Devon.

If you have any questions, or would like help in selecting legal representation, please contact this office. We work with many fine attorneys, and would be pleased to provide a recommendation.

"I'll bet they'd *love* to recommend one," Devon snickered. A brother-in-law, maybe. Or a racquetball partner.

Then she arrived at the closing line: *We appreciate your prompt attention to this matter, as my client wishes to pursue legalization of another relationship.*

Devon was tempted to laugh about the request for her *prompt attention* until she realized her heart had stopped beating when she'd read the last line: *my client wishes to pursue legalization of another relationship.*

She sucked in a whoosh of air through her teeth.

The letter was signed: *Sincerely, Davis Bachman, Esq.*

She sipped her water again, that time as if it were wine. Or scotch-on-the-rocks, her father's favorite drink after her mother had died and he had shut himself in his study, losing himself in his books and his bottle. She wondered if Julie knew that Josh now wished *to pursue legalization of another relationship.* That he wanted to be married. To someone other than Devon.

A cramp twisted in her gut. She supposed the "other" woman was prettier. More society-savvy. And, of course, younger, much younger. Early thirties, perhaps. Or late twenties.

The cramp cramped again.

Devon had always felt she was decent-enough looking. Tall, lean, almost-athletic. With charcoal hair, clear skin, and violet eyes that her father once said looked like Elizabeth Taylor's. During those airless months when Josh had first left, she'd stopped having manis and pedis and facials and hair-crops. She'd packed on more than a few bloaty pounds from too much take-out pizza and chicken fried rice. She hadn't intentionally let herself go; she had merely let herself be. Getting up in the morning, taking a shower, and pulling on the fleece had seemed like victory enough.

But that was before the long journey toward her new life, from which she'd emerged an independent, whole woman who looked great again and felt great again and should now throw down the letter, open the window and shout from the twenty-seventh floor: "I'll sign your damn papers when I'm damned good and ready!"

Instead of shouting, however, Devon felt a slow glimmer of hurt rise in her heart.

Another relationship.

One without her.

Her gaze drifted from the paper down to the zebrawood floor. Perhaps she had not completely evolved, after all.

Then she noticed her cell phone, sitting softly beside her, hinting at gentle distraction. She thought about Libby and about Julie's plea. Then she thought about Candace and Emmie. The women rarely answered their phones, but an urgent message might get their attention.

3

Candace discreetly unsnapped her ivory clutch and peered inside at her phone. At least she'd remembered to switch the ring tone to vibrate, a setting she thought seemed pornographic. She glanced at the Caller ID: GREGORY, DEVON. She frowned. Why on earth was Devon phoning? It was four-forty-five. Wasn't Devon at work? Hadn't Candace told her she'd be at a fundraiser at the Botanical Gardens this afternoon? That she'd be "working the room," as her husband called it, or, in this case, the Victorian glasshouse, the centerpiece of the landmark place? Didn't Devon know how important this was?

Rrrr, rrrr, the phone replied from her purse.

On the other hand, Devon rarely phoned anymore. Perhaps this was important.

"Excuse me," Candace said to Mrs. Halston Derberfield who used these fêtes as opportunities to showcase her absurd hats. Today's offering was too wide-brimmed for her age-spotted face; its silk pansies were a washed-out shade of purple and looked as if they needed watering. "I'm afraid this is urgent."

She escaped Mrs. Derberfield, stepped to a corner, and looked outside at a bountiful magnolia whose buds had been timed to bloom for the occasion. "Devon," she said, foregoing hello. "I'm at a function."

"Sorry to interrupt. But my daughter just called. Alana has backed out of their trip, and the girls are upset."

17

Candace examined her newly gelled nails that her manicurist had accomplished between lunch with Emmie and Devon and the festivities now going on. "The girl's family is broke. It's no wonder she doesn't want to trot off to Europe. Especially now that our daughters have money and she no longer does." She brushed a piece of lint from the swell of her right breast that rose from the asymmetrical neckline of her Michael Kors. She'd chosen the pewter-colored stretch sheath because it matched her eyes, and because it complemented the pink sapphire necklace she'd recently purchased in honor of spring. Plus, the snug fit nicely flattered the fact that she'd had a few fat cells moved from her belly up to her breasts, not to enlarge but to restore firmness and youthful *esprit*, though she wasn't sure if the latter objective had been met.

"My daughter wants us to help," Devon continued. "You. Emmie. Me."

Oh, no, not again, Candace thought. "Devon, we can't save the world." She thought they'd all learned that lesson years ago when Devon had convinced them to house supposed eastern European ballerinas for the holidays, and Devon's and Emmie's had made off with the silver. (Candace, however, had locked up or tied down all items of value. She had, after all, been raised on the other side of society's tracks, and was instinctively wary of strangers.)

"We could at least go to the Vineyard for the weekend," Devon continued. "Alana might change her mind if she feels her Mom has support."

Leave New York? *For the weekend?* Candace felt a sudden jolt as her heart lunged up to her throat.

"No. This is not a good time for me." She could have told her about the Art League election that was scheduled to take place on Tuesday. She could have said that Peter, her larger-than-life husband, was vying for the even larger, coveted position as Chair of the league board, and that he needed Candace to make a number of schmoozing appearances among the voters until then. But since Devon and Josh had separated, Candace did not like to flaunt the benefits of married life. Despite how Candace might occasionally act, she tried not to hurt her friends' feelings. Which must have been why Devon had felt free to interrupt her this afternoon—because Candace, simply, hadn't told her how vital the event was.

"Why?" Devon asked. "Because of the Art League thing?"

She supposed she should not be surprised that Devon had already known. New York could be such a small, tittle-tattle town. Then an icy wave rippled from Candace's heart in her throat down to her toes. She wondered how long it would be before she could leave the city for anything other than tomorrow's graduation. She wondered if staying home could even guarantee that no one would learn her horrific secret, the real reason she had to stay put. Rubbing her arm with her free hand, Candace wished she had worn a cashmere shawl. One of the hand-woven ones that she'd plucked from a vendor on a recent trip with her husband to Dubai. "The Art League is hardly a *thing*," she unintentionally snapped. "Peter is up for Chair of the Board. The election is going to be Tuesday."

"Yes. I know." Devon's tone sounded flat.

Candace supposed it was for the best that their daughters would be going in different directions, to different colleges, in the fall. After so many years, familiarity among the mothers had become tedious. Besides, it now appeared that the only one with whom she had anything in common with was chatterbox Emmie. Perhaps it was time to foster new female connections in circles that mattered. The Mrs. Derberfield types notwithstanding.

"Then you understand why I can't leave," Candace said. "My *husband* needs me here." She wasn't proud of the way she'd stressed the word *husband*. But Candace never behaved well when she felt she'd been backed into a corner. She gripped the back of her neck, aware that was how she'd been feeling since her brother, Gil, had called last week; since he'd told her he was being released. She locked her eyes on a magnolia blossom. Thanks to the godawful Internet, he'd found out she'd moved to the city, married Peter, and had taken up residence in one of his family's elegant brownstones.

Thank God Peter hadn't been home.

Devon made a small clucking noise now. "If Alana won't go to Europe, I'm afraid the others won't, either."

Candace jerked her head. "What?"

"If Alana stays home, our girls might not go. That would be a shame, don't you think?"

The temperature in the room flared. Candace dabbed the sudden outbreak of moisture that threatened to clog her derm-abrased forehead. "Of course our daughters will go. Tiffany is ready. They will leave for the airport after graduation. Right after our brunch. As planned."

"Maybe not. You know how teenage girls are."

"But . . ." Candace didn't know what to say next. The thought of her daughter missing out on her pre-college adventure was overshadowed by the prospect that she'd come home instead. That was not possible. Not until Peter had won the election, not until he was in a blissful mood, high on the manic side of his manic-depression, swinging from the North Pole of his bipolar disorder, or whatever the condition was that could plummet his mood and then peak it, often making the dramatic swing in an instant. (He would not see a therapist or ask his doctor for proper medication: people with real money, he'd once told her, can work things like that out by themselves. Unfortunately, he typically employed a hefty bout of obsessive-compulsive behavior in order to "work things out.")

After the election, Peter was sure to be energized by success and acceptance. Candace knew that would be the perfect time to tap him for a large sum of money, to pretend she wanted something celebratory like stunning emerald earrings, for which she could quickly, secretly, have a pair of reasonable imitations made. It was a hastily conceived plan, but a foolproof one, albeit sad testament to the fact that Candace had perfected the art of fast thinking and lies. Once she had the funds and paste jewels in hand, she would flash the new earrings at her husband and then send the cash to her brother, thus enabling him to relocate north, south, east, or west. Anywhere, but New York City.

Then, and only then, would the proverbial coast be clear for Tiffany to come home whenever she wanted. And for Candace's world to continue as if nothing had happened.

She hadn't explained all that to Gil. She'd only said she could help him, but not right away. He'd said he didn't want money, that they still were a family, and after twenty-five years he only wanted to see her.

But Candace had come to believe that all things were about money. Money and respect. Life was good when you had them, not so good when you didn't.

She'd told him to call back in a few days. So far, he hadn't.

With her luck, he'd surface on the day of the election.

Or worse, he'd show up at Miss Porter's.

But yes, Devon was right, Candace did know how girls were, especially Tiffany, who Candace could easily persuade to get on the damn plane—with or without Libby's daughter—if she granted her unlimited credit for the fine shops in Paris and Rome. Good or bad, right or wrong, Candace had raised her that way.

Flashing her eyes back toward the gathering in the prestigious glasshouse, Candace saw that High Tea was ending, that the ladies were dispersing. "Ultimately, Devon, I'm sure our daughters' main concern will be for themselves, not for Libby's daughter," she said with a touch of sadness. "As you said, they are teenage girls." She smoothed the front of her sheath again. "I suppose we won't see Libby at graduation. So if you go to the Vineyard, please tell her I said, 'Hello.'" In spite of a slight prickle of guilt, Candace knew it was the best she could do. She clicked off the phone, resurrected her practiced smile, and went in search of farewells.

It wasn't that Candace didn't feel any less sorry for Libby than she supposed Devon or Emmie did. It wasn't that she hadn't been disconcerted when she'd heard the tragic news of Libby and Walter's financial demise. But there had been so many stories in recent years of friends in their circle losing it all, blaming Wall Street, the president, and, in one case, an alien intervention. Late that afternoon, as she stood in her bedroom, shedding the Michael Kors, Candace wondered if anyone took responsibility for their own greed anymore.

She would have engaged Peter in that conversation, but he hadn't yet come home from his daily visit to the club. With their hectic social calendar, he spent little time at the busy law practice that boasted the name "P. Cartwright" at the top of the brass plaque on the door. Thankfully, his inheritances were more than sufficient; though he made occasional office appearances, he did not have to actually work for a living.

Candace glanced at her watch as she unclasped it; she knew Peter would be home any minute, he would not be late for drinks at the Algonquin.

Slipping into her vintage 60's Dior white robe with the hand-crocheted edge lace that she'd bought new at auction and paid a damn fortune for, she bypassed the four-poster bed and the working marble fireplace and the exquisite rosewood armoire that had been in Peter's family for over a century. She double-checked the new lilac summer suit that she would wear for graduation and zipped it into a garment bag. Then she made her way into the master bath, deliberating what shoes she would wear this evening, and wondering if they could do double-duty at Miss Porter's tomorrow.

Tonight she and Peter were going to meet one of his old Yale Law School buddies whose name she could never remember but who now lived in San Francisco. Unlike Devon's and Libby's and even Emmie's daughters, Tiffany—who, despite an insatiable hunger for shopping—was going to forego an Ivy League education for pre-law at Stanford. Connections on the west coast were therefore essential.

After their drinks, Peter's driver, Sergei, would bring Candace and Peter to Connecticut where they would spend the night at Avon Old Farms Hotel in order to make the 9:30a.m. Commencement.

Candace was tired just thinking about it all.

Still, she knew she was fortunate. At forty-six (though she claimed forty-three), she had a fine, healthy family, now that Tiffany had stopped binging-and-barfing (as kids today called it) and had actually gained twelve pounds in the last year. Marrying into Peter's family had not always been easy. But though Candace had not started out as one of *them*, over the years, she had managed to garner approval and, perhaps, even envy. She'd "made her own luck," as her mother would have said, by getting out of Jamestown, New York, when she had. The truth was, if it hadn't been for Gil, or rather, Gil's conviction, she probably would never have left.

She slid from her robe and pulled back her multi-highlighted blonde hair that was, in her stylist's words, "As straight as a southern Baptist." She stepped into the shower and tried to focus on her daughter's graduation. She did not want to think about Gil.

And yet, there he was, stuck in her mind, like a price sticker on crystal that you couldn't scrape off.

She twisted the faucet on, tapped her foot while the water turned warm, then flicked the lever for the twelve-headed shower.

The wet heat did not dampen her thoughts.

Gil was Gilbert Martin, her kid brother. From early on, it had been Candace's job to protect him. Their father had left them before Gil started kindergarten; their mother had pulled double shifts as a hospital nurse in order to make their endless ends meet. Candace had taken Gil to Cub Scouts, to swimming lessons, to see Santa on the sixth floor of Bigelow's Department Store. When Gil showed an interest in photography, she bought him a camera with her babysitting money. She loved her kid brother. She still had trouble believing it was her fault that he'd gone to prison.

"*Guilty*," the jury foreman had read. She could hear the word resonate in the shower now as if she were back in the cold, hollow courtroom and the years in between hadn't happened.

A familiar, dull ache rose in her chest. She turned up the water pressure, wanting the harsh pelts to pummel her flesh, punish her soul, scold her for telling the hideous truth. She tipped back her head, prepared to let out a wail, when Peter's massive body suddenly stepped into the shower as if he owned it, which of course he did. The shower and everything else in her life.

"You live around here?" he asked with a tentative smile that belied his commanding physique. Even at five-five-and-a-half, Candace was nearly a foot shorter than he was.

She drew in a small, quiet breath. Through the wet haze, she looked at her husband. Large-framed yet muscular, he was still handsome with his dark brown eyes, his Tom Selleck-type moustache, his dentist-whitened teeth. By the obvious look of his nakedness, he was primed to have sex.

She moved to one side, turned down the water, and tried to regain her emotional balance. She could have told him there was not enough time because they had to be at the Algonquin for seven. She could have told him she was not feeling well, or that she had too much on her mind.

She could have told him about Gil. But she'd been over and over this a thousand or more times in her head: Peter would be angry with her for having kept silent all these years; he would be angry with her for the embarrassment it would cause the family and him, not to mention their friends who knew they were judged by the company they trustingly kept. And he would no doubt lose his bid for the chair. He would plunge into depression, his yang succumbing to his yin. There would be no state of bliss and no start-up money for Gil.

God only knew what he'd do about her. The prospect of divorce would not be out of the question.

So, instead of sharing the secret from her past, Candace looked back to her husband and returned his smile. Then she leaned against the Patagonia stone tile and slowly submitted. Life, after all, held no guarantees and, yes, making one's luck often started at home.

4

The sun shined down upon Farmington, Connecticut, as if it had been invited like the esteemed parents and friends of the girls in the white sleeveless dresses. Only girls, young ladies, actually, as Miss Porter's still did not admit boys.

Emmie fanned her face with the program and wished she'd worn something other than the rose-colored, raw silk suit that wrinkled like one of those odd Chinese dogs and revealed every droplet of perspiration. At least there was brunch to look forward to at the Old Mill after the pomp and circumstance. The company of her friends always helped cheer her up.

Hopefully, they'd discuss the possible trip to the Vineyard. Devon had left Emmie a lengthy phone message yesterday afternoon, but after their lunch, Emmie had dashed out to Long Island and had been too busy to answer her cell. Too busy to do anything, really.

She straightened her spine and adjusted the little pink scarf she'd looped softly around her neck in a last-minute attempt to camouflage the plum-colored, crescent-shaped hickey.

"Jennifer Lynn Adams," a dark-robed scholar announced from the podium that had been erected under a tent that kept out the glare but did nothing to stave off the heat. A girl in a tiny dress marched up the side stairs of the dais and extended her right hand toward the diploma. The scholar paused; Jennifer looked befuddled. Then he bent down and whispered something

27

inaudible; she quickly switched hands, taking the lambskin in her left and shaking the scholar's right hand with hers.

Emmie fanned again, grateful the young woman was not her daughter, Bree, that Bree—although serious and not terribly pretty—took after her smart, steady father and was not scatter-brained like her mother.

Perhaps reading Emmie's thoughts, her husband, Conlan (named after an Irish Lord, a sixteenth-century ancestor), patted her knee as if it were a poodle. She rotated her eyes, not her head, in his direction. "Too bad we didn't give Bree your maiden name," he whispered. "We would have been able to dart away early."

Though he'd been born in Westchester, Conlan had adopted a European affect to his language in the late nineties when he had learned he'd inherited a castle in County Donegal, Ireland, not far from the sea. It was then he'd suggested they assume Emmie's maiden name, *Ainsworth*, because it sounded more regal than his *Malloy*. It had not seemed to matter to him that Ainsworth was Welsh and not Irish.

When Emmie told him she thought his idea would cause confusion, he'd encouraged her to at least begin using Ainsworth as her middle name. He said it might open doors to the world of the royals when they went abroad.

Conlan wasn't a snob, merely playful, as his twinkling blue eyes, carrot-and-gray-colored hair, and elfin-like size (not much bigger than Emmie) often suggested. They both knew he was far from titled, that, in truth, he was also the heir to a nation-wide chain of fast-food family restaurants. In spite of his substantial net worth, he went to work every day at the firm's corporate headquarters downtown. He was as humble as he was playful. He was also a good dad. And a good husband, in the ways that should matter, not counting the stuff in the bedroom, because in the big picture, that didn't count, did it?

Emmie shifted uncomfortably in her chair.

She knew she had been lucky to land *His Highness,* as she now called him in private. Two decades older than Emmie (and therefore "much wiser," he often teased), he indulged her and the children: Bree and her twenty-one year old brother Brandon, who, unlike Bree, was much like his mother in thought, word, and often misguided deed. Lighthearted yet romantic, Brandon (who had failed out of Brown) had a crush on Libby's girl, Alana, and was currently in Ireland, preparing the family castle for the girls to visit on the first leg of their post-graduate jaunt. He thought hospitality might be his vocation and that he'd enjoy living in Europe.

"I think I can turn the castle into a destination resort," he'd said before heading there two months ago. He believed that the greatest attraction could be that the place was out of range of cell tower signals and WiFi satellites. "More and more travelers want to get away from technology," he rationalized. "Instead of 'Free WiFi,' let's build a 'WiFi-Free' hotel campus. I think half of Manhattan will make reservations."

Emmie admired his enthusiasm, but winced at the thought that soon she would be a true empty-nester. With Brandon in Ireland they wouldn't even be texting—a communications tool she ordinarily detested but might welcome now. The troubling fact was that her children would no longer give her life form or purpose, and Emmie had learned long ago that she didn't do well on her own.

"Rebecca Ann Chilton."

Applause. Handshake. Applause.

"Carrie Jane Doty."

Applause. Handshake. Applause.

"Miriam Ruth Farnsworth."

Applause. Handshake. Applause. Most of the names sounded like they were being read from a list of WASPish, Mayflower descendants.

Emmie fanned herself again while the string of blushing girls ascended the dais and accepted the wings to their future.

"Julie Louise Gregory."

Oh! There was Devon's daughter, tall and elegant like her Mom, walking with the confident stride of a pure Porter's girl. Until now, Emmie was the only one in her small circle who could claim that she was a Miss Porter's *Ancient*, the school's coveted word for "graduate." Emmie was not, however, inclined toward bragging, humility being one of the attributes she'd been taught right there, on those hallowed, well-mannered grounds, where she'd also been taught to embrace the next stage of her life.

The younger generation of Emmie's inner circle certainly were prepared for their next stage. Devon's girl would be going to Princeton in September; Tiffany to Stanford; and Alana to Mount Holyoke, unless Libby and Walter had lost her tuition along with the rest. Bree had been accepted to Wellesley like Emmie had once been.

She'd hoped that her daughter would go elsewhere: Wellesley held such unfortunate memories for Emmie, who had dismissed her studies before she had started because, to the bewilderment of her shocked parents, she'd been convinced she'd found her soul mate.

Then again, Emmie pondered now, her studious, head-on-her-shoulders daughter would hardly succumb to that kind of behavior. The girl intended to major in business, with a goal set on taking over the family fast-food dynasty. Emmie had never liked academics, let alone business. She had only loved horses; and, as her mother had cried, what kind of life could she have with *that?* What kind of life, indeed.

Emmie could only have had the magic of Boyd Madigan, who'd been the young groom at the stables where her parents had boarded Miss Trouble, the sleek, chestnut Morgan, and where Emmie had spent most of her time when she was at school in Farmington.

"Alana Susan LaMonde."

Lifting her chin, Emmie held her breath. She glanced around the well-heeled audience, yet failed to see Libby or Walter. She'd tried calling Libby several times since hearing the news; so far, she'd only reached voicemail. She wanted so badly to tell Libby that she understood, that she knew too well what it was like to wake up one morning and know that your whole world had gone topsy-turvy. It had happened to Emmie, though her friends didn't know it. She'd never told them that, at age eighteen, before she'd met Conlan, Emmie had eloped with the stable hand.

"Brittany Ainsworth Malloy."

Conlan leapt to his feet and clicked his Nikon in proud fatherly fashion, while Emmie laughed lightly, amused that her daughter had apparently adopted the coveted "Ainsworth" as a surprise to her parents. It was a good distraction from the gnawing worry about Alana and Libby and Walter, and from the dizzying exhilaration that last month—when Emmie realized her children would soon be officially out of her charge and she'd be left with only Conlan—she had tracked Boyd down at Belmont Park off the Van Wyck Expressway, and that she had seen him two or three times. Actually, four. Counting yesterday.

Yesterday.

The first time they'd reunited they'd exchanged long kisses and familiar touches in the back of a horse stall. Then they had sex on the hay. It had been quick, surreptitious, and totally divine.

The next time they met at the Courtyard Marriott on Route 47. Boyd said she deserved clean sheets and a mattress, but as it turned out, she'd preferred the horse stall. It had been so reminiscent of when they had loved so innocently, so fiercely, so wonderfully well.

They met at the barn two more times. For the first time in years, Emmie was treated to the wonders of romance. Of sex. Of no-holes-barred passion. The kind that made her ooze with wetness in places she'd forgotten knew how to ooze. The kind that made her feel . . .

Ahhh.

No wonder she was so warm now.

She wriggled in her chair again and forced herself to refocus on the issues at hand. Empty-nester or not, Emmie wanted her children to be happy, wanted the girls to go to Europe so Brandon could court Libby's daughter on his quest for true love, as long as they could convince Alana to go. But that was only part of the reason Emmie had relished Devon's suggestion of going to Martha's Vineyard. The truth was, she was dying to blurt out her decadent, *OhMyGod, I'm having an affair with the love of my life* shocker to her fabulous friends.

She could hardly stand keeping such a secret.

But did she dare? She only knew that she needed to tell *someone* before the seams of her heart simply split open from all the love that was growing, swelling, in there. Who better to tell than

Candace, Devon, and Libby? And where better to do it than on the Vineyard where no one would overhear, because no one who mattered was there at the beginning of June?

⌣⌐

As soon as Julie received her diploma, Devon needed to use the Porta-Potty. Excitement, she supposed. Or merely frayed nerves. She stepped inside the molded plastic booth, relieved her bladder of an entire bottle of water, washed her hands with the medicinal chemical, then quickly stepped out in time to see Libby's daughter who, with her head down and her stride purposeful, was marching toward the parking lot where the potties had been discreetly placed.

"Alana," Devon called before she considered that Alana might have preferred to dodge her mother's friends.

Alana stopped at the edge of the pavement. "Oh. Hello, Mrs. Gregory."

Devon laughed. "Please! Call me Devon. I'm no longer with Julie's dad."

The girl hesitated. "Right. I'm sorry."

"No problem. And congratulations! You girls finally did it. You did Miss Porter's proud." She wanted to ask how Libby was holding up. She wanted to ask Alana if she would reconsider bailing out of the trip. But before Devon had a chance, the slightly plump, always cheerful, attractive brunette burst into teenage-tears. "Oh, honey," Devon said, "are you all right?" She cupped an arm around the girl's shoulders and escorted her to the shade of a giant oak tree that was often photographed in the autumn and used as a colorful foreground in promotional brochures for the one hundred-plus year-old school.

"Oh, Mrs. Gregory, it's awful," the girl cried. "I thought I could come here today and pretend nothing was wrong. But it's awful. I mean, I *graduated*, and my mom and dad aren't even here. They're on the stupid Vineyard."

Devon was glad she already knew about the predicament. "Oh, honey, I am so sorry," she said. "But I'm here, and I clapped for you. Did you hear me? Did you hear Tiffany's mom and dad? And Bree's?" Devon hadn't yet seen Candace or Emmie in the crowd: They'd reserved a table together at the restaurant and planned to meet then. But saying they'd all cheered was a good bet and seemed to help Alana's sniffles abate.

"My mother texted me yesterday," Alana then said. "She told me they couldn't come. That it would be too humiliating for Daddy."

"I'm so sorry, Alana. That must have been hard."

The girl picked at what might be a hangnail or nothing at all.

"Do you have plans for lunch?" Devon asked. "Will you join us? Julie's dad isn't here, either. He's in China, I think. Or Timbuktu." She'd added the part about Timbuktu in an effort to lighten the mood.

A corner of the girl's mouth almost smiled. "Will Bree's parents be there? And Tiffany's?"

"I expect so."

The half-smile dissolved. "Then I can't go. It would be . . ." She started to cry again.

"Oh, honey," Devon said, "it's okay. The Cartwrights and the Malloys love you. And they love your parents. You girls have grown up together. Over the years we've all had troubles. We've gotten through them together." She hoped Alana didn't ask her to elaborate, because other than mentioning the divorce again, Devon didn't know what "troubles" she could possibly fabricate. As close as the women appeared to be on the surface, the only deep, dark story that had ever been shared was the abridged report of the bulimia, and only then because Candace's daughter had grown so noticeably, startlingly, thin.

Alana didn't answer.

"Alana," Devon continued, her two feet jumping in before her brain was fully engaged, "I couldn't imagine any worse humiliation than when Julie's dad walked out on me. I wanted to run away from everyone I knew. I never told anyone, but I thought about going to the South Pacific, where I could claim that I was from Iowa and my husband had been killed in an accident that involved farm machinery." The surprising thing was, Devon hadn't manufactured the tale for Alana's benefit. It had been her plan—well, one of them, anyway, having constructed a number of similar fantasies as she'd slouched in her fleece on the couch.

"You're kidding." Alana's adorable dimples now lightly etched her rosy cheeks.

"I wish." Devon reached over and brushed a lock of hair from the girl's forehead. "Have lunch with us, honey. At the very least, it will give everyone a chance to try and convince you not to miss out on your trip."

"But . . ."

Devon held up her forefinger. "Wait here," she said. "I'll round up Julie, and we'll drive to the restaurant together."

Alana nodded. "Okay," she said, "I guess."

Devon walked back toward the jubilant crowd, telling herself that though she'd never believed in coincidence, and that the obvious reason she'd needed the potty at that precise moment was so she could accidentally meet up with Libby's daughter.

They feasted on calamari and crab-boursin fritters, pan roasted scallops and delicate spears of grilled fresh asparagus. Conversation was lively and guided by Peter and Conlan; Devon admitted to herself that sometimes it was nice to have men punctuate a group of women; sometimes it was nice to have men simply take charge. Chances were good that they, too, now knew about Libby and Walter, but had the man-sense not to bring up the subject in front of the girls.

As for Alana, she was quiet but seemed content enough, under her parentless-circumstances. She hadn't cried any more.

Since no one else broached the subject, Devon waited until the dessert trifle was served and the men sipped on single malt scotch though the hour was just after noon. Then she dabbed the corners of her mouth with her cloth napkin and said with quiet caution, "Alana, I'd like to make a deal with you. If you go to Europe, I'll go to the Vineyard to visit your mother."

Silence fell like a hemline in winter.

Alana didn't respond.

Devon braced for more tears.

Then Emmie cleared her throat. "I'll go, too! Your Mom needs her best friends, so the three of us will go, won't we, Candace?"

Candace's mouth seemed to freeze halfway open and her fork stopped in mid-air as if someone had hit her *pause* button.

"What a superb idea!" boomed Peter, not Candace. He reached over and touched his wife's unmoving arm. "I'm sure Libby would love to see you."

Candace cleared her throat and set down her fork without tasting the trifle. "But the Art League election . . ." she began, though Peter quickly interrupted.

"If I haven't impressed the members by now," he said, "I never will. No, go with your friends. You always have such a good time when you're together."

Candace's cheeks flushed. "But the election is important."

"So are Libby and Walter."

Candace propped her elbows on the table, tented her fingers, pursed her lips, and directed her comments to Alana. "My husband sometimes forgets the importance of finesse. As much as I would love to see your mother, my place, right now, is in New York. Perhaps I can go after the votes have been tallied."

"No, Candace," Peter interrupted again, that time jovial and insistent. "I'll take care of everything. You can leave in the morning. Good friends, after all, are the backbone of society!" He took another robust sip of the malt. "Yes," he mused loudly, "the Vineyard is a superb idea."

Candace twittered a moment then said, "Oh, all right. But I must come home Sunday night. Monday morning at the latest."

Devon wondered why Candace was so hesitant. Ordinarily, she seemed to enjoy submersing herself in other people's business. It was doubtful her presence with the folks at the Art League was really a life-or-death matter. It wasn't as if they didn't already know "Madame Candace," as Josh had often called her with his tongue in his cheek and his nose in the air.

Josh.

Devon thrust her fork into the trifle. Being reminded of her soon-to-be-ex completely negated her earlier thought that sometimes it was nice to have men around.

5

Candace examined her bags at quarter-to-ten the next morning to be sure she'd left nothing out.

"Martha's Vineyard is not a third world country!" Peter informed his wife, as he leaned around her and zipped her suitcases. "If you forget something, you can buy it on the island. Speaking of which, I've put a few one hundred dollar bills inside your purse. You never know when you'll need cash!" Whenever he was on the cusp of his mania, he tended to act with more bravado than usual.

Peter was a master at controlling people and places and situations, and Candace had learned a lot from him. Yesterday, after the limousine had whisked all four grads—*Ancients*, Emmie had kept insisting—from Miss Porter's to the airport to begin their trip, Peter had whipped out his iPad and made all the arrangements, starting with hiring a driver to escort the ladies for two or three days in his Town Car. (He had already given Sergei the time off and could easily have put them on a flight out of Teterboro, but he reminded Candace that Emmie was reluctant to fly in "teeny-tiny" planes, as she called any aircraft smaller than a 29-passenger jet.) He also made ferry reservations because he said a bridge had yet to be built from the mainland, *ha ha*, and he'd booked hotel rooms for the three women and the driver because it would be rude to expect Libby and Walter to host them, uninvited, given the situation and the fact that the season hadn't yet started.

39

For an attorney with a trust fund, Peter would have made a great personal assistant. As long as he kept his depressive side under invisible wraps.

The doorbell rang.

"Ah!" Peter said, hoisting Candace's bags as if he were a valet, "I like it when a driver arrives early!" Then his big voice called out, "Coming!" and he trundled down the stairs from the third floor of their brownstone.

Taking a last look in the full-length mirror, Candace was glad she'd amassed a collection of linen jersey separates that were suitable to wear anywhere. She tied back her barely shoulder-length hair with a small scarf, then abruptly changed her mind and switched the scarf for her three-inch platinum Van Cleef barrette with its subtle line of petite pavé diamonds. If she had to be on an island she might as well have some style. With a final look of approval, she collected her purse and her cell phone and went into the hall.

A murmur of voices drifted up from the foyer.

"I'm here to see Candace," a low, throaty, male voice said.

"Certainly!" Peter replied. "You're right on time!"

Candace heard the jangle of keys as she moved from the third floor down toward the second.

"I'm right on time?" the other voice asked, and that's when she knew. Her leg muscles, her arm muscles, every one of her muscles became paralyzed on the fourth step from the top. She sucked in her breath.

"Punctuality is a quick-dying virtue!" Peter expounded. "Here are the keys. The garage is around the corner. The attendant's name is Danny. Just give him my card!"

Candace couldn't move. Her Calvin casual flats stuck to the mahogany floor like hairspray to fingernail polish that hadn't yet dried.

"But . . ." the other voice muttered.

"These are her bags! Here's a folder with all the info you'll need: reservation numbers and directions in case the GPS goes haywire. By the time you bring the car around, my wife will be ready. She believes in punctuality, too!" Peter guffawed the way Candace remembered hearing his late father guffaw. "The addresses of her two friends are in the folder. You'll probably have to wait for Mrs. Malloy. She's sweet and perky, but a little high maintenance, if you know what I mean. The other one, Mrs. Gregory, will be on time. If you have any questions, my wife will be able to answer them. Don't forget to drive safely!"

The front door closed, the one-hundred-and-twenty-year old stained glass inset quietly quivered. And Candace remained steadfast, glued to the step.

"Candace!" Peter bellowed, then looked up into the stairwell. "Oh, there you are. Well, hurry up! The driver has gone for the car."

She could not, of course, tell him that the driver was not a driver at all but her brother, Gil Martin. Just as Peter's guffaw had sounded like his father's, Gil's low, throaty voice had haunting echoes of the man who had been theirs.

⌇⟶

"Suddenly I don't feel well," she said from her perch on the stairs. It wasn't a lie.

"What is it?" Peter asked, as he climbed up to meet her. "A migraine? Your stomach? Oh!" he added when he reached her, "you do look a bit pale."

"I can't go," she said. "I need to go back to bed." She turned and headed to the bedroom.

"But Candace, your friends are waiting."

She waved her hand without looking back. "I can't, Peter. I'm going to vomit."

"Well," she heard him say. "That isn't good."

She went into the bedroom and shut the door. She snapped on the lock, then leaned against the wall. Her breath went in and out in short little bursts. Her thoughts tumbled together. She might be able to convince Peter that she was sick, but what would happen when Gil returned with the car? What would he say?

"I'm your wife's brother. I've been in prison for twenty-five years. Didn't Candace ever mention me?"

She closed her eyes and tried to breathe slowly, evenly. *Think, Candace. Think, dammit.*

Peter would be livid.

She'd have to call Devon. And Emmie. She'd have to lie to them, too. At least their daughters had already landed in London and were a safe distance from the fallout of gossip. It would be bad enough if Tiffany learned she had an uncle who also was a former convict. But what about the rest of . . . *New York?*

The doorknob jiggled. Then Peter knocked. "Candace? Open up. Please, let me in. Would you like tea?"

He was a good man, despite the fact he was a capitalist. At least he had come by it through an honest birthright, not like Emmie's *nouveau riche* husband, the burger-baron Conlan Malloy.

Oh, God, she thought. *Who cares about Emmie's husband? Get a grip, Candace,* she demanded.

"Candace?" her husband asked again. "Please?"

She knew she was making this worse. She'd always hated when one of her friends became overly dramatic.

She struggled to take a deep breath. There was only one way to take charge of this situation. She could start by hoping that Gil had been honest when he'd said he only wanted to see her, and to trust that he wasn't there to disrupt her life.

No matter what had happened, he'd been right about one thing: they were still family. But that didn't mean she had to tell anyone, including her husband or daughter. Things would become far too complicated for that.

Breathing, at last, a long, steady breath, she adjusted her diamond barrette and unlocked the door. "I'm fine," she said to her husband who stood in the hall, his face noticeably perplexed. "It was a strong wave of nausea, but it's passed." Without further comment she brushed past him and rushed down the staircase before her sanity could reappear.

Peter opened the door to the backseat and saluted his wife with trumped-up bravado. Candace slid onto the seat and pulled the door closed. "Not one word," she spat at Gil. "Not one word." Then she smiled a tight smile and waved at her husband through the tinted glass.

Gil pulled into the sparse Saturday morning traffic while she remained staring out the window, trying to think. She could not bring herself to look in his direction; she did not want to catch his reflection in the mirror.

He maneuvered the big car onto Park Avenue as if a sixth or seventh or forty-third sense had reminded him how to drive after twenty-five years, three months, and two days.

It was easy for Candace to remember how long Gil had been incarcerated. On the day he'd been found guilty, she'd turned twenty-one. The previous morning, she had testified against him. He'd been eighteen, old enough to be tried as an adult.

"I heard him go out around one o'clock."

"In the morning?" the prosecutor had asked.

"Yes."

"And did you hear him return?"

She'd paused.

"Did you hear him return?"

"Yes."

"At what time?"

She had not looked at Gil. She had not looked at their mother, who was seated behind him. She knew their eyes were fixed on her, boring into her with anticipation. She shifted her attention to the portrait of Ronald Reagan that hung on the wood-paneled wall opposite where the jury of Gil's peers awaited her answer.

She lowered her eyes, her chin, her voice. "After sunrise." She waited for a gasp to shiver throughout the courtroom. But there was only silence.

On his re-direct, Gil's lawyer asked if Candace thought her brother was capable of such a heinous crime. She said, "No," but, by then, most people in the courtroom seemed to disregard her opinion.

The prosecution *rested its case*, closing arguments ensued, and the judge ordered the jury into deliberations.

After that, Candace had not had a decent night's sleep for years, not until long after her mother had died of a *broken heart* (or so Candace had presumed, and she carried the burden of guilt for that, too), not until time and distraction eventually quieted the bedtime image in her mind's eye of Gil resting his head on a thin pillow and drawing a scratchy blanket up to his neck while she fluffed sweet-smelling down and smoothed a thick comforter.

Yes, it had been years before she'd been able to sleep. And now . . . this.

She closed her eyes. "Pull over," she said to her brother. "I can't breathe."

It was another few seconds before the car stopped. They sat, Candace with her eyes still shut, Gil still silent as she had requested.

Then he quietly asked, "Are you all right?"

She felt tears well up. "No," she said. "I am not." She opened her eyes, reached into her purse, located a tissue and dabbed her wet cheeks, all without looking at him.

"I saw you on the stairs," he said. "You let your husband think I was a chauffeur. Am I right—he was your husband?"

She unbuttoned her cardigan and straightened the folds. "I asked you not to come to the city." She didn't know why she'd said that. She didn't know why she just didn't let her tears flow, tell him she'd missed him, tell him she loved him.

"I thought you'd change your mind if you saw me." Father's square-jawed, low, throaty voice jarred her again.

She twisted the band of her gold watch and glanced at the diamond-dotted face as if she gave a damn what time it was.

"Will you at least tell me why I'm driving this car? And where we're supposed to be going?"

She laced her fingers together and looked out the window again. "I'm going to the Vineyard to visit a friend."

"Martha's Vineyard? The *island?*"

Her eyes flashed on his: grey upon grey, brother and sister. She uttered a small sound that was like a cry. "Please, Gil. Don't make this so hard."

He ran one hand around the steering wheel. "This isn't exactly a picnic for me."

She looked out the window again. A bakery truck had double-parked next to them. "Maybe it's best if you get out here. I'll drive the car. I'm sure I'll remember how." *The way you seem to have*, she could have added, but did not.

He turned his face toward the bakery truck. "You always hated driving, Candace. I can bring you to the Vineyard. You and your friends."

"No. Absolutely not."

"Because they don't know about me, either?"

"Gil, please. It's too complicated." The tears lodged somewhere near her heart. She didn't want to try and justify her life or her behavior, not then, not ever. What she wanted was to tell Gil he looked good, that the neat, trim cut of his tawny hair framed his handsome face nicely, that his eyes still sparkled, that the years and the circumstances and his abrupt transition into maturity had, in no way, harmed his appearance.

She wanted to ask if he was okay.

She wanted to say she was so glad to see him, that she was so glad he was finally free.

But all those words were bunched up in her throat, and then, her cell rang.

Fumbling with her purse, she tried not to tremble as she found her phone. She considered not answering it; maybe she should fling the damn thing out the window. No matter who was on the other end of the line, she knew she would have to lie.

Gritting her teeth, she checked the read-out. It was Peter. If she tossed the phone, Candace knew he would be worried. He might call the police. Or the National Guard, depending on which way his mood swung.

She sighed. She answered.

"I don't know what's happened," Peter said in a rush, "but another driver is here!"

Candace pressed her fingertips to her forehead. This was not the right time to tell him the truth. She stared at her lap. Life was much easier when all she'd needed to do was show up for High Tea or cocktails or an occasional lunch. "The service must have made a mistake." She wondered how she could sound so calm.

"But Conlan recommended them! He said they're always reliable!"

"Sending two drivers is better than sending none. Don't make an issue out of it, Peter. Give him a good tip and tell him to go."

"Well, I'll at least give Conlan a call. I'm sure he'll want to know."

If Peter called Conlan, Conlan would no doubt tell Emmie about the mix-up in drivers. If Gil got out to let Candace drive as she had demanded, Emmie would wonder why there had been two drivers and now there was none. She would probably call Conlan, who would call Peter, who would call Candace back . . . then what would she do?

Besides, Gil was right: Candace had always hated driving.

She clenched her jaw. "Peter," she said as steadily as she could manage. "The driver we have is fine. Please thank that one for his time and send him on his way. There is no need to involve Conlan."

If Peter disagreed, he didn't say. He merely said, "All right," then he hung up.

The bakery truck eased into traffic. Gil flashed his eyes back to his sister. "To the Vineyard?"

She looked out the window again. She tapped her fingernails on the leather seat. "As far as anyone knows, you're simply our driver." She sucked in another uncomfortable breath. "And you must call me Mrs. Cartwright, not Candace."

He pulled the car away from the curb. "Okay," he replied. "But I would like to add that you look good, Mrs. Cartwright. The years have been good to you."

She closed her eyes so more tears wouldn't leak out, mess up her mascara, and alert her friends that something, indeed, was direly wrong.

6

Emmie couldn't remember when she'd been this ecstatic. She was sad for Libby, but realistic enough to know that life was an ongoing balancing act, and that usually when one friend was down, another was on top of the world. And vice versa. There was no way to hide that, right now, Emmie was the one who was happy, Emmie was the one up on top.

She couldn't wait to tell them. But she would have patience, a virtue she detested, and hold back her news about her horse-trainer-lover until they were with Libby. That way, they could celebrate Boyd's return to her bed together, and Libby would be reminded that things could get better, they really could.

Gazing out the window in search of Peter's Town Car (with two facing bench seats in the back, it was really a modest limo), Emmie knew that the others would be shocked. She knew they already felt Emmie's life was perfect, which it was from the outside looking in. She had Brandon and Bree, and Conlan was devoted. She had health and wealth and "maids up the whatever," as Candace once commented after several glasses of wine. She also had her "special work" as she called it, though no one, not even Conlan, knew about that.

All in all, Emmie sometimes felt that the definition for the word *pampered* should be *Emmie Ainsworth Malloy*.

While Emmie was musing, Wallace, the butler, stepped into the foyer—the "reception hall" her mother had called it the last time she'd visited from Palm Beach on the third anniversary of

Daddy's death. Wallace raised his chin. "If you'd like to wait in the parlor, I'd be glad to watch for the car."

Emmie shook her head. "No, thank you. I'm fine." She couldn't very well tell him she was so excited to have this time with her friends that she'd wait on the curb if she could be certain no one would see her.

Boyd!

It was astounding how often and how quickly his name popped into her head, even when she wasn't thinking about him. Yesterday it had happened in the middle of the post-graduation luncheon, and she hadn't been sure if she'd blurted it out loud. Just at that moment Conlan had leaned over and requested that she pass the bread and Emmie had to fan herself then ask to be excused so she could duck outside for air.

Resurrecting Boyd had been delightful, yet it could get awkward if she weren't careful. Awkward, dangerous, and terribly upsetting to Conlan, who really *was* a devoted husband and father. Emmie knew she should be ashamed.

No! she cried to her goodie-two-shoes self. She could not let her conscience interfere with her heart—she'd done that already and had lived with the nagging regret of *what if.*

A thin sheet of dampness crept over her face now and moistened the fringes of her reddish-blonde, pixie-like hair. Adjusting the open collar of her sleeveless cotton, coral dress, she smoothed the dozens of tiny pleats on the long, circular skirt that Wallace's wife had expertly steamed, then ironed with precision that morning. Then Emmie fluffed her petticoats that danced underneath and, with her patience exhausted and her adrenaline pumping, she straightened up on her high-heeled, strappy sandals and tugged at the four-wheeled suitcase that stood on the marble floor. With the same "gritty streak" that Daddy used to say could get her into trouble if she wasn't careful, she maneuvered the bag to the front door and juggled it down the steps and onto the curbing—nosey onlookers be damned.

Devon rode down on the elevator and wondered what she had started. Yesterday she'd been lamenting time spent with Candace and Emmie, and now, there she was, heading on a weekend outing to save their other friend.

Had she lost her mind?

She supposed she could see a therapist, but that would result in a health insurance claim that Josh no doubt would see because his provider and policy still covered her. Josh might use the information against her, now that he wanted to get married again.

She blanched, and then squared her shoulders.

She could pay out-of-pocket, but that would be wasteful. She hated to be wasteful with what was rightfully hers.

The elevator stopped on the twentieth floor and a silver-haired gentleman got on. He toted a black suitcase that was similar to hers; they exchanged New York nods. The doors closed again, and they inhaled the same cube of air.

He gestured to his bag: "Cleveland," he said. He was tall and distinguished-looking. She'd seen him before, coming, going, armed with hints of his life: a laptop case, a bundle of mail, a brown paper bag from which emitted a distinct aroma of Chinese take-out. Like her, he was always alone.

She looked down at her suitcase. "Martha's Vineyard," she replied.

He smiled. "Care to trade?"

She took note of his blue eyes, and she smiled back. "Not really." Of course, part of her wanted to say, "I have a better idea. Why don't I go to Cleveland with you?" But Devon had never been an aggressor with men, which she knew was one of probably several pathetic reasons that she was dragging out the divorce. As long as she was still legally married, she convinced herself she wouldn't "feel right" if she dated.

In short, she was safe. Safe from accumulating any more man-made scars.

The car continued its descent. She turned her gaze back to the polished brass doors. Their reflections gazed back, a fuzzy pair of images, a man and a woman and two suitcases. A *New Yorker* cartoon without a caption.

"I'll be back Friday," he said. "I could take you out for a glass of wine and tell you about my adventures in Cleveland." He had a nice voice. Crisp, authoritative without being arrogant. "Unless, of course, you'll still be on the Vineyard."

The elevator halted and the brass doors glided open.

"I don't know how long I'll be there," she replied.

"Well," he said, catching her eyes once again, "perhaps another time."

They moved through the lobby and out the revolving door. Just then, Peter's Town Car pulled up to the curb. Emmie jumped out and waved with childlike glee. "Here we are!" As if Devon could have missed them.

The driver emerged and took Devon's suitcase; the silver-haired man strolled off to her right, then disappeared into the parking garage before she could manage to say, "Yes, another time."

Not that she would have been bold enough.

For four hours and twenty-eight minutes (one pit stop included), Emmie babbled more than usual. She'd said that talking helped take her mind off getting carsick, which did not work very well because somewhere outside of New Haven she needed to use one of the plastic sandwich bags that she'd tucked in her purse. Throughout the entire trip, Candace sipped wine. When Devon broached the subject of Libby and how they might help her, Candace pursed her lips and said, "We're going for a visit. I see no need to overthink this."

It was clear Candace felt she'd been hoodwinked into going.

So Devon did her best to smile and pretend to enjoy their company, even Emmie's, whose mouth barely stopped moving though her face remained a light shade of puce. Mostly, Devon looked out the window. When they were east of Providence, a text arrived from Julie: Emmie's son had surprised them at Heathrow and had whisked them up to the Lake Country that was *awesomely gorgeous* and they were all having a blast, even Alana.

"Brandon is in love with Libby's daughter," Emmie said, which presented a new topic for her to natter about.

By the time they reached Woods Hole and the driver steered the car onto the ferry, Emmie was clearly exhausted, Candace was drunk, and Devon just wanted to get out of the car.

"I'm going up on the deck," she said.

Candace nodded; Emmie fell asleep.

Devon opened the door and squeezed between the Town Car and a vehicle that was parked only inches away. In the damp, concrete cavern, she threaded her way around tightly packed rows of SUVs, delivery trucks, and late model BMWs and Jaguars with oval MV stickers on the back. Finally, she located the steep iron stairs.

It was surprising how quickly she remembered the layout of the ferry. She had not, after all, been to see Libby and Walter on the island since Josh had left her: the absence of an invitation hadn't been a shock. Though an occasional ladies' lunch was still acceptable, Devon knew that once a woman (or a man) was no longer part of a couple, paired-off friends retreated like cowards on a playground. It did not matter whether the loss had occurred through death or divorce; it did not matter how long the parties had had cordial, or even close, relationships. An unattached person was simply too awkward for group interaction among those who were still together.

Law of the jungle, Devon thought, as she heaved open the heavy door and drew in the sea air.

Not that her memories of the Vineyard were limited to trips with Josh. As a child she'd come every year with her parents: her mother took part in a popular, annual concert that blended opera with classical music and rock and was held at the rustic, open-air Tabernacle in Oak Bluffs. Her mother often said the island held a special magic, that it was her "heart home," and that if only someone would start an opera company there, they could relocate. Her father always laughed and said someone would also need to build a university so he could teach.

To Devon, the idea of living there had been delicious, like the sweet scent of a daydream.

Stepping onto the upper deck now, she went to the railing and looked out at the freight boats and research vessels in the harbor. Beyond them stood a cluster of red brick buildings that belonged to the Woods Hole Oceanographic Institute. The buildings looked deceptively insignificant—not like the home of the world-renowned organization that had become famous for its underwater explorations of marine life and science, and for finding the wreck of the *Titanic*. But it wasn't all academics: Woven among the buildings, hugging the water, white-trimmed fishing shanties wore large, hand-painted signs that boasted fried clam plates (whole-bellies and strips) and draft beer in 32-ounce glasses. Devon closed her eyes, letting the afternoon sunshine warm her face and the familiar cries of seagulls soothe her nerves. Then, from below, the big engines rumbled to life.

"Well," a man's voice said from beside her. "That was a long drive."

She opened her eyes. She blinked. The man turned his face toward Vineyard Sound. It took Devon a few seconds to realize he was their driver. Drivers, after all, didn't typically dress in khakis and white golf shirts. Nor did they have strong-looking arms that suggested frequent trips to the gym. She brushed a strip of hair from her eyes and said, "Yes. It was a long ride."

At that moment, she would have expected him to nod, perhaps say something like, "Have a nice crossing," then walk away. But he remained standing as if he weren't a driver but a date, like the man in the elevator had wanted to be. She turned back to the water.

"I'm Gil," he said, extending his hand toward hers.

"Devon," she replied. She shook his hand lightly because it seemed like the polite thing to do. His touch was strong, his skin tight and toughened. She wondered if he also worked at manual labor.

"I know who you are," he said. He had nice gray eyes and a gentle smile. "Your name is on my manifest."

She withdrew her hand. "Well," she said, "thank you for getting us here safely."

He gestured toward the stairwell. "I think the other ladies have passed out."

"As you said," she replied, "It was a long drive." She was uncomfortable—*ill at ease,* Candace would have said—to be making idle conversation with a man Candace had hired.

"She must be a good friend. The one you're going to visit."

"She is."

"Does Mrs. Cartwright come to the island often?"

No matter how often Devon heard any of them referred to by their married surnames, she still thought it sounded pompous. However, she did know she would not—ever—reveal personal information. She supposed she should say that Mrs. Cartwright's activities were none of his business, but Devon couldn't be that blunt or bad-mannered. So she merely smiled and said, "I really couldn't say how often she comes here. Now if you'll excuse me, I must find the Ladies' Room," not because she needed to, but because she did not want Candace to surface from the bowels of the boat and find Devon cavorting with the help. Their trip was already thorny enough.

Gil leaned against the rail and looked down at the churning water as the big boat pulled from the pier. He was forty-three years old, but he'd never seen the ocean until now. He'd written it on his list, right under "never flown a plane," "never owned a home," and "never slept with more than a total of two women," neither of whom had been old enough to vote because he hadn't been, either. Having been locked up since he was eighteen had sure put a crimp in his lifestyle.

The list had started out as the social worker's idea.

"If you write down the things you feel you've been cheated out of, it might help you let them go." She'd had on eyeglasses that she'd kept pushing up to the bridge of her too-broad nose. She'd worn tweed, even in summers, and, on occasion, she'd had bad breath. Gil had ruled her out as a woman who might enable him to remove item four from his list.

Once in a while, he'd reviewed the list to see if he'd let go of anything. But after a couple of years, he'd given up and thrown it away. He had learned to live without, not because he'd let go, but because what choice had he had?

Candace, however, had been able to make lots of choices over the years. She'd chosen to move to Manhattan, hide her true identity, pretend that her family had never existed. His sister now lived in a world that wasn't remotely like the one that they'd grown up in. He wondered how many lies she'd told to protect her secrets, to keep herself in fancy clothes, living at the fancy address, riding in the back of a fancy car. He wondered if those were the reasons why she hadn't been to see him, why she'd never sent a Christmas or a birthday card, why she'd decided to act as if her brother no longer existed.

As the boat moved from the harbor out into the sea, Gil wondered most of all why, now that he'd seen her, he didn't tell her friends who their driver really was.

Wouldn't it serve his sister right?

Saltwater sprayed like needles on his face. He closed his eyes and remembered another thing that had been on his list: "Never feeling like it was okay to cry."

7

Libby and Walter's house was seven miles from the Steamship Authority pier, eight by way of the beach road, according to the GPS that Devon ended up setting because, oddly, their driver had not known how.

"Make sure we take the beach road," Candace said. "We'll have something nicer to look at than small houses with old cars parked in the yards. You know—the kinds of places where year-round residents live." In the forty-five minutes it had taken to cross, she'd ratcheted her nose up another notch, which she tended to do when she was in a sour mood. At least she'd stopped drinking wine.

Gil rolled the car out of the ferry, went left as the GPS voice instructed, then zigzagged through the web-like intersection. He followed the arrow on a signpost marked "Edgartown." They rode past a boatyard where wooden sailboats awaited the season; past gray-shingled shops that were close to the road and sported bright new geraniums in long window boxes; past a large chalkboard that stood on the tree belt of a seafood restaurant and announced the daily special: *Crabcake Sandwich w/tartar, $3.99.*

"Let's dine somewhere elegant tonight," Emmie chattered again, as if her catnap had recharged her spirits. "I'll pick up the tab so Libby won't be embarrassed. I wish it weren't June; I'm dying for scallops." For someone who had only been to the Vineyard a few times since Devon had known her, Emmie surprisingly remembered that Vineyard scallops were freshly caught during the months that contained an "r" in their name: September, October, and the rest.

"The street looks uninviting without people," Candace said. She must not have considered the driver of the pickup truck in front of them or the man and woman walking on the side of the road toting fishing gear.

"So people actually live here year round?" Emmie asked.

"Yes, can you imagine?" Candace said.

Devon nearly shared the story of her mother and the dream to relocate on the Vineyard. But she was too tired for pointless conversation.

They continued along the beach road, where Emmie made predictable comments about several tourist sights, which Devon tuned out. They rode through Oak Bluffs, past the old wooden carousel, past the park that Devon remembered from one August night when she, Josh, and Julie had been visiting Libby and Walter. The pastel-painted gingerbread cottages had been decorated with bright paper lanterns, music from the gazebo had filled the air, and laughter had risen up from the mass of people crowded on the grass. She'd bought Julie a glowing necklace, and they eaten hot dogs on a stick, and Josh had held her hand.

Turning from the park now, Devon looked out to the sea. She closed her eyes and let the minutes pass as Emmie chattered in the background.

They rode for a few more minutes, then stayed right at the fork on Main Street. Devon knew that once they reached South Water Street, they would go right. *Then three streets down on the left,* she thought. *Last house on the street, by the harbor.*

Gil followed the GPS instructions, carefully navigating the narrow lanes of white picket fences that shielded stately white houses and wore eager spring vines as if they were bottle green shawls. Within minutes, he pulled into the long, clamshell-coated driveway and parked behind Libby's silver Mercedes.

The three women waited for their driver to get out and open the door.

⌒

While his driving seemed fine, Gil's chauffeuring skills definitely needed work. After a short, action-less pause, Devon looked at Candace who rolled her eyes, yanked on the handle, and got out. Devon and Emmie slid across the seat, as if they were in Manhattan and needed to depart curbside in order to avoid being clipped by a cab.

"Stay here," Candace ordered Gil through the car window. It was a strange command to a driver. What else would he do? Go inside for cocktails?

Devon headed toward the sun porch that overlooked *Down Harbor*, as she recalled the water south of Main Street was called. Emmie tottered on the clamshells in her inappropriate heels; Candace walked ramrod straight as if she hadn't consumed half a winery.

"Look how beautiful this place is," Emmie whispered. "It's such a shame . . ."

"Hush," Candace warned, then pushed past Devon and knocked on the porch door.

They waited.

She knocked again.

"Jeepers," Emmie said. "She isn't here."

Devon winced at Emmie's favored word "jeepers" that made her sound as if she were still in fourth grade.

"Of course she's here," Candace said. "Her car's here."

"She must be napping," Emmie said.

"Or," Devon offered, "she's depressed and does not want to see anyone."

Candace and Emmie exchanged perplexed looks. They were no doubt clueless about depression.

"Maybe she's with Walter in Walter's car," Devon added. As far as she knew, Walter still owned his matching, yet dark blue, Mercedes.

Candace knocked with insistence again. She tried the door handle, but it remained fast.

They stood for a moment, then Candace called back to the Town Car. "Driver? Do you know how to pick a lock?"

"Candace," Devon said, "we can't." She did not watch as Gil crouched at the screen. "It's called breaking and entering."

"Don't be ridiculous. You're the one who said Libby might be depressed. What kind of friends would we be if we didn't check up on her?"

Refusing to witness the felony, Devon folded her arms and stared past the gardens and out at the water. She wondered what kind of burglary tool Gil had found stashed in the car. As for Candace, Devon thought her motive for wanting to get into the house was completely transparent: since she'd come all this way, she probably wanted to damn well be able to claim that she'd tried to help Libby. Maybe she thought Peter would gain Art League votes for her humanitarian efforts.

The lock clicked open. Candace and Emmie scampered onto the porch.

Candace checked the inside door: the handle turned easily and she stepped inside. "Emmie and I will go upstairs," she told Devon. "You can canvass the main floor."

Canvass the main floor. As if they were detectives, *Charlie's Angels*, older and wiser.

Still, Devon supposed it was good that at least one of them wasn't afraid to take charge. She walked past pretty, yellow-cushioned porch furniture that seemed fresh and new and so very Libby. Devon tried to push down her anguish for the road that lay ahead for her friend, one that probably wouldn't be paved with lovely décor.

She slipped into the whitewashed paneled foyer. "Libby?" she quietly called out.

No answer.

She surveyed the enormous kitchen with its spotless marble counters, stainless chef's appliances, and rack of gleaming copper pots. She moved through the dining room, where the windows sparkled as if they'd been shined yesterday, where the tall linen drapes were crisp and white and the long, black walnut table was adorned with two crystal vases that held balls of fat peonies. This did not look like the home of the *nouveau poor* or of anyone who was depressed.

"Libby?" Devon whispered again, as if whispering would help disguise the fact that they had intruded.

She bypassed the glass-walled living room and took two steps down into the sunny library. The room was painted in pale blues and white—had that been the color the last time Devon was there? Two walls held bookcases; another held a massive stone fireplace. A cherry desk sat in front of the bookcase that faced the fireplace. A high-backed, upholstered chair behind the desk had been turned around, as if the last person to sit there had not been looking at the fireplace, but had been examining books. Devon glanced to the large bay window on the opposite wall. She remembered sitting on the pale blue window seat—yes, she remembered, it had been blue then, too—surrounded by pillows, reading a mystery, the last time she had been there.

With an idle sigh, she moved behind the desk, over toward the bookcase, as if to locate the mystery she'd been reading back then.

That's when she saw Libby sitting in the desk chair, eyes closed, unmoving.

Devon drew in a sharp breath and screamed.

8

Devon had never been skittish about spiders or snakes or things that went bump in the day or the night. When she'd been a very young girl, before they'd moved into Manhattan, her family owned a small country house in Sleepy Hollow, New York—*yes, that Sleepy Hollow,* she often explained. She'd grown up tip-toeing through the famous village cemetery, listening wide-eyed to legends of headless horsemen, and dealing with field mice who insisted on invading the space under their kitchen sink every autumn when the first frost loomed. But Devon hadn't been afraid, not really, because, while her father had professed the wonders of 19th century literature, he also had instilled the importance of sorting fact from fiction, reality from imagination. In short, she knew that spiders and snakes and other nasty nuances of life in general would probably not kill her.

Still, when unexpectedly faced with the lifeless image of her friend now, Devon screamed.

Libby's eyes flew open; Devon screamed again.

Libby screamed. She leapt up from the chair.

Devon jumped back and fell into the bookcase, sending volumes of novels and biographies, histories and self-helps tumbling out, careening onto the gleaming hardwood floor in a hodgepodged heap. An oversized coffee table book titled *Cape Cod & The Islands* bounced off Devon's left foot.

"Jesus!" Devon shrieked.

"God!" Libby shrieked.

Neither of them noted the irony of the religious references coming from two women who had not been inside a church in at least a decade, except for several weddings of the children of friends.

A door banged open; footsteps clambered from different directions.

Candace's voice shouted, "Devon! Devon! Are you all right?"

Gil raced into the library. "What's going on?"

For some ludicrous, strangely timed reason, Devon noticed that Gil was wearing sneakers, which, though matching his khakis and polo, also seemed out of place for a driver.

"It's okay," she said, once her heart slowed down enough so she could speak. "It's okay, Libby's okay."

Libby had her hand to her throat as if she, too, were trying to slow her pulse. "Devon," she said breathlessly, "you scared me half to death." Her eyes moved from Devon to Gil, then over to Candace who stood on the top step that lead down to the library, and to Emmie who had just skittered in behind Candace. "Why are you here?" Libby asked, turning back to Devon. "Is it summer already?"

Devon paused for a moment, then laughed. "Not quite. Though it did feel like it took several weeks to get to the ferry."

Moving from the chair and the desk and the clump of books on the floor, Libby knitted her fingers together. She looked thinner than she had the last time Devon had seen her. Thinner, paler, smaller overall, as if losing her money had caused her to lose physical stature, too. Not that she'd ever been very big. Not as tall as Devon, certainly. None of her friends were.

"What time is it?" Libby asked, while the three women and Gil stood still and watched. She went to the bay window and looked out toward Chappaquiddick. "I must have fallen asleep."

"It's after four," Devon said, picking up *Cape Cod & The Islands* and setting it back on the shelf. "Look at the mess I've made."

Libby didn't look. She just stared out at the water and rubbed the back of her head.

"Where's Walter?" Candace inquired from the doorway. She looked at Libby, then Devon. She scowled; Devon shrugged. It was apparent they both sensed something was out of sync.

Libby frowned. "Walter's still in the city, isn't he? Is it the weekend yet?" Her voice sounded as small as her size had become. "Is it?"

Emmie spoke up. "It's Saturday, Libby. You totally missed out on yesterday. Our girls were amazing. But I do love what you've done with the sun porch."

"Yesterday?" Libby asked in the kitten-like tone. "Was there a recital?" She turned back to her unexpected guests. "Oh, please don't tell me I missed a recital. Alana will be so disappointed."

They all fell silent, even Emmie.

Gil left the room, perhaps having decided he was no longer needed now that the screaming and shrieking had stopped. Devon and Candace and Emmie stood still as his sneakered feet padded through the entry hall then out onto the sun porch. No one spoke again until the back door closed.

"Libby?" Candace asked. "What recital are you talking about?"

Libby didn't answer.

"We should call Walter," Devon said. "Libby? What's his cell number?"

Libby looked confused.

"The number," Devon repeated, "for his iPhone." Devon assumed Walter still had an iPhone. At Josh's business-savvy suggestion they had all bought them around the time Apple's stock had started to soar.

But Libby raised her hand to her head once again and dropped her eyes to the floor. "What's an iPhone?" she asked. Then she blinked a few times and scanned the room again. "And why do you all look so old?"

⁓

Emmie stepped back, Devon stepped forward, and Candace stood mute, as if she were assessing the pros and cons of getting involved.

"Libby?" Devon asked. "Are you all right?"

"I'm fine," she said. "But I wish someone would tell me what you're all doing here. And where are the men? Devon? Where's Josh?"

Devon looked at Candace then back to Libby. "Do you have any wine?" she asked. "I think we could use a drink."

Libby laughed. "Since when do you drink, Devon? I thought iced tea was your favorite."

The comment might have seemed benign to many people. After all, Devon had once been the lone abstainer in their social group, the one who preferred iced tea over vodka gimlets or wine, because of her headache issues. But that had been in the early days of her marriage. After that, she'd slid into those years of trying to be like them, one of the *wives who lunched*, one of the perfect domestic partners who entertained as if they were all stars of *Mad Men* before the TV show had existed. Devon hadn't had iced tea with her friends since Julie was in pre-school.

"Emmie?" she asked. "Why don't you and Libby go into the kitchen and get us some drinks?"

Emmie agreed: fixing cocktails was a task she'd always professed to enjoy. Candace once remarked that Emmie's middle name should have been Hostess.

Once Emmie and Libby had left the library, Devon looked at Candace. "We have a problem," she said.

"What the hell's going on?" Candace snarled as if Devon was part of a conspiracy and she'd been left out. She marched to the window seat and sat down. "What was that comment Libby made about us looking old? Has she looked in her own mirror lately?"

"It's something else," Devon said. "Something's wrong. For one thing, she asked me about Josh. And when was the last time the girls had a recital?"

Candace pressed the index and middle fingers of her right hand to her brow and stretched the skin back as if to prevent a line from settling in. "Do you think she's lost her marbles? God, that's the last thing she needs right now."

"We have to find Walter," Devon said. "He must be somewhere on the Vineyard."

"We're obviously not going to get his number from Libby."

"It must be in her phone. Which must be in her purse." Their eyes quickly surveyed the room. "I don't suppose Libby knows where it is."

"We can text Alana," Candace said. "She must have Walter's number."

Devon thought for a moment. "No. I'll call Julie. Maybe she can get it off Alana's phone. I don't think we should scare the girls yet."

Candace didn't seem poised to argue. Devon and Josh, after all, had been closer to Libby and Walter; Candace and Peter, to

Emmie and Conlan. Even best friends often had a pecking order. "What will you tell Julie?"

"I'll think of something. But my phone's in my purse, which I left in the car." Devon left the library; Candace followed closely behind. Pecking order or not, it was always hard for Candace to let someone else be in charge.

⌒⟶

Emmie often said she wasn't as dumb as she looked. She supposed that might be more believable if she didn't giggle each time she said it. Still, she'd been accepted at Wellesley way back when. Her grandmother on her mother's side (the Lexington people) said they would have taken her anyway, and been damn glad to have her, even if she weren't the granddaughter of one of their favored patrons, Emmie's grandfather, who had provided funding for the astronomy lab. He had chuckled and said it was appropriate because Emmie usually had her head up in the clouds.

He'd been joking, of course. She'd been her parents' only child, which she'd never minded because she knew she got more attention than her friends who came from big families. Her grandfather always said she was his favorite grandchild, which was funny, too, because she was the only one he had. More than once he'd said she was just like her grandmother whom the man totally adored throughout 60 years of marriage. (She supposed it helped that she'd been the "good girl" who could be counted on to set the table with the right forks and spoons in the right order, who politely remembered the names of her parents' friends, and who was seen and not heard when it was required.)

Not surprisingly, her grandparents had died within days of one another.

Emmie did not know from whom she had inherited her gritty streak, her determination to do special, secret things off the narrow grid of her upbringing, things like sneaking into the gospel church on Lenox Avenue because she loved the music; doing her secret, "special work" rocking sick little babies at the hospital two mornings a week; and having the nerve to meet up with Boyd again. Her streak, as it happened, was not always noble.

"I'm having an affair," Emmie whispered to Libby now as Libby stood in the kitchen holding a bottle of unopened wine, looking befuddled.

"That's nice," she replied. "But where is my Waterford? Has someone stolen my Waterford?"

Emmie sighed. "You changed your Waterford for Orrefors, remember? You said Waterford had become ordinary."

Libby was busy examining cabinets and didn't respond.

Reaching for the shelf above the built-in, 58-bottle wine cooler, Emmie withdrew four wine glasses and set them on the counter. "Libby, didn't you hear me? I said I am having an affair. So far you're the only one who knows. Except Boyd, of course. Boyd knows. He's the one I'm sleeping with. Do you remember him? He was the groom at the stables at Miss Porter's . . ."

But Libby was scurrying around the U-shaped room, ripping open the cabinet doors. "Where is my Waterford?" she cried again. "I would never have gotten rid of my Waterford! Someone has stolen it, Emmie. Who is that man in the driveway? Did he steal my Waterford?"

"He's just a driver, Libby. He didn't steal anything." She was deflated, of course. Why wouldn't she be? She'd had the perfect opportunity to test her hush-hush revelation on one of her friends, but Libby must have decided that crystal was more important than true love. "I am sleeping with a horse trainer," Emmie said sternly, because she couldn't help it. She planted her hands on her hips to underscore her annoyance.

Libby dragged a stool from the corner and climbed atop it, peering into the cabinets over the Sub-Zero refrigerator. "If you're trying to shock me, it's not going to work. We all wondered how long it would take."

Emmie opened the wine cooler and grabbed a bottle. She pulled on a drawer and plucked out a corkscrew. She knew her way around Libby's kitchen better than Libby seemed to, not that it was terribly difficult. They all had the same doodads and gadgets, china and silverware. And crystal, except for the Waterford. "How long what would take?" Her voice sounded timid again. She felt her cheeks flush. How could her friends have known she was committing adultery?

Libby climbed down and swiveled her head from one end of the room to the other. "Conlan," she said, and Emmie felt a sudden rush as if Libby were going to tell her that Conlan had a girlfriend, had had a girlfriend all the years they'd been married. Or, even worse, Libby was going to ask Emmie what she expected, given the vast difference in their ages.

"What about him?" Emmie knew her tone was edgy, but she couldn't help it.

Libby started to investigate under the sink. "All along," she said with obvious, distracted agitation, "we've assumed Conlan is gay."

Time stood still for a moment, the earth stopped turning, and several other trite clichés occurred, the ones that described what happened when someone stopped thinking. Or went into a coma.

"What?" Emmie squeaked. "*What?*" Conlan was gay? *Her* Conlan was gay?

Libby looked squarely at her, planted her hands on her hips, reflecting Emmie's pose, and cried out, *"Where is my goddamn Waterford?"*

Emmie dropped the wine and the corkscrew and dashed from the kitchen, down the hall to the powder room where she locked herself in and promptly threw up.

9

"Don't tell Alana," Devon said into her phone as she sat in the backseat of the Town Car. She'd left the car door open to ensure better reception. "Something's wrong with Mrs. LaMonde, and I need Walter's phone number. Tell her I'm your Dad. Say I lost the number and want to get in touch with him."

"Mom . . ." Julie said.

"It's okay, honey. We just need to find Walter. Alana's mom is a little confused. She's probably worn out from all the stress she's been under. I'm sure she'll be fine, but we need to find Walter. Mr. LaMonde."

"But, Mom . . ."

"Oh, honey. I'm sorry. What time is it over there? Were you sleeping?"

"No, Mom, I wasn't sleeping. But it's after ten. And I'm in a pub. I can't get the number for you right now."

Devon closed her eyes and tried not to picture her eighteen-year old daughter sitting at a bar in an English pub, hoisting a pint with the local lads. "Just ask Alana for the number, honey. It will only take a minute."

"I can't, Mom. Alana isn't here."

"What do you mean, she isn't there?"

"Well, she's not."

Heat rose in the back of Devon's neck. "You girls are supposed to stay together. You promised you would stay together. That was one of the conditions when we let you go on this trip."

"It's okay, Mom. We're all fine."

The image of a pub came back into her mind: one with a timbered ceiling, rowdy sounds, and a dartboard hanging slightly off-kilter on a dark wall. "Are you there . . . alone?"

Julie laughed her sweet laugh. "No, Mom. Tiffany's here. And Bree."

Devon blinked. "Then Alana is alone? Alana went off by herself?"

"She's not alone, Mom. She's with Brandon."

At least Libby's sweet-faced daughter was with Emmie's son and not one of the strangers. "Well, call her," she said. "Hang up and call her right now. I need Walter's number, honey."

"I can't, Mom."

"What do you mean, you can't?"

A small sigh trickled over the line. "Mom, she's with Brandon back at the guesthouse. The place where we're staying. It's so beautiful in the Lake Country. Did you and Daddy ever get up here?"

"What do you mean, she's with Brandon back at the guesthouse?" But even as Devon said, she knew the answer. She had pulled her head out of the sand after Josh had left.

"Mom . . ." Julie said.

"Well," Devon replied. "That didn't take long."

"It's okay, Mom. He's being real nice to her."

Nice. Right. Devon might have been born at the end of the nineteen-sixties, but she'd never been comfortable with the openness of kids having sex wherever, whenever, and with whomever. Still, Brandon had been with his sister and her friends on many occasions—more in the last couple of years. Devon thought he was a happy, congenial young man, though not exactly an intellectual. For all she knew, he was a perfect match for Alana. "Never mind, honey," she said. "Try to get the number in the morning. In the meantime, maybe Walter will show up here at the house. Or we'll stumble across Libby's purse."

Devon rung off and stared down at the driveway, wondering how on earth they could find Walter on the island and where they should even start. She glanced up to ask Candace her opinion, but for some reason Candace had walked away and was strolling toward the croquet lawn that cupped the waterfront. Their driver was keeping pace beside her.

"What's going on, Candace?" Gil asked. "I haven't seen you in all these years, and I find out you're living in a soap opera."

Candace tried to relax. She tried to tell herself this was a lot like the old days, with her kid brother tagging along. The trouble was, she'd never been good at pretending, not in her heart anyway. She folded her arms and kept walking. "Most of life *is* high drama, Gil. But there's no need to worry. Everything's fine." She meandered to the wooden park bench that sat on the edge of the garden and served as a viewing post in the summer. Viewing the croquet matches. Viewing the garden. Viewing the harbor. Not that anyone actually sat down and viewed anything. There had usually been too much socializing for that.

"Well, it's a nice place," Gil said, gesturing back toward the house, then sitting next to her.

"The grounds are exquisite in the summer. It doesn't look as if they've started on them yet this year." She didn't add that Libby and Walter would probably not be hiring gardeners this season.

Despite his mention about the soap opera, she doubted that Gil wanted to chat about landscaping and gardens—any more than she did. "I'm sorry," she said, "if I've been a bitch. Please understand. My life is so different now. I had to make it different. I had to . . . change."

He didn't comment.

She wanted to take his hand. She wanted to press it to her cheek. She wanted to cry for the brother she had lost for so many years. "Why did you want to find me, Gil? Why don't you blame me for all you've gone through?"

"Did I say I don't blame you?" She couldn't tell if his tone was serious or teasing. It had been too long since they'd talked.

Then he reached out, touched her shoulder, but quickly withdrew his hand. He must have remembered he shouldn't do that, not with her friends nearby. She felt a small pang of sorrow for that.

"Well, I'm sorry for everything," she said. "Including dragging you here. But it happened so quickly . . ."

"There are worse places than this to go after prison." A gull flew overhead emitting a vigilant cry into the sun-sparkled sky. "Is your friend all right?"

Candace snickered. "Which one? They're all a little bit nuts."

Gil rested his hands on his knees. "Tell me."

She reached down to a small patch of bluebells. She pinched one between her thumb and forefinger and studied the tiny blossom. When they'd been young Candace had entertained him with tales of her friends and people in town that she didn't know but had heard snippets about. It had started as a ritual at naptime and bedtime, a way to help ease him into sleep. Over time it had evolved into daily doses of little kid gossip. "Our private stories," Gil had called them.

"Devon is our bleeding heart," Candace said now as if this were then, as if they still were close. "She's in the middle of a divorce, but for some reason it's taking forever. She won't tell us why. Emmie is just, well, Emmie. We've never been sure if she's on the same planet as the rest of us. As for Libby, I have no idea what's going on with her. Libby has always been fairly tepid. She came from a big tobacco family, married 'fairly well,' and has never been anything other than perfect. She's from the South, though, and I think she's kept her accent by choice. It can be annoying but, other than that, she's okay."

"I wonder," he said, "what they say about you."

She paused, then laughed. "Plenty, I'm sure! Imagine how much more they'd have to talk about if they knew . . ." She stopped herself. "I'm sorry," she said again. She slipped out of her flats and touched her feet to the thick grass. "We played croquet here," she said wistfully. "But Libby and Walter have lost all their money, so I guess those days are over now."

"They've lost their money?" Gil asked without noticeable concern. After all, why should he care?

Candace nodded. "But what about you, little brother? Have you thought about the future?" She suddenly felt solemn. "About where you might go? About what you might do for work?"

He stood up, put his hands in his pockets and paced a small area. She wondered if that was a habit he'd developed in prison. She looked away, back toward the water.

"I've ruled out medical school," he said. "And rocket science." If he'd meant that to be humorous, Candace could not laugh. "I'd been thinking about teaching, though."

"Teaching?" She raised her chin.

"I've been taking college courses in business online. I need six more credits to get my degree. I planned to go on for my

Master's. But when I was being processed out, the counselor said most schools don't want former inmates—even innocent ones."

"Teaching?" she repeated. "I didn't even know you liked school. Or business."

"I didn't. But a few years ago I was tagged to assist in the GED program. In addition to working on the chain gang, I helped convicts get their high school diplomas." He walked to the wild-flowers, then back to the bench. "Just kidding about the chain gang. Though I did get pretty good at sanding and painting walls in the pods. *Pods* is the cool word for cellblock, in case you were wondering. Anyway, I put the money I earned into my account and paid for my courses with that. It took a while, but the years weren't a total waste."

Candace stood up. She touched his arm. She wanted to tell him maybe she could help, that with her husband's connections they might be able to find a school that would welcome him. She wanted to tell him so many things, but the words were balled up once again in her throat. "Gil . . ." she started to say, but he was looking back toward the house and not at her.

Libby stepped from the sun porch onto the lawn. She stared at Candace who was down at the croquet lawn with the strange driver-man. Then she looked toward Devon who was sitting side-ways on the back seat of the car with her legs sticking out and her feet on the clamshells.

How dare they show up unannounced?

Friends didn't do that, did they?

They certainly weren't acting like friends, sneaking up on her, causing all kinds of commotion. They didn't look like her friends, either. They *did* look older. Less stylish. More severe. Something was wrong. Very, very wrong.

But where was Walter? And precious Alana?

Standing on the grass, she felt a low ache in the back of her head. She started to tremble. Then she realized her friends had stopped doing whatever it was they'd been doing. And now they were staring. At her.

She nibbled her lower lip, trying to think, trying to think, but only one thought formed in her muddled mind. She tipped back her head, cupped her hands to her mouth, and shouted, *"Which one of you stole my goddamn Waterford?"*

Then she dropped onto the ground.

10

"Libby? Libby?" Devon tossed down her phone and sprinted from the car. She knelt next to Libby, grabbed her thin wrist and felt for a pulse. Thankfully she found one beating under the two-tone band of Libby's Ladies' Rolex, the one reserved for outdoor activities such as croquet and tennis.

Candace froze. "Is she . . . ?"

"She's fine," Devon said. "Gil? Can you help me get Libby onto the porch?"

"I've got her," Gil said, then scooped Libby up as if she were a dollop of airy whipped cream.

Devon followed them inside, adjusted the pale yellow cushions on the wicker sofa, and stepped aside as Gil lay Libby down. "Candace," she asked, "can you get her a glass of water?"

Candace sighed. "This is too much theatrics for one day." She marched away in a huff as if Devon had suggested she jump off the roof in the Dior nightgown ensemble that she'd boasted about buying last fall.

Devon pulled a chair up to the sofa. "You'll have to excuse Mrs. Cartwright," she said to Gil. "She's been under a great deal of stress." Devon didn't know what was going on with Candace, but between her snarky remarks and the excessive wine she'd consumed, she wasn't her typically charming self.

"I understand," the driver replied.

There was no chance that he did, but Devon appreciated his kindness. She took Libby's hand and lightly rubbed it.

"I know it's none of my business," Gil continued, "but it seems like your friend has a problem that's bigger than Waterford."

Devon didn't respond.

"Shouldn't you call her doctor?" he asked.

Her doctor? How could she call Libby's doctor? "I don't know who her doctor is, let alone how—or where—to find him. In fact, right now, we don't even know how to find her husband." There was no need to mention she couldn't get Walter's number from Libby's daughter because the girl was in bed with Emmie's son. Then Devon realized Candace had been right: this was too much theatrics for one day.

Libby stirred. She put her hand to her forehead but did not open her eyes. Still, that must be a good sign.

"Libby?" Devon whispered. "Where's Walter?"

Libby slowly shook her head but said nothing.

"Walter is the husband?" Gil asked.

Devon thought she should thank him for his help and remind him that he'd been right, this was none of his business. But Candace still hadn't returned and she didn't know where Emmie was. And this whole mess was frustrating. "Walter is her husband, yes," she said. "We think he's on the island, but he's not here at the house."

"Maybe he's off yachting, or whatever these people do."

Libby's lips began to move. "The boat is in Bermuda," she murmured.

It was a relief that she'd spoken. Her comment, however, made no sense to Devon. As far as Devon knew, it had been a long time since Walter had sailed in the Newport/Bermuda Race.

Propping herself up on her elbows now, Libby looked slightly dazed, as if she were waking up from a long nap. "Where are my cigarettes?" she asked. "May I please have a cigarette?"

The four women had gone to a hypnotist-guru in Boston almost twelve years ago when the girls started elementary school, "real school," Julie had called it, "not pre-school." The guru had tranced the ladies into quitting smoking without gaining an ounce. Since then, only Candace admitted to having indulged "once or twice" in the nicotine habit. Between that, the Newport/Bermuda Race comment, and the mentions of Josh, Devon suspected her friend had no clue about anything in the present.

"I'll get your cigarettes in a minute," she said. "But first, can you tell me the name of the president?" It seemed ridiculous, but it was the first question that came into her mind.

Libby frowned, though the Dysport she must have had recently injected held fast and didn't reveal the tiny crow's feet that had been there the last time Devon saw her. "The president of what?" she asked with veiled annoyance, then held her hand to the back of her head.

"The country. The United States."

"Please, Devon, don't make fun of me. Of all our friends, I count on you to be practical."

"I'm not making fun of you, Libby. But you could have fallen and hit your head. Does it hurt?"

Libby pulled her hand away and looked at her palm, as if it held the answer. "No," she said. "Well, maybe a little."

"Okay then, who is our president?"

A few seconds ticked. Devon watched Libby. Gil watched Libby. Libby watched her hand. "Bush," she finally replied. "It is 2003 and George W. Bush is our president." She paused for a long breath. "So you see, I am perfectly fine."

⌣⁓

85

Candace returned, a glass of water in one hand, a purse in the other. "I found Libby's purse. There's no cell phone inside. I called her number; nothing rang in the house."

"Stop talking about me as if I'm not here," Libby said.

Devon stood up and motioned Candace to the other end of the room. "We need to take Libby to the hospital. She thinks it's 2003. She must have some kind of amnesia."

"Amnesia isn't real, Devon. That only happens in the movies." She set down the water and the purse.

Devon ignored the comment. "Gil can drive us. I know where the hospital is. You can stay here with Emmie in case Walter comes back."

"No. I'll go." Candace pushed past Devon, went back to Libby, hoisted her up, and headed toward the door. Gil followed them to the car.

Libby and Candace usually got along like sparring partners in heels. Devon knew it wasn't wise for them go off without a referee. Grabbing Libby's purse and sighing a slow sigh, Devon followed the group, climbed into the backseat, and sat down across from the women. But as Gil started the engine, Devon suddenly remembered Emmie. "Stop. We need to tell Emmie we're leaving." She reached for the door handle, but Candace brushed it away.

"She'll figure it out."

Gil put the car in reverse and crunched down the driveway, over the clamshells, when Emmie suddenly tore from the house. "Where are you going?" she cried. "Wait for me!"

So Gil slowed the car and Emmie jumped in the back next to Devon and said, "I can't believe you were leaving without me," and Gil backed out to the street and they rolled toward the hospital while Candace found a half-empty bottle of wine and poured herself a tall glass.

The waiting room was empty. On the way to the hospital, Candace had suggested they drop Libby and Devon off there, then Gil could take Emmie and her to check into the hotel. Peter had booked them at the Harbor View that was up by the lighthouse. "It might take a while for Libby to be examined," Candace had reasoned. "We won't want to lose our reservations. Besides, it will probably be close to dinnertime when you're done. If we're settled into our rooms at least we'll be able to change." God forbid Candace should wear the same attire to dinner that she'd worn on the drive from New York.

Devon hadn't argued. Aside from the fact that no one, to her knowledge, had ever won a discussion with Candace if it involved travel arrangements or accommodations, she welcomed the chance for some quiet time. She had a feeling this was going to be a long weekend.

Libby had been escorted through big double doors over half an hour ago. Devon had settled into a comfortable chair to wait, but now she was antsy. She got up, went to the vending machine, and bought a bottle of water. Then she walked to the big window that overlooked Vineyard Harbor.

The hospital was still fairly new: Devon remembered Walter had said he'd donated a "hefty sum" toward the construction because, though they were there only in summers and had actually only needed medical services once when Alana sprained her foot

playing volleyball on the beach, supporting the new hospital had
been the right thing to do. "The year-round people need us,"
he'd explained, "and we need them in season." She'd supposed
he had a point.

Devon wondered what had constituted a "hefty sum" and
how badly Walter must now wish he could have it back.

Taking a long drink, she looked out at the water and thought
about how quickly, indeed, life could change. That last time
she'd been on the Vineyard with Josh, she'd thought everything
had been perfect. They'd golfed and gone sailing and dined at
the boat club and made love with the windows of the guesthouse
wide open to the rhythmic night sounds of the surf. They'd had
a marvelous time, because she hadn't yet known that by autumn
he'd be spending nights at The Pierre, or that a few weeks later
Devon would wind up on the sofa by day and sneak out of her
apartment at night. Yes, she'd snuck out in her fleece and her
sneakers. Smart, stable Devon Gregory, had found no shame in
lurking around midtown after the sun had gone down, stalking
her husband to see if he had a mistress. The night she'd been
leaning against the streetlamp and Josh had come from out of
nowhere, she knew she had ruined any chance of reconciliation.
It had been ugly.

"How dare you?" he'd growled.

"How dare I? How dare *I*?" she'd responded. "How dare you.
How dare *you*." Of course, she'd been unable to accuse him of
anything specific because she'd been the one who'd been caught
red-handed, red-faced.

"We are separated, Devon. I have filed for divorce."

It could have been because of the way his nostrils flared just
a little, or the way those killer turquoise eyes had narrowed into
angry slits. It could have been because he wouldn't deny the

questions that she couldn't vocalize: *Are you seeing someone? Are you having an affair?* Or it could have been because of a quick flashback to that summer on the island, when they had made love as the waves kept gentle time with their movements. It could have been for any number of reasons, Devon supposed. But standing under the streetlamp, as Josh uttered the word *divorce*, she'd pulled back her arm, the one holding her JW pocketbook (an as yet unknown foreshadowing of her career to come) and wailed it at his groin, leather upon penis, buckle upon balls.

He'd doubled over.

She'd laughed, then walked away.

Yes, she thought now, that incident, indeed, had ruined any chance of reconciliation.

Not that she'd ever want to reconcile.

Looking out at the view, at the sun's rays that yawned across the water and hinted that a creamsicle tint would come with the sunset, Devon wondered if, indeed, there had been a woman that night at The Pierre, and if she was the one with whom he now wanted to *pursue legalization*. Perhaps, thanks to his duplicitous charm, he'd found another since then.

"Mrs. Gregory?"

She blinked back to the present. A young man dressed in green scrubs stood next to her.

"Your friend will be ready to leave in a few minutes."

"Is she all right now?"

"She's the same as when she arrived. I can tell you she is medically stable."

"But her brain is screwed up."

He looked down at his shoes. "I'm sorry, but I can't discuss her condition further. HIPPA regulations, you know. If you were related . . ."

Devon assumed a Candace-kind-of-stance. "For all intents and purposes, I *am* her family right now. Her husband is missing, and her daughter is out of the country." She did not mention Libby's cousin who had squandered their fortune or Libby's parents who lived somewhere out West as Devon recalled. "I appreciate your regulations, doctor, but it's quite obvious something is wrong with Mrs. LaMonde. If you're telling me her condition is the same, but she's 'ready to leave,' I need to know how I can help her."

He paused for a moment, then raised his eyes to meet Devon's. "I can tell you there is no obvious medical problem. She's behaving like she's suffering from retrograde amnesia, but there isn't any evidence of a concussion or head trauma that usually accompanies that. She says she has a slight headache, but that's all. She might have a dissociative fugue, but those are rare, and I'm not a specialist. Do you know if she's had any recent psychological shock?"

Was losing one's money considered a shock? And was it Devon's place to share the situation with the doctor? "I'm not sure," she replied.

"Well, under any circumstances, your friend should see a neurologist. There aren't any on the island, but I'm sure we can arrange an appointment for her in Falmouth. On Monday."

"Monday?"

"Sorry. Of course, if her condition deteriorates, we can airlift her to Boston."

"What are the chances of her condition 'deteriorating'?"

He shrugged. "As I said, she is medically stable. She should be fine until Monday. But I don't think you should leave her alone."

Devon looked back to the peaceful harbor, then took another drink. "What do we do in the meantime? Do we tell her she has amnesia? Or do we act as if she's right to think it's 2003? Is it like when someone's sleepwalking—you're not supposed to wake them up, are you?"

He flicked off his glasses, closed and tucked them into the pocket of his white coat. "My best guess is that you should keep her quiet and be kind. But if you notice any change in her symptoms, please consider having her airlifted to Boston. We have a helipad here at the hospital."

"I hope we can find her husband before it comes to that."

He nodded. "Well, if he's on the island, it shouldn't be too hard to find him. But she should come back here on Monday so we can take another look, then, if necessary, make the appointment in Falmouth."

"Yes. Of course." If Walter didn't surface, they'd have to do that. Candace wouldn't be happy about extending their visit, but she'd get over it. Eventually. Or she could always take the damn car and the driver and go back to New York on her own.

The doctor handed her a small packet. "Here are a couple of sedatives to help Mrs. LaMonde get her through the rest of the weekend."

Devon thanked the doctor, dropped the pills into her pocket, then watched as he disappeared through the big double doors. For the first time in a long time, she felt anxious about what to expect and what to do. Josh would have known. He had always known how to handle everything. Among other reasons, Devon had loved him for that.

11

"Do you think Conlan's gay?" Emmie blurted out after she and Candace had checked into their rooms and reconvened in the hotel restaurant to await word on Libby.

Candace scanned the area for any sign of Gil. She hoped he'd decided to stay in his room away from them. Far away. Not exactly a sisterly attitude.

"Candace?" Emmie whined again.

"You've been married how long?" Candace asked wearily. "And suddenly you think Conlan is gay?"

"Not me. Libby. She said you all think he is."

Satisfied that her brother wasn't nearby, Candace returned to the Pinot Grigio that she didn't really want. She'd far surpassed her quota of wine for the day. Peter would be disappointed in her: "Nothing's more unattractive than a drunken woman," he'd often said. Nonetheless, she gulped again.

"I don't believe I ever thought Conlan was gay. But I certainly would never have said it."

"Well," Emmie said, staring into her lemon drop martini, "it's not a very nice rumor for Libby to be spreading."

"Libby is not exactly in her right mind now. Go easy on her, okay?" If Emmie was surprised by Candace's compassion, she didn't show it. She was too busy fiddling with the small, square napkin that peeked from under her glass the way her petticoats often peeked from her hemline.

"Well," she said, "he isn't."

"That's nice," Candace replied. Her gaze resumed traveling, that time out the tall, wide windows to the sweeping veranda where several high-backed rocking chairs swayed back and forth in the breeze coming up from the harbor. Then she saw a solitary figure walking down the narrow, sloping path that lead to the Edgartown Lighthouse. Even after all these years, she recognized her brother's walk. Not everyone would notice the slight limp on his right side, the deformity that had been the result of a fall off his bike and a subsequent broken leg. She'd felt guilty about that, too, because protecting him had been her job.

They'd been riding to the First Ward to check out the new Soap Box Derby track; Gil caught his tire in an iron sewer grate and jammed his foot into one of the openings; three bones cracked when he tried to yank his foot out.

Candace had been terrified but had tried to act calmly. "Don't you dare move," she'd ordered. "Don't even breathe." She ran to a stranger's house, banged on the door, and shouted for them to call an ambulance. Later, the doctor said if it hadn't been for her smart thinking, Gil might have lost his foot.

Smart thinking? Hardly. It had been her fault for not watching him more closely. But he'd never blamed her for that either. At least, not that he'd said.

He limped as he walked toward the lighthouse now. His hands rode in the pockets of his pants; his head was tipped toward the sky. She wondered if he were reveling in the clear, clean air—such a contrast to that in the stale cells in the *pods* of the prison. She wondered if he was smiling. Then she realized she had not seen him with a suitcase. Did he have clean clothes? Did he have any toiletries? A toothbrush? A razor? When he'd showed up at their front door in the city, had he been toting some type of bag? Peter had said the Vineyard wasn't a third world country. Surely Gil would be able to pick up clean underwear and a shirt. But did he have any money? Should she give him her credit card? She started to get up. She needed to go to him.

Then Emmie touched her hand. "Candace? Where are you going? Aren't you listening to me?"

She hesitated, then sat back down. "Of course I'm listening."

"Well, then, what do you think? Should I or shouldn't I?"

"Should you or shouldn't you what?" Gil might have to go back to Vineyard Haven to find a store that sold men's underwear. As far as Candace remembered, Edgartown had mostly high-end tourist shops, stores with golf shirts and ties with small green whales embroidered on them.

"Should I or shouldn't I take a test?"

She pulled her eyes back from the lighthouse. "A test for what?"

"To see if I'm pregnant! You really *weren't* listening!"

"You're pregnant? Well then, Libby will have to stop spreading those rumors about Conlan."

"But I told you, it won't be Conlan's! He had a vasectomy years ago. If I'm pregnant, the baby is Boyd's."

The first twinges of a headache crept around the back of Candace's neck. "Whose?"

"Boyd's!" Emmie exclaimed. "Boyd—my old lover! He was the stable boy when I went to Miss Porter's!" She pushed away her martini, burst into tears and bolted from the restaurant.

~

While Libby shed the hospital gown and got back into her clothes, Devon called a cab. There was no point bothering Candace or Emmie; this weekend was already fraught with enough consternation.

As she walked back toward the lobby of the emergency room, Devon tried to figure out what Josh would have said, what Josh would have done.

The doctor had said to keep Libby quiet. That would mean she'd have to omit the forces of nature that whirled around chattering Emmie and controlling Candace.

Devon looked down at her cell phone. She should call Candace and say she was going to go back to the house with Libby and that Candace and Emmie could stay at the hotel. Surely, at some point, Walter would show up at the house and Devon could leave and join them. After all, now that the LaMondes' problems had escalated beyond a lack of money, it truly was a family matter. With any luck, the quiet evening would work some magic, and Libby would be better in the morning. Then the women could go back to the city.

Yes, she should start by calling Candace.

Shouldn't she?

But what if Walter didn't show up by . . . what time? Seven? Eight? Midnight? How could they find him? What if he'd left the island? What if Libby didn't get better? Should they bring her to Falmouth without Walter? The doctor had said she was medically stable, but what if . . .

Her brain cells were hyperventilating. She closed her eyes and tried to think slowly.

If Walter wasn't at the house, Devon could call Candace and tell her to go to the boat club. Or to start asking around at some of the upscale restaurants in the village. Surely someone would know Walter. Surely someone would be able to help.

She opened her eyes. Josh, of course, would know where to look. After all, Josh and Walter had been golfing buddies. Every year, they'd traveled their favorite circuit: Talega in San Clemente, Royal Palm in Boca Raton, Grand Dunes at Hilton Head. Not to mention a couple of courses in Scotland and England whose names Devon never remembered. She had not, after all, been raised in a house filled with jabber about fairways and doglegs and water hazards. Her childhood conversations had revolved around less physical pastimes like Mozart and Verdi and Dickens.

Josh would have Walter's cell number, no doubt on speed dial. Over the past couple of years, Libby hadn't mentioned if the men still got together, but now that Josh was half of a couple again, re-connection was probably inevitable.

Could she, should she, call Josh?

Why not?

Chances were, when he saw her name on Caller ID, he wouldn't pick up. She could leave a message.

"I don't want to bother you," she could say. "But this is an emergency. Please call me back and leave Walter LaMonde's cell number."

How hard could that be?

When he called her back she would not have to answer; he could just leave the message and that would be that.

Wouldn't it?

She looked at her phone as if it could offer guidance.

Then she thought, *No.* She'd have to be more specific. After all, Josh knew that Julie was in Europe with Libby and Walter's daughter and the others. He might think something had happened to the girls, theirs included. A cryptic message like that wouldn't be fair.

Fair? She should worry about what was fair when it came to him? Had he been fair the night he sat down on the pre-Libby sofa and said he was leaving?

Her jaw tensed; heat flared in her cheeks. She stared at her phone. Then she hit the button for *Contacts* and scrolled down to his name. She looked out to the harbor again and quickly tapped the number. Somewhere—in New York or China or Timbuktu—Josh's cell started to ring.

"Devon?" Libby's voice called from behind her. "Is Walter going to pick us up?"

Devon hit "End." She turned and produced a hasty smile for Libby, who sat in a wheelchair that was being steered a young woman in a cherry pink smock. "I'll bring her outside to the curb," the girl said.

Devon nodded and slipped her phone back into her purse.

Candace remained in the Harbor View restaurant, pondering her situation. She wanted to walk down to the lighthouse. She wanted to ask Gil if he had enough money, if he had brought any clothes. But Emmie had fled after her meltdown and was probably in her room. And because Peter had made their reservations, they had the best rooms at the resort: front, harbor view, like the name promised. If Emmie, indeed, was in her room, she might look out her window and see Candace strolling with Gil. She might think Candace had decided to cheat on her husband the way Emmie had cheated on hers. She might think Candace was going to get pregnant, too.

Pregnant! By a stable boy?

Good Lord, Candace thought as she nursed the glass of club soda she'd ordered to replace the wine. What had Emmie been thinking? It was one thing to have a dalliance with her former lover, but pregnant? She'd have to abort, of course. Conlan—gay or not gay—would be devastated by the news. Everyone knew he adored Emmie. And he did have that marvelous castle now.

She shuddered a little and wondered when her world had become rife with castles and art leagues and devoid of the things that really mattered in life, like taking care of her kid brother. She supposed it had been a slow, conscious process.

When she'd first left Jamestown for New York City, Candace had taken a job as an assistant to a caterer. One semester shy of a degree in occupational therapy, she would have had a fine, respectable career if life hadn't knocked her in the courtroom that day.

Luckily, she had worked her way through much of college doing prep work for a food service company in Buffalo. Candace knew the basics. She also knew that caterers often worked parties for influential society people. She decided to use her job as a steppingstone. It wasn't long before she stepped right into the gilded path of Peter Cartwright. Candace had hung up her apron and never looked back.

Until now.

Not that this was her choice.

She looked outside again, but dusk was quickly settling in, and she couldn't see where her brother had gone. She wondered why she had not heard from Devon. Waiting around was giving her too much time to muse, to ruminate, to think about thoughts she had wisely submerged long ago.

Enough!

Signing the check with a flourish, Candace hurried from the restaurant, clipped down the long hall, and stopped under a sign for Henry's Bar. She took out her phone and called Devon. "Where are you?"

"In a taxi," Devon said. "I was going to call when we got to the house."

"How's Libby? The short version, please." The sooner she knew what was going on, the sooner she could deal with her own situation.

Devon gave her the rundown then added, "If Walter's not at the house, maybe you and Emmie can go out and look for him." She suggested a few places she thought he might be.

Candace said she was too tired to start hunting for Walter. Then she thought about the alternative: going to her room, worrying about Gil, wondering what she would do if her—their—secret leaked out. "On second thought," she said, "I suppose we might as well." She told Devon to let her know if Walter was at the house, then she hung up and decided to have a quick drink before she rounded up Emmie.

But when Candace turned the corner and stepped into the bar, there sat Gil, nursing a beer.

He looked up at her and smiled. "Good evening, Mrs. Cartwright." A gourmet-looking burger sat on a plate in front of him.

Her stomach growled: when had she last eaten? She was tempted to sit down next to him, order a burger, and slide back into her role of the big sister. She wanted to pretend that the past years had never happened. It would have been easy except, of course, for Peter. Except, of course, for her future, for Tiffany, and for all the upset Candace would cause if she revealed who Gil really was and how she had ruined his life.

So instead of becoming a big sister again, Candace simply said, "Do you have the car keys? I need to run an errand."

He frowned as if wanting to challenge her. Then he reached into his pocket and pulled out the keys.

She grasped them then said, "Have a good night." She left Henry's Bar to find Emmie, then, hopefully, Walter. Some problems, after all, were more easily resolved than others.

⌒

Half of one lousy beer and he was lightheaded. Gil picked at the burger, wanting to delay tasting it. In his early years at Attica, he'd fantasized about burgers: a Big Beef from Friendly's with lettuce and tomato or a medium-rare creation from Johnny's Lunch. Then, like everything else, he trained himself to forget, forced himself to accept that life on the outside was no longer his, that Pod 17, Cell 3-F was his home. Louis D. had suggested he do that. He had been more believable than the tweed-loving social worker.

"Train your brain," Louis D. had repeated to him more than once.

They'd met in the cafeteria when Gil had been too afraid to look one way or another. He was scared, scared and cold, and his legs were numb. At his first mealtime, he picked what he'd thought was an invisible spot in a corner of the big, noisy room. He sat down on one of the round metal seats that was attached to the long metal table. The next thing he knew, a big muscled leg flung itself over the seat next to his and a lard of a man sat down. From the corner of his eye, Gil could see gray hair, ruddy cheeks, and an armful of tattoos. If Gil had been scared before, he was terrified then.

That first time—lunch or dinner, Gil couldn't remember— the man scarfed down a large bowl of pasta, mopped the sauce with his roll, and never spoke a word. There was no way to tell then that Louis D. would become important in his life. More than important. Vital.

"Something wrong with the burger?" A great-looking redhead who could have been twenty-five or forty-five, Gil had no clue, grinned at him from behind the bar.

"Nope," he said. "Just taking my time."

She nodded. "First time on the island?"

"It's obvious?"

"Actually, no. But your wife looks happier to be here than you do."

"My wife?" Gil laughed, then shook his head. "She's not my wife. She's my . . . employer."

"Oh. My mistake." She winked, then she moved to the opposite end of the bar where a new customer had appeared.

Gil wondered if a woman might consider him reasonably good-looking, if he were one of those men that a woman might say she wouldn't kick out of bed. When he'd been in high school, he hadn't had any trouble getting a girl. His last girlfriend had been Mindy Gleason. Mindy had said he was really cute, but what the hell had that meant? And how did that translate into today's standards, when the cute eighteen-year old was now forty-three?

Louis D. hadn't warned him about how to act on the outside; having been found guilty of murder, the outside hadn't seemed like an option for Gil. When it was over, it happened fast.

"Martin, you're done." The guard had stood outside the cell. He'd motioned to the things Gil had taped onto the wall over his makeshift desk of a wooden plank set atop cinderblocks. "Get your stuff. It's official." He'd tossed him a small duffel bag and waited in the doorway. "You'll get your clothes on the way out."

The lines in Louis D.'s forehead had crumpled together, his thin lips curled back, revealing uneven, brown teeth. "What the f . . .?" They were cellmates by then, lifers. Louis D. was pushing seventy and had been the closest thing to a father figure Gil ever had.

"Wow. Cool," Gil said, his heart starting to pound, his brain trying to absorb what he'd heard. He swung his legs off the mattress and stood up. He'd known that a few people had been working on his behalf—pro bono, do-gooder people—but he'd never let himself believe anything good would come of it. He grabbed the duffel before anyone could change their minds; then he stuffed it with his books and his papers. When he was done, he turned back to Louis D. and quietly said, "Thanks, man. Thanks for being here for me."

Without another word, Louis D. gave him a strong bear hug; when he let him go, there were tears in the big man's eyes. Then Gil was gone, into the bright sunlight where no walls, no barbed wire coils, no tall guard towers would cast shadows on the rest of his life.

He looked at his burger now for another half-second, then he picked it up and took a big bite.

12

Emmie lay on the four-poster bed in the beautiful room at the Harbor View and wondered why she felt as if her life was coming undone. A while ago she'd been startled—then elated—to think she might be pregnant, that she might actually be able to have the life she should have had all along.

It had taken all the courage she could muster first to tell Libby about Boyd, then to tell Candace that she might be pregnant with Boyd's baby. But neither had seemed interested. Without her friends on her side, how could Emmie survive?

Of course, she didn't know for certain that she was pregnant. She'd thrown up in the car, then again at Libby's, then one more time when she'd come to her room. She often threw up when she was under stress, but she'd also done it a lot when she'd been pregnant the first time, when she'd been eighteen, when she'd been married to Boyd. It seemed like a century ago. It was the reason that they'd eloped, that they'd driven Emmie's blue Chevy Camaro convertible (a graduation gift from her parents) across the border into Poughkeepsie. Boyd's uncle Jack lived there, and he'd had a friend who was a Justice of the Peace.

They were married in Uncle Jack's living room surrounded by overstuffed furniture with lace doilies on the armrests and framed pictures of family members scattered atop mahogany side tables. Jack and Aunt Martha were witnesses. Emmie was happier than she could have ever imagined.

They drove to her parents' house and told them the news. The aftermath remained a turbulent blur: shouting and tears; the annulment, the abortion.

She had not argued loudly or strongly enough. She was, after all, her parents' one-and-only, their treasured child, the one gift they'd received that had nearly cost her mother her life, and had definitely cost her the ability to bear more children even though she'd once told Emmie that she'd always wanted a family of seven. Emmie had grown up feeling guilty about that. She knew she'd sneaked off with Boyd because they would have disapproved, because he brought out her "gritty streak" that would deeply disappoint them.

In the end, pleasing them had won out over loving him.

But she was a grown woman now.

She turned onto her side now and cupped the teeny swell of her tummy.

What to do, what to do?

She loved Boyd so much, but this news would crush Conlan.

Her father was gone, but her mother—well, her mother would be sad and distressed. She would not point her finger, she would not raise her voice. She would simply say, "I am ashamed of you." And, on the inside, Emmie would crumble to dust.

She knew she'd have to think of her kids, too.

Bree would side with her father, Emmie had no doubt of that.

Brandon was so much in love with Alana perhaps he would understand his mother's emotions.

The family would be divided. Her wonderful, loving family.

And then there was Boyd.

Being with him again had been harder than she'd imagined. Oh, it was truly romantic and sexy. But it had been painful to tell him she was married. And even worse when he told her he was married, too, that he had three children, two boys and a girl, and that his girl was a champion equestrian who rode in the last Olympics.

Emmie's tummy started to roil again; tears formed in her eyes. How could something so joyous hurt so much and be so confusing?

Just then there was a knock on her door. "Emmie?" It was Candace. "Emmie, open the door. I've just spoken with Devon. Our plans have changed."

Oh, Emmie thought, *right*. They were there, after all, to prop up Libby. Not to help Emmie untangle her life.

⌒

"What do you mean, you don't know if you're pregnant?" Candace asked once she and Emmie were situated in the front seat of the limo. Candace was behind the wheel, skillful or not, and headed toward the boat club. Devon had phoned again and said Walter wasn't at the house, so their mission was to find him. *Pronto*.

"Well, it feels that way." Emmie hushed her voice as if she were afraid someone was listening. "But it's been eighteen, almost nineteen, years since I've been pregnant. It's hard to remember, you know?"

Candace wove the big car through the one-way streets of Edgartown. She noted that the restaurants had changed and, sadly, the Scrimshaw Gallery was gone. But the bookstore still seemed to flourish with bright flowerpots on the front porch and what looked like new, welcoming furniture and a sign that promoted a café around the back. The island, she supposed, was not much different from a small town, not unlike Jamestown, perhaps, with its ups and downs, its old, its new. Ultimately, it survived.

She pursed her lips, hating that she'd thought about Jamestown more often in the past dozen hours than she had in the last twenty-five years. Her fingers gripped the steering wheel more tightly.

"I'm forty-one years old!" Emmie continued. "Is it harder to have a baby at forty-one? Does it hurt more?"

Candace wondered what she'd ever done to turn into the person that others looked to for answers. Was it because they instinctively sensed she was older? Or was it due to all those years she'd spent trying to build her own confidence, trying to act as if she belonged in places she didn't? Had her manufactured know-it-all attitude been more successful than she'd realized? "Maybe it's menopause," she said.

"Menopause? I'm forty-one!" Emmie screeched, as if Candace hadn't heard her the first time.

"Well, okay, then, you're pregnant. How would I know, Emmie? I'm not a gynecologist." She drove through the intersection at Water Street (North and South) and wedged the car down Dock Street to the boat club. She stopped in the middle of the street because it was easier than trying to park. They got out. Candace straightened the fabric of the honey-colored sheath that she'd changed into. With a white cashmere cardigan draped over her shoulders, her Calvin casual flats (those were white, too), and her Van Cleef barrette for added effect, she knew she could pass for an Edgartown summer resident. Plus, with Emmie's natural flightiness coupled with another of her trademark sleeveless dresses with a playful, circular skirt, they created a respectable presentation. Two women who were obviously well-connected albeit driverless tonight.

"We're here to meet Walter LaMonde," Candace announced to the polished maître d' who stood inside the door of the gray-shingled building that jutted out over the water.

"Is Mr. LaMonde expecting you?" He was charming in his best yachtsmen attire. Hopefully he didn't know that the only people Walter might be expecting would be bill collectors.

"I'm Mrs. Cartwright. Mrs. Peter Cartwright. Of New York." She'd learned long ago that those who were truly entitled felt no need to add the word *City*. "And this is Mrs. Malloy. Her husband is Conlan Malloy, heir to Donegal Castle in Ireland."

Emmie curtsied; Candace blanched. Okay, she thought, so the part about the castle was a bit much, even for her. But it was important to get past the gatekeeper. Once they found Walter, they could go home. And Candace could get back to the real world. Well, *her* world, anyway, such as it was.

The maître d' nodded as if he were the guard of the palace. "How nice of you to join us," he said. His tone had changed, however, from inviting to cool. She should have remembered that the Vineyard was less impressed with name-dropping than Nantucket. "Are you planning to join Mr. LaMonde for cocktails or dinner?"

"Either," Candace said. "Both."

He glanced down at a book that stood on a lectern. Apparently there was no techie computer-based reservation system at the good old boys' boat club. "Is Mrs. LaMonde coming too?"

"Not tonight," Candace said.

"She's not feeling well," Emmie said with a sheepish grin as if she were twenty and flirting. *Pregnancy hormones?* Candace wondered and refrained from giving her a swift little kick.

"Well," the young man said, returning the grin with one of his own that had turned caustic, "I'm afraid Mr. LaMonde isn't here at the moment. Perhaps you'd care to wait?" He gestured toward a wooden bench that probably was reserved for those who did not measure up.

"No," Candace seethed, "We do not care to wait." She spun on her flats and exited the club, angry that she wasn't on her own turf where the name Peter Cartwright always gained admission.

Back in the car, she gunned the engine. "I can't believe you flirted with the maître d'. And you curtsied! When we get to Main Street, we'll stop at the corner."

"Do you think Walter will be there?"

"I doubt it. But the Edgartown Paper Store is there. You're going to go buy a pregnancy test."

Devon was in the library putting the books back into some semblance of order and reminding herself that she hoped one of her so-called friends would be there for her if she ever went through what Libby was going through now. Then Candace called.

"Walter is not at the boat club. I don't suppose he showed up at the house."

"Not yet."

"How's Libby?"

"The same. I made mushroom omelets. Then I gave her a sedative and a glass of sherry and sent her to bed. Hopefully she'll sleep through the night."

Candace sighed. "How the hell are we going to find Walter?"

"I don't know. Where are you now?"

"Sitting in front of the Edgartown Paper Store. Emmie ran inside to get something."

Devon dropped onto the desk chair where she had found Libby. "Maybe we should call the police."

There was a brief pause, followed by a solid, perfunctory, "No. No police."

"This could be considered an emergency, Candace. A medical emergency. The police might have better luck finding Walter. For one thing, they probably know him, or know people who know him. They might have a better idea about where to look."

"*No.*"

That time, Devon pictured Candace's jaw as stiff as a clay facial. She was too tired to ask why.

"All right," Devon said. "Then I think I should stay here tonight. I'll sleep in the room next to Libby's in case she needs me. Is my suitcase still in the trunk?"

"No. It's at the hotel. In your room."

"Can you have Gil bring it over?"

At first, Devon thought they'd been disconnected. She supposed that dropped cell service wasn't uncommon on an island. But as she was about to hang up, Candace said, "You don't need your suitcase, Devon. Libby has everything in every one of her guest rooms. Toiletries, a robe, whatever. Besides, the Mercedes is there if you need anything. Or if anything happens and you need to leave."

Over the line, Devon heard the limo door open and close. Then Emmie exclaimed, "Damn! They don't have any! They told me to go to the pharmacy, but it's already closed for the night."

Candace said, "We'll go in the morning."

"What's wrong?" Devon asked, and Candace said, "You'll know soon enough. Believe me, you'll live until then." She clicked off, and Devon was left staring at the library bookcases wondering again why, if Candace had always been such a pain in the ass, she kept her as a friend. Devon's phone rang again: she figured it was Candace calling back. But when she glanced at the screen the callout read: GREGORY, JOSH. She tossed the phone on the floor as if it were an envelope loaded with anthrax. What in God's name had she been thinking when she'd called him?

13

Though Emmie wanted to have dinner at the hotel, Candace fibbed and said she wasn't hungry, that she was going to order a bowl of chowder from room service and take a long bath. The truth was, she did not want to listen to anymore of Emmie's tale of infidelity and her potential state of maternity. Not tonight. Not after this long day. Besides, she had other plans.

Once she was certain Emmie had gone to bed, Candace went downstairs to the cozy, fireplaced-lobby and slipped out the back-door. She tiptoed toward the motel-like building that was pleasant but missing a prime view. Peter had booked their "driver" there instead of in one of the pricier rooms.

She knocked on Gil's door as if she were a call girl sent up from the streets, though she supposed there were few, if any, of those on the Vineyard, and, in any case, they would not be welcome at the Harbor View.

He opened the door without asking, "Who's there?"

"I could have been anyone," she scolded as she moved past him into the spacious, nicely furnished room that had been decorated in the soft hues of sea glass.

"Anyone sinister wouldn't have knocked."

She walked toward a small table in the corner. "Devon wanted to call the police," she said. "Under the circumstances, I don't think that's a good idea."

"Under what circumstances, Candace? Under *my* circumstances?"

She sat in a well-upholstered barrel chair. "They could recognize you. Maybe your picture has gone over the wires."

He laughed. "I'm the one who's been locked up. But even I know they don't do things by 'wire' any more."

"You know what I meant."

He cocked an eyebrow as if he were surprised at her abrupt remark.

Candace closed her eyes. "Sorry, little brother. But Devon knows your name. She asked me if you could bring her suitcase. If *Gil* could bring her suitcase. How the hell does she know your name?"

"I have no idea. Maybe you told her. Maybe I did."

"It wasn't me." She watched as he crossed from the door and sat on the edge of the bed. She folded her arms, feeling foolish for grilling him. "When did you talk to her?" Tension rippled through her body, but she was so godawful tired she barely felt it.

He shrugged. "I don't know. Oh. Wait. On the ferry. Right. I introduced myself to her on the ferry."

She inhaled. "Did you say your last name, too?"

"Jesus, Candace, I don't know. No. No, I'm sure I only said 'Gil.' I didn't think you'd make a federal case out of it."

She let out her breath. "You promised," she said. "You promised you wouldn't say anything."

He stood up again, walked to the glass doors, and pulled back the drapes. Outside, it was dark. He did not seem to care. "What kind of a life do you have, Candace? Where you have to hide from things that used to matter?"

He had no way of knowing that was a question she'd asked herself more than once over the years. But how could she explain how frightened she'd been when she'd first moved to the city? How alone, how lonely, how frightened she'd been living in a fourth floor walk-up that looked out over an alley where rats ran freely and grown men often peed? She could not tell him because surely he'd experienced worse. And he'd had no caterering job, no wealthy people to dupe, no way out—literally or figuratively.

"I did what I had to," was all she could say.

She sat in silence; he stood without moving. Then he said, "You thought I was guilty, didn't you? You never came to see me because you thought I killed him."

Candace supposed there were many things in life that people wished they could go back and change, things they could do differently, say differently, respond to differently. She wished she could have gone back to that courtroom and lied. She wished she had said, "Gil came home at ten o'clock that night. He was sound asleep when I checked on him a few minutes later."

Another thing she wished she'd done differently occurred in those moments right then, right after he'd asked: *You thought I was guilty, didn't you?*

But Candace sat there too long, waited a couple of heartbeats too long to respond. By the time she opened her mouth to deny it, Gil had moved outside onto the balcony with his back to her.

"Close the door on your way out," he said.

Emmie stood at the window in her room, gazing out at the *flip-pause-flip* of the lighthouse signal. She texted Bree and asked if the girls were having fun, which of course they must be. Tiffany would be shopping, Julie would be sightseeing, Bree would be monitoring what they were spending, and Alana would hopefully be falling in love with Brandon, who would be taking good care of them all.

Bree hadn't answered the text. It was late in Europe now: all the children must be sleeping soundly.

She wondered again how her son and her daughter were going to feel when they learned about the sins of their mother. Were they old enough to understand true love? Would they forgive her for loving Boyd more than she loved their father?

"Mommy, how do you know when you're in love?" Emmie had asked her proper Lexington-born mother not long after she had met Boyd. Her mother had been in her dressing room, getting ready for the Daffodil Gala, the annual hospital charity ball. Spring break had arrived. Emmie had longed to stay at Miss Porter's, spend her days riding, and her nights hanging out in the stables. Her protective parents, however, had said no, that she was too young to be alone while her classmates had gone home.

Her mother sighed and straightened the shoulder pads of her long, sequined top. "You will know, Princess," she said, then kissed Emmie's cheek. "When you find love, you will know." She checked her watch, said she was late, and left Emmie standing in front of the big, full-length mirror before Emmie could ask if it would be okay for her to have sex.

Flip-pause-flip, the lighthouse signaled again.

Then Emmie's text alert buzzed.

HI, DARLING! R U HAVING A GREAT TIME? MISS U HEAPS. XOXOX.

Only Conlan called her "Darling." Conlan. Not Boyd.

A knock came on her door, followed by an announcement: "Room Service." But Emmie was no longer hungry.

116

In the morning, Candace woke up famished. She quickly showered, dressed, and put on the walking shoes she was grateful she'd packed. She hadn't slept well; her thoughts had kept tumbling, trying to devise a new plan. She called Emmie who said she was not only up but also out, sitting on the veranda, sipping tea.

On her way to Emmie, Candace stopped at the front desk.

"I'd like to leave a message for Gil Martin," she said. "Tell him his services won't be needed today, that he is free to do whatever he likes." She handed the clerk an envelope. "And please see that he gets this." In it she had tucked three of the one hundred dollar bills Peter had put in her purse. She included a note telling Gil to use the money for clothes or whatever he needed and to charge his meals to his hotel room bill. She could have slipped the envelope under his door, but she didn't want to risk running into him: She'd decided she could not effectively deal with Libby, Emmie, and Gil all at the same damn time. Something had to go, or at the very least, be delayed, until she could strike a few items from her Things To Do list.

"Go change your shoes," she said to Emmie when she found her on the porch. "We're going for a walk."

Emmie looked down at her red canvas stiletto sandals. "But these shoes match my dress." This morning she had donned a white summer frock with red diagonal striping from the turned up collar to the hem of the umbrella-like skirt. She looked like *Alice in Wonderland*.

"We're going to Libby's. You can't walk that in those things. Did you bring any flats?"

Emmie pondered a moment. "I don't own any flats."

"Well, something lower then? Something more . . . sidewalk-appropriate?"

But Emmie shook her head, her light curls dancing as she did.

It came as no surprise that Emmie didn't own flats, anymore than she would not be accustomed to walking. Unlike Candace, she'd no doubt had drivers since she'd been a child: people who picked her up, dropped her off, toted her from one destination to another. She'd probably never had to walk back and forth to school, to the community center to pick up her kid brother from Cub Scouts, or to the supermarket to buy groceries for the family. No, Candace thought, of course Emmie did not "walk."

"If you can make it to Libby's, she must have something in her closet. I think her feet are close to your size."

When Emmie stood up, she barely reached Candace's shoulders. Candace realized then that perhaps the woman wore high heels because she was so petite.

"Can't we go in the car?"

"No. I gave our driver the day off. The streets of Edgartown are too narrow for me to drive that monstrous car. Last night damn near killed me. And us." There was no reason to elaborate that she'd decided the Town Car drew unwanted attention. She feared they'd created too much of a scene last night at the boat club and left people to gossip about her snobby demeanor and Emmie's ridiculous curtsy. Candace knew that she and her entourage needed to cause less attention.

Slipping her long purse strap over her head, Candace adjusted it diagonally across her newly-enhanced breasts that today were concealed under a linen jersey short-sleeved cardigan (pale peach trimmed in off-white). She had buttoned the sweater and was wearing a pair of matching, white capris, which were socially "legal" now that Memorial Day had passed. Candace, after all, was a champion of Emily Post, and though she knew times had changed, good etiquette was still good etiquette. "We'll stop for muffins on the way," Candace added. "Who knows if Libby has any food in the house."

"Will we go past the pharmacy?"

"Emmie, please. You know how much I detest melodrama. Let's tackle one thing at a time." She set off down the stairs out to the sidewalk, which was charmingly red bricked but very uneven. Emmie caught up and wobbled next to her without complaint.

"You brought muffins but not my make-up? Or my clothes?" Devon was on the sun porch. She wore one of the thick terry robes that Libby always hung in the guest bathrooms; she had showered and washed her hair in a wonderful, sweet-smelling shampoo: She had wanted to ask Libby where she'd bought it, but wasn't sure if the woman would remember. According to some research Devon had done last night by squinting at her iPhone (thankfully, someone in the neighborhood must have known it was not 2003 and offered a WiFi connection), if Libby had a dissociative fugue she might repress her memory for a long time to come. Curiously, Devon read on more than one website that the victim often wandered from home. Was it possible Walter had the same condition?

"I told you to take Libby's Mercedes if you needed anything," Candace answered, but her reply seemed thin and concocted on the spot. "It's not like you're stranded on Gilligan's Island."

Under other circumstances, Devon might have found the comment amusing. Instead, she said flatly, "I couldn't find Libby's car keys. When I asked her, she just stared out the window."

Then Emmie interrupted. "We couldn't bring your suitcase, Devon, because Candace made me walk." She looked down at her bare feet. The bright red polish on her left big toe was scuffed. And she was holding her shoes.

"You walked? From the Harbor View?" Devon wasn't certain, but she thought the hotel must be a mile or more away.

"Oh, what's the big deal," Candace said. "A little exercise never killed anyone." She adjusted the diamond barrette that held back her hair. "No word from the missing husband?"

Devon decided not to comment on Candace's foul mood. "Julie sent Walter's number this morning before the girls left the Lake Country for Ireland. I called, but got voicemail. I left a message. I said it was an emergency. I'm sure he'll call soon." She was not, of course, sure of anything.

"Unless he doesn't have his phone with him," Candace remarked, then added, "Maybe it's hiding in the same place as Libby's. If we knew how, we could probably ping it." She gestured toward the mug of coffee on the end table next to Devon. "I hope you made a pot." She took the bag of muffins and went into the house.

"What's with her?" Devon asked Emmie. "She's more strung out than usual."

Emmie dropped onto a chair. "You tell me. You'd think she was the one who is pregnant."

It took a few seconds for the comment to register. They all were over forty, after all, and *pregnant* was a word they had not said in years, unless it was about other people's grown-up (or nearly grown-up) kids. Devon leaned forward. "Emmie, are you pregnant?"

Emmie set down her sandals, rubbed her feet, and started to cry. "I don't know for sure."

Devon chose her words carefully, trying to determine what she'd like a friend to say to her if the shoe—or in this case, the high-heeled red sandal—was on her foot. "Wow," she said at last, "this is amazing. You must be excited. And Conlan! He's always been so good with the kids."

"Oh," Emmie said, "it isn't his."

That's when Libby showed up in the doorway, holding half a blueberry muffin. "This is fun," she said. "I didn't realize we were going to have a girls-only weekend."

Devon shook her head and stood up. "If you will excuse me, I'm going to put on yesterday's clothes and walk to the hotel to get clean ones." She left the porch and her friends and went upstairs to change. One of them, after all, needed to stay relatively sane.

14

Candace came from out of nowhere and caught Devon on the stairs. "There's no need to go to the hotel," she said. Her cheeks were pink; her words were rushed. "Throw on something of Walter's. A polo shirt and a pair of slacks." At least she didn't comment that Devon was a size eight and Libby was a two, which would be why Walter's clothes would fit better.

"I am not going to put on men's clothing," Devon said. "I doubt you would either."

"Then wait until everyone's had breakfast and we'll go together. Libby might enjoy the walk."

Devon could have pointed out that while it might be fine for Libby, the last thing Emmie probably would want would be to retrace her steps in heels. "No, Candace. I'm not going to wait. I wouldn't have to leave at all if you'd brought my things." Enough said. She continued up to the guest bedroom and slipped into her day-old clothes. She sneaked down the back stairs then out the side door, thus avoiding Candace. She waved good-bye to Emmie and Libby, who both sat on the porch, each looking lost in thought.

Cutting around Libby's Mercedes, Devon scooted down the driveway, glad for the fresh, solitary air, determined not to waste time obsessing over why Candace was behaving exceptionally badly or who Emmie's lover was and why she'd come to the island without comfortable shoes. To Devon, being on the Vineyard was synonymous with the kind of leisurely strolls she'd had with her father when her mother was rehearsing at the Tabernacle. Years later, when she'd returned and Josh and Walter were at the golf course, and Libby was having her nails or her hair or some part of her done or re-done, and Julie was dressing up dolls with Alana and Alana's nanny, Devon recaptured the magic of those unhurried walks: she navigated the maze of narrow streets and dirt paths; she skipped among the grassy dunes and teal blue water; she let the sunshine fill her with warmth, balance, and contentment. Those kinds of strolls could not be managed in stilettos.

She realized then that since her father had died she preferred walking alone, especially on a morning like that when she could let the magic of the island—her mother's "heart home"—envelop her. Devon had missed coming here these past couple of years. She had missed the way the light stretched its long fingers through the picket fences; she had missed skipping stones across the waves at Fuller Street Beach; she had, quite simply, missed the peace of the place.

At the Main Street intersection, she crossed from South Water to North, passing the banks that flanked the corners and the shops that showcased pre-season finery through sparkling windows.

In the muddle of the last few years, Devon had forgotten how much she loved it there. Nothing had ever changed that, not even the hideous incident that had occurred the first time she and Josh visited Libby and Walter.

Julie and Alana turned three years old that summer. The girls were a delight: adorable and playful, perfect hints of the young ladies they would become. It was a wonderful trip. Together the families went sailing, rode bicycles, and scoured South Beach for purple wampum. They prowled through the bookstore (especially the kids' section), gorged on ice cream, and shucked countless ears of corn. It was a perfect vacation until the night Walter got drunk.

She winced now as she walked by the art gallery and the fudge shop. She remembered the ugly scene. The two couples had gone sailing at dusk. They'd had cocktails on the boat, then trundled back to the house and talked about making dinner. The nanny had already tucked the girls in for the night; Libby said she'd check on them then jump into a comfy caftan before making a salad. Josh said he needed to make a business call from the library (dependable cell service was still spotty on the island); Walter went into the kitchen to spin a blender of margaritas and find the lighter for the gas grill.

Devon decided to use the outdoor shower. Having grown up in Manhattan and Sleepy Hollow, neither of which had such unique, open-air plumbing, she'd always felt that an outdoor shower was a wonderful indulgence.

Slipping out of her swimsuit, she turned on the water: It was delicious, smooth and cool; she closed her eyes and let it trickle through her hair, down her neck, her shoulders, and the rest. And then, an arm encircled her waist. She thought it was Josh. But a voice that wasn't Josh's whispered, "Ssssh. I'm supposed to be starting the grill."

She opened her eyes. Wide. She wanted to scream. Walter was naked. He laughed and held his hand over her mouth. "Don't wake up our babies." With his other hand he grabbed her breast. He bent down and grazed it with his tongue. She tried to pull away. He grasped her butt and jerked her close. "I've wanted you all day," he said. He pushed himself against her; she felt his penis. It was small but bouncing with anticipation.

She smacked him across the face. "You are a filthy pig," she hissed. She grabbed the towel she'd draped atop the stockade fence enclosure, threw it around her trembling body, and stormed across the lawn.

Moments later, she tried to tell Josh. At first, he laughed. Walter LaMonde would not do such a thing, even if he'd had too much to drink. He was far too dignified. Maybe it was Devon who'd had one cocktail too many (she had not).

Then Devon began to cry. The lines that skirted Josh's brow grew deep; his eyes grew dark and angry. "Wait a minute. *Are you serious?*" His fingers curled into his palms.

Her anxiety multiplied. She thought about how much she loved her husband, how much she loved their marriage, how much she loved their life. If she made a big deal out of this, everything would crumble. Josh would erupt at Walter. They would tear out of the house and off the island and Julie would lose her playmate and maybe the other girls, too, because who would believe the word of the daughter of an English professor and a minor opera singer against the word of a respected man whose family had been well-connected for generations?

If she ratted Walter out, sooner or later, Josh would be angry with her. Men had a way of doing that, Devon knew, of turning the tables to avoid putting any potential blame on themselves. He'd be angry with her; he might say that she'd led Walter on. The incident—and its earthquake of an aftermath—would be perceived as having happened because of something she had said. Or done. Or misunderstood.

Besides, she reminded herself, Walter had been drunk.

All those things had sped through her mind at Star Trek speed as Josh stood beside her with his darkened eyes and balled fists.

"You're right," she finally said, averting her eyes. "I must have overreacted. I am too sensitive."

His hands relaxed. "Well, geez, Devon, don't do that again. Walter is my friend."

They rejoined Libby and Walter; they ate steaks and salad, but neither Devon nor, she noticed, Walter, had a margarita. And no one mentioned the outside shower.

Her eyes stung now, as she thought of how, for so many years, she'd been pretending that the incident had never happened. She wondered what Josh would say today if he knew the truth—not that he'd recall the situation, he'd become so self-immersed. When she'd tried calling him from the hospital last night, her name must have showed up on his Caller ID, which was why he'd called her back. But he hadn't left a message because things always had to be on his terms, when he had time.

Well, she thought, screw him. Screw all of them.

Shaking her head as she walked, Devon folded her arms around her waist to keep the hurt of Walter and Josh and the life she'd once loved deep inside her. Then she looked up and saw Gil walking toward her. He looked freshly-showered and shaved; his gray eyes glimmered in the new morning sun; his smile was soft and gentle and kind.

"Good morning," he said. "I'm looking for a cheap place for breakfast. Any suggestions?"

That's when Devon—sturdy, independent, in-control Devon—dissolved into pent-up, aching tears.

Gil put his arm around her and guided her from the sidewalk down a slight slope to a bench outside the old tavern, The Newes. Devon was glad it was too early in the day for it to be open: she loved everything about the place, from its great, fun food to its authentic eighteenth-century charm complete with brick walls, a wide, shallow fireplace, broad floorboards, and low-beamed ceilings. It was sociable, snug, and romantic—all the kinds of adjectives she didn't want to think about just then.

"I am so sorry," she said, once she regained her composure. "It's been a long couple of days. Please forgive me."

"Nothing to forgive. If I'd been stuck with your friends for very long, I'd wind up in tears, too."

Devon laughed. "You push a lot of boundaries for a driver."

He shrugged. "Few things are often as they appear. But I'm sure you know that."

"I don't know much of anything right now. Other than I came here to try and help a friend, and I've wound up feeling sorry for myself." She studied the landscape: The Newes was attached to the Kelley House, a white clapboard hotel trimmed in forest green shutters that dipped in perfect harmony with the terrain of the street. The pub had served guests of the hotel since Edgartown's vibrant whaling days when massive, wooden boats had clogged the harbor and rum-thirsty fishermen required frequent hydration. She'd once heard that the hotel was haunted. She wondered if that was what was wrong with her now: her spirit was being haunted by her past.

Gil touched her shoulder. "Take it from an expert. Feeling sorry for yourself is a total waste of time. Even if you have all the time in the world." Then he crossed his legs and folded his hands atop his knee. "As for me, I am very hungry," he said. "Which brings me back to my original question. Do you know a good breakfast place around here? Even better, why don't you join me? My treat."

Devon laughed again. Around the corner was the café, Among the Flowers. She'd often stopped there after her solitary morning walks. "There's a nice place on the next block." She pointed south. "And thanks for the invite, but I'm still in yesterday's clothes." She did not elaborate. She'd probably said too much already.

"Ah," he said. "Well, I can't leave you until I'm sure that you're all right. It's the first rule in the Driver's Code of Ethics."

She smiled again and looked down at the sidewalk. "I'm fine, now. Thank you. I'm sorry if I caused a scene."

"I'd hardly call it a scene. If this were the middle of summer, I'd expect you'd have had more witnesses. But I'm betting that today there weren't enough people around to have noticed or cared. Candace will be grateful for that. I'm sure you know how she detests public displays of emotions." With that, Gil stood up.

"Candace? I didn't realize you were on a first name basis with your employer." Her words had jumped out before she'd edited them.

Gil put his hands into the back pockets of his khakis. "You'll have to ask her about that. If I say anything else, she'll have to shoot me." He nodded once. "Have a nice day, okay?" Then he strolled away.

Devon watched him go, sensing one thing was for certain: as Gil had said, few things were often as they appeared.

15

Emmie was in the kitchen, putting ice on her bare feet. Candace leaned against the chair rail in the hallway that linked the sun porch to the kitchen. She wondered if Emmie was really pregnant, and if so, if her husband really wasn't the father. Candace had never cheated on Peter; she never would. Their marriage parameters, although unspoken, had been clearly defined: she supported his love of charities and functions and his quirky brain-wiring; in return, he supported her need for security, both financially and emotionally. She knew that today the concept seemed old fashioned, but she couldn't help it. She would do anything to keep her marriage successful, anything to avoid having to work two shifts the way her mother had.

But Emmie? No one should blame her. The woman might insist that Conlan wasn't gay, though with his recent inclination to wear Irish kilts on special occasions, Candace supposed it wouldn't be out of the question.

Then she wondered why she was worrying about Emmie when there was so much to do.

Looking out toward the porch, she saw Libby sitting, facing the harbor, staring vacantly as if she were in a coma. As much as Candace wished she hadn't made this trip, she reminded herself that Peter had forced the issue. He'd said that good friends were the backbone of our society, or something equally corny. But, corny or not, she actually liked to please her husband. She needed to stop acting as if helping Libby was a waste of time

131

and patience. After all, she was hardly qualified to judge another woman's situation.

With a long, resigned sigh, Candace decided to try and talk to Libby. Maybe instead of being coddled, the way Devon had been doing, the woman simply needed some no-nonsense conversation. Something to jolt her back to reality. Besides, between getting Libby to a neurologist in Falmouth and trying to find Walter, they could be tied up for days. No matter how important good friends were to Peter, Candace had her limits.

Meandering onto the porch, she sat down across from the woman who thought George Bush was still the president. "Libby?" she asked. "How are you feeling today?"

Libby smiled. "I'm fine. How are you?"

She looked fine enough. She wore a little eyeliner and lipstick and was dressed in newly pressed beige pants and a short-sleeved, chocolate silk shirt. She looked fine enough to attend a luncheon at the boat club. Devon must have seen to all of that.

Candace leaned forward. "Libby, what the hell is going on?"

Libby's eyes widened. "What do you mean?"

"Please cut the crap. Be straight with me."

"Oh, Candace, you worry too much. You always have." She fanned herself as if it were August. "The girls will be fine. They went with Walter, didn't they? To the beach? To the park? To the carousel?" She blinked several times. Her small shoulders squared. Candace braced herself in case Libby erupted. "Oh, that must be it!" Libby suddenly yelped. "Walter has taken them to the carousel!" She seemed to relax then, perhaps having found solace in her explanation.

"No, Libby," Candace said, keeping her tone decisive and firm. "Our girls are eighteen now. They are no longer three.

Walter didn't take them anywhere because they are in Europe. And Walter isn't here."

Lowering her gaze, Libby picked at the pretty yellow cushion on the white wicker chair.

"Libby," Candace continued, "where is Walter?"

"Stop it, Candace. Stop bothering me."

Bothering her? Apparently Libby had no clue that she was the one being the bother. Candace sat back in the chair and rubbed her temples.

"Listen to me, Libby, I did not want to come here. I should be in New York. Supporting my husband. But we thought you were in trouble. We thought you could use some moral support. But you seem to be surviving in your own little world." She stood up again. She'd had enough frustration for one morning.

"Go ahead," Libby said quietly. "Leave if you want to. You never did like playing games unless you were sure that you could win."

"Games? Is that what this is? A charade? Have you been acting all along? Trying to make us believe you've lost your mind as well as your money? Well, I'm here to tell you that you can save your breath. We know you're broke."

Libby laughed. "I'm afraid you're mistaken. Croquet will be the only game played today. As soon as Walter comes home with the girls. But what a strange thing to say, Candace. Walter and I are hardly, as you say, *broke*." She tipped her head back and giggled as if she were Emmie. Then she sat up straighter. "Oh, wait. We *did* lose some money."

Finally, Candace thought. She expelled a small, hopeful whoosh into the salt-dusted air.

"That roofer, you know? The one who was going to tend to the guesthouse. We gave him a deposit, but he never came back.

Marshall said we hadn't signed a contract so we could kiss our money good bye. That, and the fact the man left the Vineyard and who knows where he went. Once they're off the ferry they can disappear to Boston or Rhode Island or even up north. Almost anywhere."

Marshall was an attorney who, unfortunately, had been dead for a decade. Candace covered her face with her hands.

"Is that what you mean?" Libby asked. "Did you find the roofer? Did you get our deposit back?"

Hopeless. It was hopeless.

"Libby? Where are your car keys?" Maybe Candace could still succeed where Devon hadn't. If she had the keys she could at least begin to search for Walter. She'd comb every restaurant and bar in Edgartown if she had to. Someone must have seen him in the last couple of days.

"Walter must have taken the car. It's not here."

"Of course it's here, Libby. It's parked right outside."

Libby cocked her head toward the window. "That isn't our car. Ours is black. And it's a whole different style."

Candace would have ranted, but she knew it would have been pointless. Instead of ranting, she turned on one heel and stomped from the porch back into the house in what Peter would have called a "huff." "Don't go off in a huff!" he'd scolded on more than one occasion when she'd been exasperated by his emotional peaks and valleys and his OCD behavior. She certainly knew he couldn't help it, but sometimes the way he flossed his teeth over and over or lined the spice jars in the kitchen like battalions of soldiers at attention simply drove her nuts.

She huffed her way now from the hall to the library. Maybe she'd find Libby's car keys in the desk. Or maybe she'd find some of Walter's papers: a calendar or an address book, if anyone used address books anymore and did not rely solely on their smart phones or tablets. Surely she might find a clue—local names, numbers—*something* that would suggest his whereabouts.

Ripping open the center desk drawer, she quickly rifled through a smattering of papers that seemed to have been tossed willy-nilly: a receipt from Donorama's for several new shrubs not yet delivered, an estimate from a window cleaner, a propane delivery slip. She found pens and paper clips, a pack of chewing gum and . . . a key! But, no, it was a small brass key, not the kind that worked in an ignition.

Damn.

She wondered if it were possible that Libby's car had one of those keyless entries she'd heard Peter talking about with one of his business cronies. "A damn nuisance," the crony said. "Must have been invented by a Democrat."

It would be like Libby and Walter to have something that was a damn nuisance.

She slammed the drawer then yanked at the one on the left. It was locked. She suppressed a growl. Then she wondered if the small brass key might gain her entrance. Not that the car keys would be in there. Not that she'd find an old-fashioned address book.

In a flash she retrieved the brass key and, *voila*, it opened the large drawer. At least the contents seemed well organized: file folders stood in hanging racks, stickers on the tabs were neatly labeled.

Candace supposed she shouldn't comb through Libby and Walter's papers. She would not, after all, want anyone doing that with her things. But still . . .

The first file held bank statements, the old fashioned, printed kind, not downloaded from the web. Candace sucked in her breath. Should she steal a look?

Of course she shouldn't.

But, of course, she did.

Savings account: balance $682.43.

Checking account: $213.31

Morgan Stanley account: $0.00.

Goldman-Sachs: $0.00.

Fidelity: $0.00.

Zero. Zero. Zero. There was no indication what the balances had been before the zeros.

A sick feeling swelled in Candace's stomach. She wished she hadn't seen the numbers; the reality was as disturbing as if she'd come across a wounded animal that had been a friend's beloved pet. She did not want to see more.

As she pushed her knee against the drawer, it stopped halfway. Something seemed lodged in the track. Jiggling the drawer open again, she reached inside and snatched a folder that had been jammed. A letter slid out. Well, not exactly a letter. It was a note, scrawled on a crisp, half-sheet of stationery. The words read: *Dear Libby, Forgive me?* It was unsigned.

Candace shivered. She wondered if the note was from Libby's cousin Harold from the South, the one who had trashed their fortune.

Families, she thought, can wreak so much havoc.

With a final forlorn look, Candace shook her head, shoved the note back into the file, then put the file back. No matter what her own problems were, she would not trade them for Libby's. No way. No how.

Devon had had enough walking—and musing—for one morning. "I was hoping you'd give me a ride back to Libby's," she told Gil. She'd found him sitting at an outdoor table at the breakfast café she had recommended; she hoped she looked better in clean clothes and make-up. Not that she needed to look good for a driver.

He pushed his coffee aside. "I was awarded the day off."

It took her a second to realize he was teasing. It had been a long time since she'd noticed when a man was acting playful with her. Except, perhaps, for the man in the elevator of her building, if saying he was *en route to Cleveland* could be considered being playful.

"I'll pay for your time," she said.

"I noticed there's an island bus." A twinkle in his eyes belied what he was saying.

"With my luck I'd end up in Nantucket."

"That could be a slightly damp trip," he said, draining the coffee from his mug. "But it could be an adventure."

Devon pulled out a white wrought iron chair and sat down. "Being here is enough of an adventure. I don't know what's happened to Libby. I don't know if or why her husband has disappeared. I also don't understand your relationship with Candace, but I do know it isn't my business." She had no idea from where she'd gotten the nerve to bring up *that* subject. Maybe he'd opened the door by having been so friendly. Too friendly.

The left corner of his mouth turned up ever so slightly.

"Ah, yes" he said, "Candace."

"The point is," Devon said, "I don't know everything, nor do I need to. I used to think I was pretty perceptive. But lately, I give up." It was a ridiculous conversation, but now it amused her. As her mother had often said, "You'll never know how well you can sing unless you step onto the stage." "But," she added, "I do need you to drive so I can stop at the pharmacy."

"You don't drive?" he asked.

"Not a limo."

"Coffee?" A young woman stood beside them, a silver pot in hand.

Devon kept her gaze fixed on Gil.

His gray eyes narrowed but his smile widened. "Check please," he said. "It seems that I'm on call."

They went back to the hotel, and Devon followed Gil to the Town Car. He opened the back door and gave a little flourish with his hand, signaling her in. She laughed, stepped around him, and opened the door to the front passenger seat where she quickly planted herself. Candace and Emmie could do whatever they wanted, but Devon was not going to be chauffeured around the island as if she were Prince William's Kate and the Vineyard was downtown London.

He circled to the driver's side and got behind the wheel without commenting on her defiance.

She directed him around the hotel and out the back streets toward Upper Main.

"You know your way around," he said, though it seemed more like an observation than a request for conversation.

It was true, she thought, fighting the inclination to slide into her memories again. She did know her way around the Vineyard, certainly well enough to know how to get to important places like the hospital and the pharmacy. During one of their summer visits with Libby and Walter, Julie had come down with strep throat and the pediatrician had prescribed antibiotics. Another year Devon had intentionally left her birth control pills at home, then had a wave of guilt and was able to obtain an emergency supply to get her through the trip. Josh had made it clear he did not want another child. He loved Julie very much, but he said another child wasn't necessary. Devon often wondered if he'd been fearful she would have a boy who'd compete with him at sailing and golf. Josh had never liked losing.

She wondered if his new woman was, indeed, much younger, and if she would succeed at getting him to agree to have more children. She gripped her hands around the strap of her handbag.

He'd called her again about an hour ago. He'd texted twice. She hadn't responded, so he'd stopped trying. He wouldn't have wanted her to think he cared about her anymore.

"Which way?" Gil asked.

Devon blinked. They had reached the fork that split the beach road from the inland route that crossed to Tisbury, the road Candace had wanted to avoid due to the small houses with old cars in the yards.

"Either," Devon said now. "The pharmacy is in the middle of the 'V.'" She pointed to the triangle of land that bisected the road.

He stayed on the right, then made a left into the parking lot.

"I'll only be a minute," she said.

Inside, the compact store looked as she remembered it, with aisles that were crowded and too narrow. She wound her way toward the back where she thought she'd find the pregnancy tests. She was right: they were on the shelf at eye level, displayed next to the condoms. Apparently a store clerk had a sense of humor.

She scanned the shelf, then glanced around, as if she were still a mortified teenager and was buying tampons. Or worse, like when she'd been a college student picking out condoms because her boyfriend—a sexy young poet named Danny McDonnell—had been unreliable about that. He would not have minded if Devon had gotten pregnant.

She grabbed one of the tests without inspecting it. *Good grief!* she scolded herself. *Why the heck was she thinking about Danny McDonnell now?* He'd been long gone from her life before she'd met Josh. The last thing she'd heard, he headed a creative writing program at the university of a midwestern state. Not that she cared! She quickly went to the checkout and plopped the box on the counter. But as she dug out her money, she realized why she'd thought about Danny: he'd had gray eyes, the same color as Gil's.

Stop!

She must have said it out loud because the girl behind the counter looked slightly startled. "Do you want something else?"

Devon dropped her gaze to the shelves below and moved her eyes from the candy bars to breath mints. Then she saw the Sunday *New York Times*. "This," she blurted out. "Yes. I want this, too." She quickly paid for the items. Then she stuffed the tiny parcel into her purse and, with newspaper in hand, she threaded her way back through the aisles and headed for the front door.

⌣⟶

A lot of the guys in Attica saved up the pittance that they earned from working in the kitchen, the laundry, the heads, or wherever, and spent it on magazines and cigars. Once in a while Gil splurged on a stogie and slowly puffed out in the yard, the only place where smoking was allowed. He'd never much liked the taste or the way it burned his throat, but he'd found it provided a decent way to pass some time. "Makes for good, contemplating time," Louis D. often said.

As he watched Devon come out of the pharmacy now, all Gil could think of was what he wouldn't give for one of those stogies. Not that he wanted to think too long or too hard, but he sure would enjoy the pleasure of sitting back, contemplating the view, and reminding himself how damn happy he was to be out, to be free, to be part of this beautiful, though sometimes fucked up world.

16

"I didn't find anything," Candace told Emmie who was in the kitchen continuing to swab her red toes with a towel-wrapped bundle of ice. "I ravaged the desk in the library. No car keys, no address book. No calendar to offer one lousy hint as to where the master of the house has vanished."

Emmie didn't answer; she simply glared at Candace, then returned to her swabbing.

"Look," Candace said, softening her tone, "I said I'm sorry I made you walk here." If they were going to solve this problem they had to stick together. Libby, after all, was clearly not going to be any help. Through the kitchen window that looked out onto the porch, Candace could see Libby still sitting like a terra cotta warrior, staring toward the croquet lawn as if she were on drugs, which, Candace remembered, she now was.

"I'm not surprised there was no calendar or address book," Emmie said quietly. "Most people put everything in their phones now."

Candace decided not to mention she'd already thought of that.

"So?" Emmie asked. "Should we call the police?"

Candace jerked her neck so quickly it should have snapped. "The police? Why should we call the police?"

"Because Walter is missing."

Her pulse sped up. Her palms went as cold as the ice atop Emmie's toes. "We don't know for sure that Walter is *missing*. We

143

only know he isn't here." She did not want the police around. Not with Gil close by. What if they asked questions? What if they insisted on seeing identification? They might figure out who he was and where he'd come from—then what would happen? She tried slowing her heart rate, but the air was too shallow, she was inhaling and exhaling too fast. "We don't need the police, Emmie. For all we know, Walter's in New York."

"No," Emmie replied. "He's here." She removed the towel and examined her pedicure. "Devon said Alana told her that her parents were here. She wouldn't have said 'parents'—*plural*—if Walter wasn't included." She dumped the ice down the sink, squeezed the towel, and draped it across the faucet. "Alana heard from her mother on Thursday. If something had happened, Libby would have told her then."

Sometimes Emmie could be perfectly exasperating. Just when one thought she wasn't paying attention, she remembered the damndest things. At last, Candace's anxiety eased. "Well, if Walter's on the island, where did he sleep last night?"

Emmie raised both thin, recently threaded eyebrows. "Maybe he stayed with a lady friend."

Candace raised her brows in return. "No, Emmie. Walter wouldn't sleep at another woman's house. Especially now, with their future so . . . questionable." There was no point in saying she'd often wondered about Walter, that on occasion he had seemed a little too friendly toward her.

"People cheat on each other for all kinds of reasons," Emmie continued. "After losing their money, maybe having an affair was the only way he could think of to prove to himself that he's still alive."

"You have sex on the brain. All this talk about being pregnant with a groomsman's child."

"So you were listening. You do remember the story about Boyd."
God help her, her face lit up as if she'd been crowned with a tiara.
"Please, Emmie. This isn't the time. We're here to help Libby, remember?"

Emmie wiggled her swollen toes and returned to her petulant pout.

Candace was relieved to change the subject. All this talk of adultery made her uncomfortable. "We should make a list of the places Walter might be. We're on an island, for God's sake. That should limit the search."

Emmie wiggled again. "Maybe he's dead."

Candace refrained from suggesting that perhaps Boyd would be dead if Conlan learned he was his wife's lover. "Quiet!" she warned, pressing her forefinger to her lips and gesturing toward the sun porch.

"She won't understand what we're talking about," Emmie said. "She's not exactly in this world."

"It doesn't matter. Don't talk like that." That said, it wasn't as if Candace hadn't considered the possibility that her friend's state of confusion would be permanent. But Emmie was Emmie and sometimes she said and did things without having thought them through.

Emmie leaned closer. "He could have been distraught," she whispered. "He could have had a heart attack and fallen off his boat and is lying at the bottom of the harbor or something." Her words accelerated. "Or he could have killed himself, Candace. God knows what any of us would do if we woke up and realized we were broke."

Well. It seemed that Emmie had *thought it through* that time. Still, it was difficult to tell if she were serious, or if she'd become as delusional as Libby.

"Which is why," Emmie continued, "we must call the police." Candace began to protest again, but she was interrupted by the sound of tires crunching on clamshells.

Emmie watched as Candace scooted from the kitchen out onto the sun porch and into the driveway where Peter's car was now parked and Devon and the driver were getting out.

"I gave you the day off!" Emmie heard Candace shout at the driver.

Sometimes, being around Candace gave her a headache.

Turning from the window, Emmie picked up her shoes. She wondered if Peter would win the Board Chair of the Art League, and if that would make Candace even bossier. Not that it mattered: bossy or not, Candace would no longer be her friend if Emmie divorced Conlan and married Boyd. She was pretty sure about that.

For the two hundredth time or more since breakfast, Emmie let the fantasy play out in her mind: if she were pregnant, they wouldn't wait. She'd withdraw money from her trust fund to buy a horse farm, maybe in Virginia; they would raise fine chestnut mares and bring them to Saratoga because she'd always loved that town with its colorful shops and fabulous restaurants, its cathedral pine forest, its magnificent amphitheater, and its public baths. Yes, Saratoga would be best. Belmont was too close to the city, Pimlico was in Maryland (who on earth went to Maryland?), and Churchill Downs was in Kentucky and no doubt had a clique that would be hard to crack.

New York would be their turf for racing.

The horse farm would be spectacular with lush, rolling hills and the finest, cleanest stables and a lovely main house perhaps of Georgian architecture. Brandon and Bree would visit them often; they would be able to stay in the cozy guest cottage if they liked, away from the commotion of a young family. There might, after all, still be time for Boyd and Emmie to have another child after the one she might be carrying now. Yes, there might still be time before she was too old.

Even better, this baby might be twins! Her mother's father had been a twin—didn't that count for something?

Excitement scuttled through her.

Emmie would finally be free from always trying to appease her friends, like Candace. She would not worry about disappointing her mother who would be fourteen hundred miles away. She'd be released from what had become a nearly-sexless marriage. She'd have no have-to-do's or ways to behave. She would have the love of her life in her life forever.

Of course, she would miss the castle in Ireland.

And she would miss Conlan. In spite of his flaws, he was caring and kind and he really loved her and, no matter what anyone thought, he was not gay. They just didn't have sex very often anymore because how many married couples did after twenty years? Yes, she would miss Conlan. But . . .

Her fantasy was cut short as Devon appeared in the kitchen, looking better than she had earlier that morning. She tossed a newspaper onto the counter and handed Emmie a small bag.

"One pregnancy test," Devon said.

Emmie took the bag. "Oh," she said. It slipped from her grasp and landed on the counter on top of the newspaper. "Oh, my."

"It's what you wanted, isn't it? So you'll know one way or the other?"

Emmie couldn't very well tell Devon that, no, it was not what she wanted, not really, not if it meant she'd learn that she wasn't pregnant, that her made-up world had merely been that. And if the test said she was—*wow!*—was she really ready to know?

"Emmie?" Devon asked.

"Maybe Candace is right. Maybe it's just menopause."

"Do the test. Then you'll know."

A thousand or more images rushed through her mind: of Conlan, of Boyd, of castles and stables. Then Emmie thought about her "special work"—the babies she rocked back and forth at the hospital nursery on Tuesdays and Thursdays. *At-risk Neonatal,* they were called. Babies that needed extra care, extra love. Emmie was one of the "cuddlers," who rocked, who sang softly, who gave extra comfort when their mothers could not. Emmie had been a cuddler for years. It was how she'd tried to make up for the abortion, how she'd tried to help other babies who might not feel wanted.

If she were pregnant with Boyd's baby again, she would not let this one be taken away.

She picked up the bag. "Yes. Of course I want to know if I'm pregnant. Absolutely."

Still, she remained standing in the kitchen, which was rather foolish, because she wouldn't very well do the damn test right there in the open. "I'll just go into the powder room."

Devon nodded. "Good idea. I'll be on the porch trying to talk to Libby."

"Devon?" Emmie added as Devon started to walk away. "Thank you. How much do I owe you?"

Devon shook her head. "My treat," which was really nice, because everyone knew Devon now worked for a living.

As she left the kitchen, Emmie grabbed the front section of *The New York Times* in case she was tied up for a while. She had no idea how long one of these tests took to work. It wasn't as if she were pregnant every day.

Candace grabbed Gil by the elbow and ushered him toward the guesthouse and the croquet lawn away from the main house and the women. "Don't you get it?" she fumed, her voice cracking a little. "I can't have you here. Please, Gil, you're making this so difficult."

"I was happy to have the day off. But your friend put me into service. Something about needing a pharmacy."

Candace rubbed the back of her neck. Devon must have picked up a pregnancy test for Emmie. Would this godawful weekend never end?

"Well, then, thank you. You've done your good deed. So unless you know how to hot wire a Mercedes, you can go now."

He laughed and sat down on the bench where they had sat yesterday. "Sorry, they didn't offer that class in prison. And, by the way, I didn't learn lock-picking there, either. I learned that from Bobby Benson back in Jamestown when we were in the eighth grade. We broke into the Dairy Mart one night and stole two cases of candy bars. I was so scared I peed my pants. So much for my life of crime."

Candace stared at him as if seeing her brother for the first time. Bobby Benson had looked even more angelic than Gil. Especially in the eighth grade.

"I was always surprised I didn't bump into him at Attica," Gil continued. "I wonder what ever happened to him."

She looked back toward the house then put her hands on her hips. She could have told him that years ago she'd learned Bobby had gone to college and gone into finance and that today he worked in the city. She could have said he probably had more than enough cash now for candy bars. But she didn't want to upset her brother. "I do not want to have this discussion," she said. "I'd like you to leave. Go back to the hotel. Go sightseeing. I see you bought clothes."

He looked down at the new chinos he wore—they were navy that day—and plucked the hem of the pale blue Polo shirt. "I didn't buy them. They were a gift from a group of sympathizers who are somehow connected to the parole board. Three pairs of pants, five shirts, and enough socks and underwear for a week. Plus sneakers. And a jacket." He seemed to enjoy running through the list of his wardrobe. "I hid my bag in the shrubbery before I knocked on your front door. I didn't want your husband to think I planned to move in."

At that point he sort of grinned, but Candace couldn't tell if he was still angry with her. "Whatever," she said. "That's of no consequence now. What matters is to find the car keys. Then I need to find Walter."

"That's right. Walter. The husband."

"Walter the *missing* husband."

Gil went silent, but remained seated. Then he asked, "Have you looked under the front seat of the car?"

"For Walter?" In spite of herself, Candace smiled.

In return, Gil smiled that half-smile she knew had always been so attractive to the girls back in Jamestown. "Or the car keys," he said. "Whichever you think might fit."

"Who would leave the keys to a Mercedes under the front seat?"

"Well, it seems that car thefts must be kind of rare here. How would anyone get off the island undetected? They checked your license plate at the ferry. And you showed your ID, remember?" He shook his head. "And not that you want me to, but I'd be glad to help look for the husband. I promise I won't ruin your good time by ratting myself out. Or you, for that matter."

She gave up. Whether or not her brother was still angry with her, he was hopeless. "First, let's see if the keys are in the car."

He leapt to his feet and scanned the flowerbeds. "And I'll pick some flowers for your friend on the porch. That way, the others might think we walked out here for flowers and not for anything suspect."

Exasperating. First Emmie, now Gil. Candace shook her head then started toward the house as Gil stepped into the newly-blossomed, purple and white phlox. Candace heard him snap one, two, then three stems. Then he suddenly cried, "Jesus, Mary, Mother of God."

She turned back. "What now?"

"Jesus," he said again. He had stopped snapping phlox stems and was staring into the dirt. "Candace, you need to call the police."

She laughed. "No. We are not going to call the police. I've already been through that with Emmie."

But he stood rigid, no longer amused. "I mean it, Candace. Call them. Now."

An ominous feeling inched up her spine. "Why?"

"I think I've found the husband," Gil said. "Face down. As in 'not moving.' Dead."

17

Candace let out a blood-curdling, hair-raising scream worthy of a John Carpenter film. She ran toward her brother: How could she not? He had crouched down and now held up his hand as if to shield her from the scene, but she had to see for herself.

Even from the shape of the body's backside, she knew it was Walter. No one still wore plaid Bermuda shorts like the ones he had on. No one, but Walter LaMonde.

"It's him."

"Go to the house," Gil said. "Call the police."

But Candace couldn't move. "Did he have a heart attack?" she asked, because she could think of no other explanation as to why a perfectly healthy (as far as she knew) man in his forties (or maybe fifty?) was lying face down in the phlox.

"Jesus, Candace. Do I look like a medical examiner?"

"There's no need to get pissy. I asked a simple question."

"And I told you to call the police."

"We can't call the police. You know that."

"Candace. A man is dead."

"Then we'll call an ambulance. We don't have to involve the authorities."

His eyes traveled from dead Walter up to his sister. "Because of me? Because you're afraid the cops might recognize me? Come on, Candace, this isn't New York."

"As I said before, you don't know who knows what. Someone might have found your story newsworthy. It might have already gone viral." She thought that would counteract his earlier, wiseass comment when she'd mentioned his picture going over the wires.

He stood up. "I am not going to argue with you. We don't need an ambulance. We need the police."

"Why? If Walter had a heart attack, why do we need the police?"

"He didn't have a heart attack, Candace. There's a puddle of what looks like dark blood that spread from his armpit and ran down his side."

"Blood?"

"Yeah. The red stuff that would have come out if he'd been shot. Or stabbed. Or whacked really hard with something sharp. Anyway, it's mostly dried-up, so my guess is he's been dead a while." He stepped out of the flowers and faced her. "I'm going to the house now to call the police."

Her thoughts raced. "No. No. I'll do it, Gil. You need to get out of here. You need to get off the property. You need to get off the island! If you aren't here they won't be able to ask you any questions."

"Candace, I was exonerated, remember? As in, they found the real murderer so I was set free?"

She chewed that morning's lipstick from her lower lip.

"Right," he said. "It's not just the cops. You're still afraid that your friends will learn who I am."

But before Candace could answer Emmie came running from the sun porch waving what looked like the front page of the Sunday *New York Times*. "Oh, my God!" she breathed in short, frantic gasps. "Oh my God! Our driver is a convict!"

Emmie hadn't seen Gil standing behind Candace. As he moved into her view, she stopped dead in her barefoot tracks. "Oh," she said. "Oh."

"Oh, indeed," Candace said.

Emmie shoved the newspaper behind her back as if that might help her take back her words.

"Don't come any closer," Candace said.

Emmie's heart must have stopped beating because everything suddenly seemed pretty fuzzy. She wondered if their driver—Gil, the newspaper said his name was, Gil Martin—was holding a gun on Candace. It was definitely him. The picture was amazingly clear: He even had on the same clothes he wore now. The article said he'd been let out on new evidence, that his conviction had been overturned, that he had been set free from Attica after having served twenty-five years for a murder he supposedly did not commit. Behind her back, her hands started to tremble.

"Walter is dead," Candace said.

Emmie wanted to respond, but her vision was growing fuzzier, and her head was feeling as if she were going underwater.

"It looks like he's been shot. Or stabbed. Or something. Suicide, maybe. Or murder."

Emmie dropped the newspaper, then fainted.

Devon yelled *"What the hell's going on?"* when she saw the commotion, dashed from the porch and caught up in time to pull Emmie up off the ground before she ruined her dress.

"Walter's dead," Candace said. "Gil is going back to the hotel, and I'm going to call the police."

Emmie started to stir. Devon stood her upright. "Walter is dead?"

"In the phlox," Candace said and gestured in that direction.

"Candace wants me to leave," Gil said.

Emmie picked up the newspaper and waved it at Devon. "It's all here," she said. "Our driver was in prison for murder. And now Walter's been killed!"

Candace turned a slight shade of parchment and Devon feared she'd be the next one to drop. Devon looked at Gil.

"We don't know how he died yet," he said. "But I didn't do it. After twenty-five years and DNA evidence, I finally was exonerated. I'm not a murderer. I never was."

The three women and the ex-convict stood in absolute silence and then Libby called to them from the sun porch. "What's happening? Did you find Walter?"

⟵⟶

Devon decided they could deal with the issue of Gil later, after they'd phoned the police, after they'd quieted Libby, after Walter's body had been zipped into a bag and removed from the premises. After they'd all had a chance to think.

It was hard, however, to picture Gil killing anyone, let alone Walter. Gil hadn't even known him, had he? But what was Candace's relationship with the "convict," as Emmie had so indelicately called him?

First, they must take care of Walter.

Gil drove off in the Town Car. Devon handed Emmie off to Candace and told them to go back to the house. Then she took her phone from her pocket, glanced at the screen and saw that Josh had called again.

"Right," she said with crisp sarcasm, then quickly called 911.

Three police officers arrived, two males and one female. They all had brown hair, pug noses and penetrating, dark eyes. They had square shoulders and square bodies and were of similar height, Devon guessed about five-eight or nine. They looked so much alike she wondered if they were related.

One of the males called for the ambulance, but said there was no rush and no need for the siren. Then the other male officer (who apparently was in charge) told them he wanted to talk to the person who found the body. He said it appeared the man had been shot straight through the heart, and that it did not look like suicide.

"I didn't find him," Devon said. "You'll have to ask Candace. Libby is in the house; she's Walter's wife." Devon supposed she should have said that Libby was Walter's "widow," not his wife. "Look, officer," she said, "you should know that Libby is not feeling well. She's suffering from a kind of amnesia. We took her to the hospital last night, but we're waiting to bring her to Falmouth tomorrow to see a neurologist. Actually, we'd hoped Walter would have been able to bring her so we could all go home and leave Libby to him." She wondered if that made any sense to the officer, who merely looked at her without expression. She cleared her throat. "We're from New York," she added. "New York City." As if that clarified anything.

He made a note on a small pad. "When did the victim's wife develop this 'kind of amnesia?'"

"I don't know. We arrived yesterday around two in the afternoon. That's how we found her. She thinks Bush is still the president."

He looked up from his notes. "What?"

"She thinks it's 2003."

His dark eyes narrowed, but he made no comment. "She's in the house?"

"Yes. Yes. Go ahead in. Our other friends, Candace and Emmie, are with her." Devon wasn't sure if she should go inside with him or stay on the lawn while the other cops scoured the flowerbeds and the shrubbery. She was surprised that they'd wasted no time in stretching yellow tape between the garden bench and the starting croquet stake and that it simply read "Do Not Cross" and not "Crime Scene."

She shifted her position and let her feet settle into the ground. She watched as the officers marked and measured and muttered about trajectories and timelines and speculation about where the weapon might have gone. She wondered how many homicides had taken place on the Vineyard—if any— and if the State Police would step in to assist. There were State Police barracks in Oak Bluffs, around the curve from the hospital. Josh had always laughed about that. "They learned their lesson from *Jaws*," he said. "The local constables don't exactly need major crime-solving skills." Humor had not been one of Josh's finer talents.

Devon sighed. She wondered how Libby was taking the news, and if Candace was at least being kind. Her gaze fell back to Walter, dead in the dirt, the backs of his arms and legs a washed-out shade of cardboard. She thought she should feel some sympathy, some sorrow, but how could she? The best she could hope for was that no one would ask her, "What was your relationship with Walter LaMonde?" She was not sure she could mask the disdain from her face.

Still, barring that single shower incident, Libby and Walter had remained outwardly friendly to Devon, not counting the understandable, "couples only" shunning when she and Josh had split up. And the girls . . . *Oh, my God,* Devon suddenly thought. *Someone will have to tell Alana! She will have to come home!*

She spun away from the body and yanked her cell phone from her pocket again. Then she stopped. The girls were in Ireland now. Hadn't Emmie once said there was no cell service at the castle? That Brandon planned to use that as an attraction for people who wanted to escape technology?

Devon groaned. She was sure Alana must love her father, the way Julie loved Josh. Still, if the girls couldn't be reached for a few days that might not be the worst thing. Maybe Libby would have returned to her right mind by then, and mother and daughter could grieve together. As Libby was now, if she thought Alana was only three, she might get even more confused when the young woman arrived. She might retreat even more deeply in time.

"Makes no sense," the female officer now said from her squatting position in the dirt. She called to Devon. "Are you ladies the only ones here?"

Devon gulped, then hoped the officer didn't notice. "Yes." She stammered, ever-so-slightly, and took a step back toward the flowers. "We'd been trying to locate Walter, but . . ." She blinked. In the last few seconds, Walter had been turned over and now lay face up in repose, as if he were basking in the warm Vineyard sun. His plaid Bermudas were covered with dirt, and a purple blossom was stuck to his yellow golf shirt right near a dark maroon stain—*Oh, God,* Devon thought. *That was blood. Walter's blood.* She cried out, then looked away.

"Well, I'm no expert," the female cop said, "but none of you ladies appear to be the type to wear sneakers. And it sure looks like a fresh, rubber-soled footprint in the soil. A big one, too. About a man's ten-and-a-half or eleven."

Before Devon could dream up an answer, the Edgartown Ambulance pulled into the driveway and parked behind Libby's Mercedes. Two paramedics got out; a man in a black t-shirt followed. The shirt had white letters that plainly, unmistakably, read: "Duke's County Medical Examiner."

18

Libby didn't know what to think or what to do. Her head hurt a little, and she couldn't remember anything. Not since . . . well, she wasn't sure when.

And now, Walter was dead.

She leaned against the down pillows that Candace had plumped up across the headboard, then straightened her legs on the crisp white duvet that she didn't remember buying. She thought her bedcover was blue—a pale blue comforter that matched pale blue drapes with tiny cranberry flowers that had once been at the windows but had somehow, sometime, been replaced with white cotton ones that hung from round pewter rings across plain pewter poles. They were elegant in a simple way, but she didn't remember them.

Candace had waited until Libby was settled before she'd told her about Walter.

Then a policeman had come into the room while Libby cried. He asked when she had last seen her husband, if he had any enemies, and how long she had been ill.

She said she wasn't ill, merely in shock, her husband was dead, after all.

Candace suggested he come back later after Libby had rested.

He left the room and Candace said she would get Libby a small glass of Bordeaux. "It might help you sleep," she said.

So Libby was alone now, with the white drapes tightly drawn, filtering the bright sunlight of the afternoon. She wondered where Walter had been, if not at the carousel in Oak Bluffs with the girls.

And where were the girls? Where was Alana? Devon and Candace and Emmie were all there, so Julie, Tiffany, and Bree must be around somewhere. Unless . . . unless . . .

No! Libby could not, must not, think dark, awful thoughts. Besides, her friends did not seem terribly upset. Surely they would be beyond consoling if their daughters were missing, too.

Walter, she thought. *Walter. Why are you dead? How will I go on without you?* An ache crept from her stomach up to her throat then pushed silent teardrops from her eyes.

Of course, she'd never really loved him. Their marriage had been arranged by their fathers, a merger that succeeded in saving the faces of both their families. Libby's father had explained it: his business was tobacco and was teetering on ruin unless he could diversify; Walter's family was from steel in the north. His parents were eager to have their son settle down with a respectable girl before he impregnated another impoverished teenager (at that point, there had already been three) who might demand not only money but also a ring.

Libby had married Walter to save her father's business; Walter had married her for daily, respectable sex that was hoped to tame his too-frequent erections. The funds had been lumped into one fatted pot.

She sniffed back another tear and wondered how it happened that she could remember all of that but had no idea of the last time she'd seen him. She knew he hadn't come home last night when Devon was there; nor had he been there the night before when she'd sat up all night in the library, though she did not recall why she had done that.

And Alana? Where was darling Alana?

Libby cried out and held onto her stomach just as Candace came back into the room bearing a tiny glass of *claret*, as her mother called the red wine in honor of their British ancestors who had also done their share of squandering the family jewels and the fortune in order to maintain a façade of looking prosperous. When her grandfather's wealth had run out, her mother had married the tobacco man, then given birth to Libby, the child who would be counted on to sustain the fortune. Libby always suspected that "marrying for the good of the net worth" occurred in the best upscale families.

"Where are the girls?" she demanded to know now. "Why won't you tell me?"

"Our daughters are safe," Candace said as she handed Libby the glass along with another pill. "Believe me, Libby. If they weren't, none of us would be hanging around."

"But where are they? Where is Alana?"

"Alana is with Tiffany and Julie and Bree. They're visiting with Emmie's family, don't you remember?"

Candace seemed sincere.

"On the island? I didn't know Emmie's family had a place here."

"Trust me, Libby. We decided that the girls should stay together right now."

Libby didn't understand, but she supposed she had to trust Candace. She really had no choice, now that Walter was gone.

Walter.

She swallowed the pill with a sip of wine. "Walter is dead," she said.

"Yes," Candace confirmed. "He is."

Libby drained the glass and handed it back. Then she closed her eyes. She didn't want to think about that anymore.

Emmie had been sitting on the toilet, trying to relax, holding the test wand in position with one hand, and the newspaper in her other, hoping that reading might distract her.

She'd finally started to pee when she spotted the picture of their driver on the front page. The headline read: CONVICTED MURDERER RELEASED. An accompanying photo showed a close up of a man leaving prison in upstate New York. She recognized everything about him right away, including his fresh pair of sneakers.

She'd shouted, "Oh, no!" or something like that. She'd jumped up, dropped the stick into the toilet, pulled up her panties, reassembled herself, and fled the bathroom with the paper still in hand.

By the time she returned to the bathroom, the test wand had sunk to the bottom of the porcelain bowl, its announcement of "Yes" or "No" fully drowned, unreadable.

Candace sat on the small boudoir chair, waiting for Libby to doze off.

The police had asked Libby what Candace presumed were standard questions. But her answers had been strange and disconnected. Mostly, Libby had admitted she wasn't sure of anything. Then she had cried, and Candace had suggested that the police come back later.

She wondered if they should contact Libby and Walter's current attorney, if, in fact, any of them could figure out who it was. She doubted she could find a name among Walter's papers. Hell, she hadn't even been able to find a damn set of car keys.

She watched her friend. She wondered what she would do if Peter and she suddenly lost all of their money, if Candace then learned her husband was dead.

But Peter was very much alive and, as far as she knew, they were still very wealthy. Her only job was to protect all that she'd worked so hard to accomplish including—and especially—her daughter's future. Tiffany's life was just getting started. Candace couldn't, wouldn't, ruin it for her.

It wouldn't have been surprising if the tabloids had latched onto his story. But *The New York Times?* Candace hadn't expected that.

Now she had to convince Devon to wait before calling the girls. Tiff could not come home until Gil was out of the picture, living in a different city and state.

She couldn't call Peter, either. He would want to come to the Vineyard and take charge of the situation and arrange all the details. He was the largest of the men in their group, in both physique and social standing. Peter used his stature to be the lead dog, the patriarch, even though that duty should really have fallen on Conlan, who was the eldest.

If she didn't call Peter he'd wonder why she hadn't.

But could she convince him to stay in New York?

Not a chance.

Which meant she'd first have to get her brother off the island. She could tell Peter that the driver had needed to return to the city, that she'd paid his ferry and bus fares and sent him on his way. Peter would buy that. He could be so gullible to her little lies, starting with the first when she'd told him she'd been an only child, orphaned at seventeen, and had moved to the city to start a new life.

God help him, or her, he'd believed every word.

She heard a whimper now, as if someone were crying. It had not come from Libby; across the room, Libby was asleep.

Candace closed her eyes, put her hands to her face, and wiped two tears that had run down her cheeks.

"Is that yours?" the female officer asked Devon as she pointed to Libby's car.

"No. It's Libby's. Mrs. LaMonde's."

"How long have you been on the island?"

"Yesterday. We came yesterday."

"How many of you?"

"Three of us. We are Mrs. LaMonde's friends."

"Was Mrs. LaMonde feeling all right when you arrived?"

"Actually, no."

"Did she pick you up at the boat?"

So there it was. A loaded question that Devon knew Candace would not want her to answer truthfully. Devon did not know why Candace had made Gil go back to the hotel. Why was she trying to protect him? Like Emmie, did Candace have a lover? Was it Gil—an ex-con? Suddenly she remembered his gray eyes, the color of the sea when the clouds hung overhead. Gray eyes. The same color as Danny McDonnell's back in college. The same color as . . . Candace's.

Were Candace and Gil related? Was Gil Martin Candace's . . . *brother?*

"Well?" the officer pressed. "Did Mrs. LaMonde pick you up at the boat or not?"

"No," Devon said quickly. "We have Candace's Town Car. It's back at the Harbor View. Candace wanted to walk here this morning." It wasn't a lie. Not really.

"You're staying at the Harbor View? Not here with your friend?" That question came from the cop who'd gone inside to question Libby but now had returned.

Devon fidgeted. It wasn't her place to tell the police that Libby and Walter had lost all their money, that the women had come to give Libby girlfriend support. Was it? But was it right to conveniently disregard that Gil had been with them? That he'd been their driver? "Libby wasn't expecting us. It was a . . . surprise. We didn't want to put her out." She had no idea if she sounded convincing.

Both officers left her and walked over to the Medical Examiner who seemed finished with what he'd been doing. He directed the paramedics to remove Walter's body. Devon turned away; she did not want to watch.

That's when Emmie emerged from the house, strutted toward Devon, wagging her cell phone in her hand. "I'm going to call Ireland."

"What?"

"There's no cell service at the castle, and I don't think Brandon has had land lines installed yet. But I can call a pub in the next town. They can get a message to Brandon to call me. Alana needs to know what has happened."

As if the situation wasn't bizarre enough, now Emmie seemed to want to be in charge. "Emmie, no," Devon said. "We don't even know what happened here yet."

"We know Walter is dead."

"But we don't know how. Or why. Or who did it."

"That's for the police to figure out. In the meantime, Alana needs to know that her father is dead and her mother has gone off the deep end. The girl is eighteen. She's a grown woman. We must not treat her as if she's a child. Believe me, I speak from experience."

Devon wondered if Emmie had used the test kit and if her new-found attitude was a side effect of the results. Then she decided she'd rather not know. Not then, anyway. "Did you call Conlan?" she asked. "Did Conlan tell you to call Alana?"

Emmie shook her head. "I don't want to talk to Conlan until . . . until I know if I am pregnant. No, Devon, it might surprise you, but I figured this out all by myself."

"Well," Devon said, "before we tell the girls, we should ask Candace for her opinion."

"Why is she always the one who ends up making the decisions? Besides, I'm beginning to think Candace has lost her marbles, too. Really, Devon, think about it. Why would she hire a driver who's a convict? A murderer, no less? It said so, right there in the *Times*."

Because he is her brother, Devon could have said, but bit her tongue. "We don't know if Candace knew who he is. Or was. Besides, he was exonerated, wasn't he?"

"Like that matters? He's spent years in prison, Devon. With all those . . . all those *other* people. He probably has tattoos. Did you see any tattoos? I think they all have them, like it's a rite of passage."

This was not the time for Devon to discuss the prison system or the pastimes of the inmates.

"Besides," Emmie chattered, "Candace shooed him out of here in an awful hurry. Which tells me she knows more than she's saying."

Devon sighed. "Emmie, let it go. If Candace is somehow connected to our driver, it's really none of our business. Besides, it's obvious he'd never been to the Vineyard until he came here with us. Whatever happened here happened before we arrived. So, please, just let it go."

Emmie opened her mouth as if to say something else just as the ambulance backed out of the driveway and another vehicle—an Island Taxi—drove in. The taxi ground over the clamshells and parked. Josh Gregory got out and slammed the door.

19

"What the hell's going on? What's with the ambulance? And the cops?"

It only took one nanosecond for Devon's stomach to knot; another for her meager breakfast to flip-flop inside her. "Josh," she said. "What are you doing here?" She would have approached him, but her better sense warned her not to.

"You tell me. You're the one who called." As he walked toward her, she could see that his jaw was set tightly. He wore a navy suit, but the collar of his shirt was open. He must have shed his iconic silk tie en route. "You didn't answer when I called you back last night. I spoke with Julie. She said you were here with Libby and Walter. She said something might be wrong." He halted a few feet in front of her, out of striking distance.

Devon supposed she should take him aside, explain what had happened to Walter in private, give him a chance to collect himself once he learned that his golfing buddy was dead. But how much of a chance had he given her to *collect herself* when he'd walked out on her? Within what had seemed like minutes he'd announced his departure to their daughter, then to all their friends. On top of Devon's shock had come humiliation. And though she hadn't sought payback, this opportunity was too ripe to miss.

"Walter is dead," she said abruptly. "It appears he's been murdered."

171

For a moment there were no sounds, not even from a lone gull or a piping plover. Josh's eyes glazed; the corners of his mouth turned stiff, bloodless, white. He touched the buckle of his belt as if he wanted to reach inside and grab hold of his penis for whatever reason men did that when they needed primal comforting. Or self-protection.

Payback was sweet.

"How?" he asked. "Who?"

"Who knows?" Emmie cried, flapping her hands. "For all we know, the chauffeur did it!"

"Emmie, please," Devon said quickly. "I can handle Josh."

That's when Devon felt three pairs of eyes—cops' eyes—drilled into the back of Devon's head. She turned to them. "This is my husband." She didn't say "ex" because he wasn't that yet, and she didn't want to add unnecessary details to the situation. "Will you excuse us?"

"Sure," the cop-in-charge said. "But I'll have to ask all the ladies not to leave the island. Not until we have some answers." It was a classic line taken straight from one of those old TV cop shows that had hypnotized Devon while she'd been prone on the couch.

She led Josh away from the activity, across the lawn, around toward the back of the house, to the outside shower where her mishap with Walter had occurred so long ago. She truly hadn't done that on purpose: She was, in fact, so rattled by seeing Josh, she might have inadvertently led him off a cliff if one were nearby. She stopped on the flagstone and leaned against the cedar enclosure that wobbled against her weight.

"I thought you were away," she said, folding her arms and trying to stand erect so the fencing wouldn't crash down around them. "I thought that was why you missed our daughter's graduation."

"Jesus, Devon. Walter has been murdered and you want to talk about Julie's graduation?"

She steadied her gaze on him, refusing to turn this into a power struggle.

His gaze shifted from her toward the harbor. "I came back this morning. After I talked to Julie, I rerouted my trip from New York into Logan. I took a limo from Boston to the ferry."

It would be nice to think he'd done that because he was concerned about her, that he thought something might be wrong with the woman he'd once married, the mother of his only child, as far as she knew. But more than likely, Josh was worried something would happen before she signed the damn divorce papers and his independence would be postponed.

"Do you know about Libby and Walter?" she asked. "That they lost their . . ." she paused, searching for a word that was of Josh's world, ". . . portfolio?"

He nodded. That's when Devon realized he'd been dying his hair. The silver threads that once dusted his temples were completely gone. *Younger*, she thought. His new woman must definitely be younger. She looked away.

"I talked to Walter on Thursday," he said. "I'd thought about going to Miss Porter's with them, but he said they weren't going."

So Josh had wanted to go to Julie's graduation. And he'd needed Walter as support. His *posse*, Emmie might have said because of all the women, she was the one who kept up on the latest, hippest conversation, thanks, no doubt to having a twenty-one-year old son—a boy who was currently sleeping with Libby's daughter. Devon pulled her mind back to the issue at hand and followed Josh's piercing gaze toward the harbor. Her eyes, however, stopped on the guesthouse where they'd been so happy the last time they had been there.

"Julie said Libby was sick," he said. "Did you fabricate that instead of telling her Walter was dead?"

Josh Gregory had been a lot of things. The "con" side of the list of his characteristics was too long and too painful for Devon to dwell on. But on the "pro" side, he'd been a good father. For a time, he'd also been a good husband, at least as far as she had known. It went without saying that he'd been a good provider. But would he have come all the way to the Vineyard because he was truly worried about his friends? She would not have put compassion or altruism high on the list. "Physically, Libby is fine," she said. "But she has some sort of amnesia. She thinks it's 2003." Devon wondered how many more times and to how many more people she would have to say that before this was done.

His eyes flicked back to her. "Do you think Libby shot him?"

Her cheeks flushed. "I don't know. Do you?"

Their eyes locked and glared. Finally she spoke again. "Amnesia happens for a number of reasons. Maybe she saw someone kill Walter and was traumatized."

"Or maybe she was traumatized because of their financial losses. As I recall, Libby liked to spend Walter's money, didn't she?" He snorted.

Devon wanted to punch him in the nose. Then she realized she'd never thought Josh paid much attention to anything the wives did or did not do. He'd usually been too consumed with himself and his own agenda.

"We have no idea what happened to either of them, Josh," she said as coolly as she could manage. "I called you last night because I wanted Walter's cell number. We couldn't find him, and we needed him to take care of his wife." The last part of her sentence came out sounding terse, as she had hoped.

"Well, that's too bad," he said, matching her brusque words with his. "I thought you wanted to talk about us."

"Us?"

"I thought you finally were ready to stop being a pain in the ass and sign the goddamn divorce papers." With that, he turned on his seven hundred dollar Ferragamo loafers and headed toward the back door of the house.

Candace knew she needed to call Peter and tell him about Walter before he heard the news from someone else, or worse, before he saw it on television or read about it on the electronic tablet of which he'd grown so fond. Now that the *Times* had the story, Peter—or someone who knew them—might read it and piece things together. Maybe the media would dig up an old photo of Candace—the girl who'd gotten her brother convicted.

She was standing in the upstairs bedroom window, pondering that, when she realized she was looking down at Devon who was standing by the outdoor shower, talking to Josh. When had he arrived? Thank God Gil had gone back to the hotel. Candace had never cared much for Josh: She'd always thought that his ego was the size of a large beach ball and just as inflated.

Still, she'd been dumbfounded when he'd walked out on Devon. She'd once thought that if a marriage in their circle went on the rocks, it was an unwritten rule that the couple stuck it out for the sake of the houses and the lifestyle and the perks that being "significant" entailed. They did not discuss their troubles with one another; they merely made their union work. Some, she supposed, stayed together for the kids, though that had become a tedious reason these days. As for Candace and Peter, well, they'd been lucky. They were—always had been—a good match, well-suited in thought and deed, if not in heritage.

Josh had apparently left Devon because it had been "time," or, at least, that was what he'd told Peter. Devon had only told Candace that he was gone.

She felt a small ache for her friend now as she saw Josh march toward the house, leaving Devon alone to watch him go. She wondered why Devon didn't just divorce the man and be done with him. *Love,* she supposed, *could be so damn tricky.*

Then Candace heard the back door open and close. What did Josh plan to do? Help himself to a glass of wine? Get clean clothes for Walter for the mortuary?

"Libby?" Josh called. "Are you here?" His footsteps clomped up the staircase. He turned into the bedroom and halted when he spotted Candace.

"Hello, Josh," she said, striking first. She quickly blocked his path to the bed and gestured him back to the hall. She closed the bedroom door behind her. "Libby's asleep. May I help you?"

He looked forlorn. She hoped Devon had taken some pleasure from that. "Walter's dead," he said.

"I know that."

"Should Libby be sleeping?"

"I don't think she's had much rest in the past few days." Candace stood firmly in place.

His eyes bore into hers as if that would make her get out of his way. "Does she know?"

"Yes."

"Devon said she has amnesia."

"She does."

"Jesus, Candace, let me go in and talk to her."

"As I said, she's sleeping. There's nothing for you to do."

He laughed. "My friend is dead. I'm not going to leave."

"If you want to help, find out what happened. Go find out who the last person was to see Walter. You must know some of the places he might have gone."

"I don't have a car. I took a cab."

"Libby's Mercedes is in the driveway, but I haven't found the keys."

"Is it locked?"

"I don't know."

"Well, it has a keyless ignition. If it's not locked, the electronic button is probably in the glove box. Walter always said the Vineyard has hardly any crime."

"I guess he'd have to eat those words now, what with the possibility that he was murdered."

"God, you were always a bitch."

She smiled with smug satisfaction. She waited a few more moments in the hallway then she heard the Mercedes' engine come to life. *That figures,* she thought. After all, things in life often came easily to men like him. Once again, Candace was reminded how lucky she'd been to have found Peter—quirky, neurotic, perfect-husband Peter.

With a small, grateful smile, she went downstairs and tried to screw up her courage to call him.

"The pharmacy is on the beach road right after the fork," Emmie told Josh as he backed out of the driveway. "I mapped it on my phone." She was sitting beside him in the passenger seat, not caring if anyone had watched her jump in. No matter the state of Libby mind or Walter's demise, no matter who had done what to whom, Emmie had decided that, whether or not anyone cared, her problems mattered, too.

It had been an easy decision.

After Devon had whisked Josh to the backyard, Emmie had not known what to do next or where to put herself. Candace and Libby were in the house; the police had asked for everyone's phone number. Emmie had quickly checked her "contacts" list and complied. She did not mention their driver because Devon had warned her that he was none of her business, and she did not want to piss Devon or Candace off. Besides, the presence of authority had always made Emmie nervous, as if she were the one who'd committed a crime. She wondered if adultery was still a criminal offense. That's when she remembered the ruined pregnancy test.

She'd quickly Google'd the drugstore. She'd been planning to call a taxi when Josh came out of the house, climbed into Libby's Mercedes, and instantly started it up.

No matter where he was going, it couldn't be too far from the pharmacy. She'd danced over the clamshells, no longer caring about the state of her feet.

"Thanks for the lift," she said to Josh now. "It's been kind of crazy around here."

He said he knew where the pharmacy was and that he would stop on the way to the golf club. "Someone there might know something about Walter."

Emmie said, "Maybe his car is there. Maybe he was murdered while playing golf, tossed into the killer's trunk, then brought to the house and dumped."

Josh kept his focus on the road and didn't reply. She hated when people did that—acted as if her question or comment didn't matter as if they were more important than she was. Maybe Josh thought he could be that way because he was as handsome as a celebrity. As far as his marriage to Devon had gone, Emmie had been glad when it ended; she'd always thought Devon could do better, though she'd never told her.

"Maybe he played golf this week," Josh finally said. "Maybe someone can tell me about his state of mind."

"I'm sure he was depressed. All their money is gone."

He laughed, but again refrained from commenting.

Conlan had once called Josh a "sanctimonious bastard." Emmie wanted to tell him that now, but she was unsure of the definition. Sadly, her Miss Porter's education was a vague memory.

So she shut up and looked out the window as the sea captains' houses and neat picket fences gave way to the pizza joints and Stop & Shop. Then Josh pulled into the pharmacy lot and turned off the engine.

"I'll go in for you," he said. "You aren't wearing shoes."

In her haste, she'd forgotten that minor detail. However, she couldn't very well tell him the purpose of her mission. "No," she said. "I'll go."

"Stores are usually strict about the policy."

"I doubt if that's true here." She got out of the car and marched into the pharmacy on her tiptoes, as if she had on heels.

Inside, a clerk greeted her. "Sorry," she said, pointing to Emmie's feet. "You can't be in here without shoes."

"I only need one thing."

"It's the law."

"Can you get it for me?"

"Sorry."

Emmie knew if she were Candace she would have found a way to wrangle admittance. But she was Emmie, not Candace, so she went back outside to the driver's side of the car. Josh put down the window.

"Give me your shoes," she said.

He laughed and opened the door. "I said I'd go in for you. Just tell me what you need."

She stood her ground because she had no other choice. She put her hands on her hips the way Candace would have done. She squared her jaw. "Just give me your damn shoes, Josh. The sooner I do this, the sooner you can get rid of me."

He slipped off his shoes; Emmie slipped them on and clunked awkwardly back toward the store, rejoicing in her small victory. But her celebration was cut short when she remembered that, though she had her phone, she'd left her purse back at the house.

Lowering her chin and slowing her pace, she returned to the car and asked Josh to lend her a twenty.

20

"How's your weekend going?" Candace said into the phone as calmly and steadily as she could manage. "Any word on the Benjamins?" James and Coralee Benjamin were sticklers for playing their opinions close to their privileged vests. The fact that they had played bridge with Peter's parents for years did not guarantee their Art-League-vote allegiance.

"Not a hint," Peter replied. "But how are things going out there? How are Libby and Walter?"

She had stepped outside and waved at the police when they'd signaled that they were leaving. She walked to the front of the house now because she did not want to go anywhere near the yellow tape that now cordoned off the garden. "Actually," she said, "that's why I've called."

"Don't tell me! They want you stay there a while. Is it true that the house is all they have left?" His tone carried a ring of genuine sympathy: Peter wasn't one who secretly smiled when others fell on hard times.

Candace sat down in an Adirondack chair and tried to form her reply. Beneath his predictable brouhaha, Peter was incredibly sensitive. "From what I gather," she said, "yes. The house is pretty much all they have left. Or rather, all that Libby has left." She paused, hoping he'd ask what she meant. It would be easier to respond to a question than to bring up the subject of murder. When he didn't say anything, Candace sighed. "Something's gone terribly wrong, Peter. Libby is out of her mind, and Walter . . . Walter, is dead."

Her husband remained mute.

"Peter? Did you hear me?"

He cleared his throat. "Well, yes, of course. You said Libby is out of her mind? And Walter is . . .?"

"Walter is dead. He was shot. We found him in the phlox—over by the croquet lawn." She supposed Peter was examining his manicure. He often did that when he was faced with stress, right before he began speaking in exclamation points. "We have to stay here with Libby. She needs to see a doctor in Falmouth tomorrow."

"Where's Walter?"

"The police must have taken him to the morgue."

"Who shot him?"

"We don't know. They don't think it was suicide. I agree. I think Walter was too impressed with himself to do that." She wouldn't have admitted that to anyone but Peter.

"Does Libby know what happened?"

"She might have witnessed the shooting. Which could explain why she thinks it's 2003." She shared the details about Libby's confused state. Then she told him the police didn't want them to leave.

"Who's planning the funeral?" Peter suddenly asked, which was no surprise, as he would certainly want to be involved.

"I think a funeral is premature."

"No, Candace! The man was a friend. We must do right by him. Besides, I believe he submitted a mail-in ballot, and he certainly voted for me!"

"He shouldn't be buried in New York, Peter. Their home is no longer there."

"But their friends are here! And all their acquaintances!" She could tell his agitation was brewing.

"Peter," she said softly, trying to temper his anxiety, "their New York friends would love nothing more than a ringside seat to the scandal. But I don't think Libby should have to go through that. Or Alana."

"Oh, Alana! Their dear girl!"

"Yes. We're going to wait to tell her until we have a few answers."

He fell silent again. Perhaps the worst of his angst had abated. Then he said, "Maybe I can help in the meantime. Who is their attorney?"

"The only one Libby mentioned is Marshall."

"Marshall's been dead for years."

"I know. I suppose I could look through Walter's papers again. He kept some here. I found them when I was looking for the car keys."

"Good idea. Perhaps you'll have found something by the time I arrive."

By the time he *arrived?*

"Let's see," he continued, "it's two-fifteen now. I can be there by dinner. I'm sure I can catch a flight out of Teterboro. You already have the car. And a driver."

"No!" Candace leapt from the chair and stumbled over the wooden slats at the base. She quickly righted herself; she tried to sound calm. "Honestly, Peter, there's no need to come. Not yet. You'll only complicate things."

"Complicate things?" He laughed. "Don't be ridiculous! If nothing else, I'm sure Libby could use a male friend. Someone to lean on, you know."

"Josh is already here. Josh Gregory."

"Gregory? What the hell's he doing there?"

So much for tempering her husband's anxieties. She'd never told Devon but Peter hadn't forgiven Josh for dumping his family. "I don't know. But, please, stay where you are. I'll keep you posted about what's going on." Then, because she knew her husband quite well, Candace added, "I'll tell you when the time is right. We *will* need you, Peter. Libby. Me. And the others. We'll be depending on your strength."

At last he agreed, and she said good-bye with a quick prayer that Gil had agreed with her plea to leave. Between the police bearing down and Peter ready to spring, it would be best if he had.

Gil went back to the hotel and retrieved his duffel bag. He drove around for a while, then ended up at the pier in Vineyard Haven. He pulled into an area marked *Park & Ride*, turned off the car, and sat there, trying to decide what to do.

He could leave the car there, take his bag, get on the next ferry, and find his way back to New York, not that anything or anyone was waiting there for him. It would be easier for Candace that way. She would not have to answer any questions. She would not have to deal with the lies she had told.

Or he could stay. Maybe he could help find whoever had killed the poor bastard who had apparently been one of his sister's friends. God knew he'd met enough murderers in Attica and heard enough tales; he should be able to think from the criminal's point of view.

Louis D. was a murderer. "Guilty as sin," he'd told Gil when he finally got around to talking to him instead of just following him around, sitting near him at meals, walking too close to him in the yard. He said he was there because of a plain old bar room brawl that had started when one guy said nasty things about Louis D.'s girl and had ended with two men dead on the floor.

All that on top of his priors (three assaults, two B & E's, five years served in Cayuga) cost him two concurrent life sentences. He'd been in since 1978, only two years after the death penalty was dropped or he might have been given one or two of those, too.

At first, Gil had thought Louis D. wanted him for . . . well, plain and simple, for sex. The fact that Louis D. was older, bigger, and so much stronger than he was, had scared the crap out of him. After a couple of months, it became clear that the other inmates also thought the big man had befriended Gil for bodily reasons. They didn't know Louis D. had a kid, a sixteen-year-old boy, only two years younger than Gil. The kid been eight the last time Louis D. saw him.

Gil heard the story after Louis D. arranged for them to be cellmates. That first night, Gil was bone scared. When the lights went out, he sat on the top bunk, shivering, wondering if he'd ever sleep again.

Then the big man whispered. "I got me what they call a bad seed," Louis D. said. "I don't know if my son has it or not. But if he ever done somethin' to have him wind up in here, I'd like to think one of the old lifers would have his back. Don't worry, kid. I'm not gonna' hurt you."

And he didn't. He always gave Gil his privacy; he never went near him. He didn't mentioned his son again for a couple of years, until a note arrived from his girlfriend's mother. She said the girl had been killed in a car wreck, and that Louis D., Jr. was now living with her in western Pennsylvania. She said she'd changed the boy's name to Leonard so things would be easier in the future. She said that, thank the Lord, the boy had forgotten his father by then, and she aimed to keep it that way.

He wasn't sure if he believed her.

Gil looked out at the water now, and wished he could talk to Louis D. now. He wondered if whoever had killed Walter LaMonde had the same kind of bad seed that Louis D. thought he had.

Then Gil wondered if his former cellmate would agree that he should stay on the island and try to help find Walter's killer, or if he would be better off to abandon his sister, especially since she'd once abandoned him.

After Devon had heard the car start, she'd gone around to the side of the house in time to see Josh back down the driveway and Emmie fly after him and spring onto the passenger seat. Devon had waited until the car was out of sight then she'd gone back to the porch and dropped onto a chair.

It had been odd, seeing Josh: even odder that the first time she'd seen him since the separation turned out to be in the last place where they'd been happy. Or rather, where Devon had been happy and Josh apparently had not.

She supposed she should not be surprised that she felt so limp.

Just then, a queer cackle rose from the back lawn.

Devon stood up quickly and looked toward the sound. A smallish man in a bright orange t-shirt and tan waders stood in the yard, staring at the "Do Not Cross" tape. He held a large plastic bag that seemed to be moving. She went outside.

"May I help you?" she asked. If he'd walked up the driveway she would have seen or at least heard him; he must have come by way of the water. He made no effort to move, so she walked closer, close enough to see that he wore salt-splattered glasses and had a mop of gray-white-brown hair that looked styled by a relentless ocean breeze.

He held out the bag. "Delivery." His voice was high-pitched in contrast to his ruddy demeanor.

Devon did not reach for the bag. "Delivery for whom?"

He scowled, revealing lines and creases on his brow and at the sides of his mouth. "Waltah."

It was a good thing Devon was well versed in Boston accents. "Walter isn't available."

His eyes drifted back to the tape. "Some kind of trouble?"

She remembered his peculiar laugh and decided not to tell him what had happened. She had, after all, no idea who might be a friend and who might not. "What are you delivering?"

He looked back to her. "Lobstahs." His accent was so thick it reminded her of the fake ones the actors adopted in films like *The Perfect Storm* and *Mystic River*. "Boat's down the hill," he said, pointing toward the water. "I'm dropping them off like usual. Every Wednesday and Sunday on my way home." If his eyes were once brown, they were bleached now, nearly matching his waders. "You must be numbah three."

"Number three?"

He laughed, revealing surprisingly straight, white teeth. Devon wouldn't have thought a lobsterman could have afforded such good dental care. "The guest. Waltah said to bring three lobstahs on Sunday, that they'd be having a guest."

She almost said no, she wasn't the guest that had been invited. She stopped herself when she realized that whether or not Libby and Walter had planned on company, today was Sunday and, so far, no one had showed up except for them. And Josh. None of whom had been expected. "Did Walter say who was coming?"

He chuckled again. "No. But he promised to settle up for everything he'd bought since they got here a few weeks ago." He pulled back the bag, inciting a small flurry of flopping from what must have been claws and tails. "Can't give you these unless I get paid. Bastahd owes me a total of three hundred and twenty."

Devon doubted if Walter would take his own life because of a three hundred dollar debt. But was it enough money for this man to have shot him? Had the man laughed because he'd realized Walter's body had been found? She took a step back.

Then Candace appeared. "What's going on?"

The lobsterman fell silent while Devon explained.

"Well," Candace said, "it seems to me we don't have much food around here and, right now, no means of transportation to get any. Unless we order take out pizza or Chinese, I suggest we pay the man. At some point, we're going to want to eat."

With the lobsterman still standing there, Devon couldn't very well tell Candace how strangely he'd cackled when he'd seen the yellow tape. "Walter owes him three hundred and twenty dollars."

"Pay the man," Candace replied tersely. "We'll settle up later." With that, she stomped off into the house.

Rather than chase after Candace and start an argument, Devon excused herself, went onto the porch, found her wallet, and fished everything out: two hundred and seventy dollars. She returned outside. "We'll have to owe you the rest. If that's okay."

"It is if you tell me what happened here. I didn't even know our cops owned a roll of crime scene tape." Apparently he watched cop shows, too.

She weighed her words for a moment. Then she supposed it wouldn't be long before the man knew, anyway. He would probably find out at the market or the post office or at the harbor when he docked his boat. This was, after all, an island. A small town. She sighed. "Walter LaMonde is dead. As of now, we don't know how or why."

He paused and let out a grunt. "Well," he said. "That's a damn shame. They been coming to the Vineyard for years." Then he handed her the bag, turned heel, and waddled off toward the water, his waders slap-slapping together.

"I need to find a bank," Devon said when she went into the kitchen where Candace was pouring wine. "Our dinner took all my cash." She put the bag in the refrigerator. Libby, of course, owned a large, enamel pot that was perfect for boiling lobsters: the pot was a staple throughout Cape Cod and the islands.

"He seemed like an unpleasant little man," Candace said.

"No kidding. You should have heard him laugh when he saw the police tape. When he didn't know I was watching."

"Maybe he already knew Walter was dead?"

"I doubt it. He's been out on his boat. The police have only been gone a few minutes. Besides, he was very curious. Nosey, actually."

"Maybe he killed him."

"Because he owed him for a few lobsters?"

"Who knows? Stranger things have probably happened."

The women fell silent. Devon dug out the lobster pot.

"Did you tell him what happened?" Candace asked.

"Yes. He didn't laugh that time. He grunted."

"God. What an unpleasant soul."

"Candace," Devon said, "he said Walter told him they were going to have a visitor. There are three lobsters in the bag."

"Who was the visitor?"

"I have no idea. I didn't know they were friendly with anyone that wasn't part of a couple." She refrained from expounding on that subject.

"Unless it was the cousin," Candace said. "What was his name? The one who lost their money?"

"Harold? Why would they entertain him? With lobsters, no less?"

"Maybe he resurrected their fortune."

"Would that have caused Libby to go into shock?"

Candace shook her head. "Doubtful."

It was clear neither Devon nor Candace knew the first thing about being good detectives. Still, Devon knew if they waited around until the police figured out what had happened, she might get fired from her job at *JW* for having taken too much time off. She might not need the money (not if she signed the *goddamn divorce papers*), but without her job, she would be miserable. What would she do all day, every day? She had worked too hard toward her independence—her *un*dependence, as she'd read somewhere—to revert back to the couch. She glanced at her watch. "Wouldn't you think whoever was coming for dinner would have been here by now?"

"Unless he was here. And left."

"Of course!" Devon said. "The lobsterman didn't say the 'guest' was arriving today. Only that he or she would be here today. Maybe whoever it was came Friday. Or Thursday, for that matter. We have to find out who it was. Call Gil."

Candace blinked. "What?"

"Call Gil. We need to start probing this island from one end to the other."

Candace flushed. "We can't leave Libby."

"We'll bring her with us. Maybe she can help."

"That's preposterous. We shouldn't bring her anywhere today. We need to wait until Josh comes back with Libby's car. And Emmie. Then you and I can leave Emmie with Libby and take Libby's car and 'probe' on our own."

During the time that Devon referred to as her "dark months," she'd learned the importance of honesty. Honesty about herself; honesty about situations. And that no matter what, in the long run, honesty remained the clichéd best policy. She reached across the island countertop now, took the half-empty glass from Candace's hand, and set it on the cool granite slab. Then she said, "Candace, if the problem is that you don't want Gil around, there's something I need to tell you. I've already figured out he's your brother."

21

Josh told Emmie to wait in the car. So she sat there and sat there as the minutes ticked by, wishing she could be just about anywhere other than sitting, staring out the car window at a big bunch of boring. She surveyed the country club grounds. Though it wasn't yet summer, the course was already littered with boney-kneed men in poplin shorts and pastel knit shirts with embroidered emblems over the breast pockets. Foursomes were stuffed into flimsy-looking carts that bumped along a narrow cart path; clumps of shiny clubs clung to the back like young children cleaved to their mothers' skirts.

Emmie was pleased that Conlan had never gotten into golf. She knew far too many women who'd lost their husbands to the links, or, even worse, had decided to take up the sport and had been transformed into unladylike athletes who wore hideous skirts that had shorts underneath. They were no doubt the same women who would be stunned that sweet Emmie Ainsworth Malloy had traded her devoted, rich husband for a meager horse trainer, even though, according to the Internet, his skills had been lauded by several stables from Lexington to Santa Ana.

She had Google'd Boyd with the hope of seeing a picture of his wife; she had wanted to assess how difficult it might be for him to let her go.

According to him, he had married Suzanne because, after Emmie, he'd thought he'd never find true love again. He said the fact that Suzanne was from Trinidad like he was had made it easier. He said her cocoa-complexion was so unlike Emmie's fair skin that he'd been able to separate them in his mind.

Her parents hadn't admitted that the real reason they'd wanted her away from Boyd had not been because they were both so young or because he was only a stable boy, but had been because of his color. She'd been ashamed of them for that shallowness, ashamed of that bigotry. Most of all, she'd been ashamed that she'd let Daddy convince her that her child would be judged all his life—that he'd be neither black nor white, that he wouldn't fit in anywhere. It was such old fashioned ignorance, and yet . . .

Boyd had said Emmie must love her father more than she loved him. She told him no, that she was just scared, afraid he might be right. Daddy had, after all, never lied to her.

And now when Emmie rocked the babies at the hospital, her favorites were those whose skin was the color of milk chocolate. She gave them extra hugs.

As for Boyd and Suzanne, they had three children, including their son, "Little Boyd," who was only six and whom his father obviously adored. She hadn't let herself think about them very often, especially when she'd been dreaming about a horse farm in Virginia and racing in upstate New York. Sometimes reality was better off tucked away.

Patting the small paper bag that rested in her lap, Emmie did not like the feeling she now felt inside. *Guilt,* she thought. Guilt about her family, and now about Boyd's, too. But what about happiness? What about love?

For the millionth time that day, her heart ached. She knew only one thing that could ease her pain. So she grabbed her phone and quickly called Boyd. He would set her straight. He would make sense of it all.

But instead of his voice, she heard a message. "This is Madigan. Leave a message." Beep.

She clicked off her phone. He must be very busy. The worst part was, she couldn't very well leave a message. What if Suzanne—or worse, Little Boyd—heard who was calling?

With a tiny sigh, Emmie felt suddenly, positively, lonely. She thought about calling Conlan: he always answered his phone when he saw she was trying to reach him.

But just as she started to touch her speed dial, Josh returned. "Walter's car isn't here. But I found out that Libby's cousin, Harold, was here during the week. I'll bet he murdered Walter."

"He told you," Candace said. She had paused a long time after Devon revealed that she knew about Gil. Then she'd taken back her glass, filled it with more Pinot, and paced the room. It was one of the few times since she and the others had visited the hypnotist-guru that Candace really wanted a smoke.

"God," she said, taking a long slug of wine.

"Candace," Devon said, "it's all right. It's no one's business but yours."

"I can't believe he told you."

"He didn't. I figured it out. He looks a lot like you, you know? You have the same eyes."

She could not help but smile. "People always said that about us."

"Well, I'm sorry if it upsets you that I know, but I wanted to be honest with you. I haven't said anything to Emmie, and don't worry I won't, if you don't want her to know."

"You saw how she reacted to his picture in the paper. Do you think she could handle the rest of the story?"

Devon conceded that she had a point.

"He didn't do it," Candace said.

"So the article said."

"Peter doesn't know that Gil even exists. Neither does Tiff." Then she told Devon how Gil had showed up at the house and Peter had mistaken him for the car service driver.

"You've shielded your family from him," Devon said. "There's nothing wrong with that."

Candace shook her head. "I'm not that righteous. I protected myself. Peter would never have married me if he'd known. His mother would have had a stroke."

"Maybe you're not giving them enough credit."

"Are you crazy? Look what happened to you. Do you think Josh would have left you so readily if you'd come from the Upper East Side and not from a family of culture and academics?" Devon, after all, was hardly naïve.

"I think the divorce is about me, not my family."

"I doubt it, Devon. Let's face it, the world of the Josh Gregorys and the Peter Cartwrights has rules. They might not be written down, but they are there. And there's not much room for tolerance." She took another glass from the cabinet, drained the bottle, passed it to Devon. "Here. I know this gives you a headache, but, trust me, it helps."

Devon laughed. "No offense, but I've noticed that you've been drinking a lot lately. Now I understand why."

"No you don't. It wasn't just that Gil was in prison. The worst part was, it was my fault." As long as she was unloading, she might as well tell Devon the rest. Sooner or later, it was probably going to come out, anyway. So Candace opened another bottle (thank

God Libby and Walter still had a full cellar) and told Devon about that day in the courtroom and all she had gone through after that.

When she was finished, Devon quietly asked, "Whom was Gil supposed to have killed?"

"My father," Candace said. "Our father, his and mine."

$$ \subset \!\!\! \longrightarrow $$

Devon had drunk half a glass of wine: It had taken several minutes to absorb all that Candace had told her, to grasp that *Candace, the Terrible,* as Josh had often called her, had secrets and feelings and a real reason for her perpetual, off-putting behavior. In short, Candace wasn't perfect. For the first time since Devon had known her, she considered they could maybe be real friends, not just those framed by expectations of others and acceptable social graces.

"And then your mother died," Devon said. They had settled in on high stools at the kitchen island, the bottle of Pinot between them.

"She lived a few more years after Gil went to prison. She visited him every week. I was never able to do that. Not that he would have welcomed me."

"Do you know that for sure?"

Candace shrugged. "Like I said, I was protecting myself. I felt as guilty as if I'd been the one who'd pulled the trigger. Which, by the way, I might have done if someone hadn't done it first. The man was my father but he beat my mother. The best thing that happened to all of us had been when he'd left."

"Why was Gil arrested? What evidence did the cops have?" Devon couldn't imagine how the police could have thought such a sweet guy had been capable of murdering his father.

"For a time, my brother was a wanna-be juvenile delinquent. When he heard that the old man had come back to Jamestown, he tracked him down in a bar. He told him off in front of a few too many people. Then he stormed out of the place. The trouble was, he didn't come straight home. He bought a couple of quarts of Budweiser, drove to Chautauqua Lake, and sat by the water, alone, until dawn. When I took the witness stand, I said he didn't come home that night. He was convicted. The cops never looked at anyone else."

In spite of herself, Devon took another drink. The wine tasted soothingly good. "So the real killer got away with it. But Gil is here now. It doesn't seem as if he holds it against you."

"If he didn't, he does now. He thinks I always thought he was guilty."

"Did you?"

"Yes. I don't think he'll ever forgive me for that."

Devon frowned. "Give him a break, Candace. He's been through a lot."

Suddenly, Candace plunked down her glass. Hard. The crystal cracked. "Forgiveness!" she shouted. "I almost forgot. I found a note in the library that asked Libby for forgiveness!"

Devon sat up straight. "Who wrote it?"

"I have no idea."

"Well, show me, for God's sake. It could be important."

They hurried from the kitchen into the library; Candace jerked open a drawer and shuffled a few files until she pulled out a note.

Devon peered over her shoulder. The words had been carefully scribed on a small piece of elegant stationery: *Dear Libby, Forgive me?* "We should take this to the police."

"Oh, God," Candace groaned, "We can't go to the police. *I can't go to the police.*"

"They need to see this note, Candace. Unfortunately, now your fingerprints are all over it."

Candace dropped the paper as if it had ignited.

"You don't want to go to the police because of Gil." Devon supposed it was an elementary assumption. She reached down and picked up the note.

"Bingo," Candace replied softly. "Everything would become fodder for the media, Devon. Gil's past. My past." She paused. "Peter." She must have felt that her life was starting to unravel. "One of the drawbacks of having money is that people tend to want to see you crash."

"The police already know Gil was here, Candace. Or rather, they know a man was here. His footprints were in the dirt in the garden. They know they didn't belong to one of us."

Candace bit her lower lip. "You don't understand, Devon. If I expose my . . . relationship to Gil, Peter's whole life will be turned upside down. I'm not talking about that stupid Art League election. Did you know my husband is bi-polar? That he also has OCD? Did you know he walks a tightrope every day of his life, doing his best to hang on? Most people think he's just a big, rich lug who used to be an acceptable corporate attorney in addition to being a Cartwright. Most people think he hardly works now because, financially, he doesn't need to, which, thank God, is true. They think he would rather be volunteering with things like the Art League. The truth is his condition has progressed, so that more and more now, it's just better for him to focus on minutia. If he has to deal with things that are out of his control, he falls apart." A quick film of tears glossed over her eyes.

Devon didn't know how to respond. She had learned more about Candace and Peter in the last few minutes than in all the years she had known them. "I didn't know," she said. "I didn't know he suffers so much." There was little comfort in finding out that someone from her former circle did, in fact, know the depths of depression. She couldn't, however, picture Peter Cartwright in fleece. "I know it's no consolation," Devon continued, "but I think Peter would like Gil. Your brother is a really nice man. And I think we could use Gil's help with this. Or, at least, we can use him to drive the car. Both of us stink at driving. We've lived in Manhattan too long." She tried to smile.

Candace closed her eyes. "Okay," she said. "I'll try to call him at the hotel." Her tears started to flow just as Libby stormed into the library.

"What the hell are you two doing now?" Libby screeched. "Why are you snooping through my private things?"

It took a few moments to calm Libby down, to convince her they were only trying to help the police find out who killed Walter.

"Well, do you have a warrant?" she demanded to know. "Don't you need a warrant to go through our papers?"

"Libby," Devon asked. "Do you know who wrote this note?"

Libby glanced at it and scowled. "No. Why should I?"

"For starters, it has your name on it."

Candace interrupted. "Libby. Do you remember your cousin Harold?"

Libby brightened. "Of course. Don't be ridiculous. Cousin Harold and I are like brother and sister."

"Could he have written the note?" Devon asked. It was a long shot, but, other than the lobsterman, she couldn't think of anyone who might have wanted to kill Walter.

"Cousin Harold is at Wharton. He's getting his MBA in financial management. Isn't that wonderful?"

Devon had never met the man, but chances were he had aged out of graduate school years after 2003. She looked at Candace.

"I'll call Gil," Candace said. She took the note from Devon and retreated to the other room.

22

Emmie was annoyed that Josh insisted on going from the golf club to the boat club. He said it might be important to check out Walter's boat. She asked him to drop her off at Libby's first.

"No," he said. "If I find anything or anyone, it will be better if I have a witness."

"But small boats make me seasick. Just like small planes. And cars, if I ride in them too long."

"We're going to look at the boat, not take a cruise."

"What if a murderer is on board?"

Josh did not acknowledge that comment. So Emmie sat perfectly still, the pregnancy test resting covertly on her lap. Then she said, "I don't understand why you think Libby's cousin Harold would have killed Walter. Harold is responsible for them losing their money. If anything, I think Walter would have had a motive to kill *him*." She loved the word "motive." Conlan often used it when telling her about this or that conglomerate that was trying to enact a hostile takeover of the restaurant chain. "Their motive is pure greed," he said. Or, "Their motive is a giant tax write-off." She wished he were there. Conlan would know how to solve the puzzle. Then she pursed her lips and wondered if she should feel guilty that she was thinking about her husband while carrying another man's child.

Josh cleared his throat and gripped his hands more tightly on the steering wheel. "Maybe Walter pointed a gun at Harold," he said. "Maybe they got into a fistfight, and the gun went off.

Maybe Walter was killed by mistake. Did the police find the murder weapon?"

Apparently, Josh had been thinking, too. "I have no idea," Emmie said. "Maybe Gil found the gun."

"Who?"

"Gil. Our driver."

"*Who?*" Josh repeated as if she hadn't heard him.

She sighed. "Our *driver*. The man who brought us here in Peter's Town Car. He's a convicted murderer. But supposedly 'new evidence' proved he didn't do it. Anyway, I'm not supposed to talk about it because Devon said it's none of our business."

Josh pulled the Mercedes into the parking lot that ran alongside the beach. Emmie thought it might be the same beach where they'd filmed the scene in *JAWS* of the families swimming on the Fourth of July. He shifted into Park, and turned to Emmie. "What are you talking about? Who the hell is Gil? And why did you have an ex-convict for a driver?"

Emmie shrugged. "I have no idea. Peter Cartwright arranged everything. If you ask me, he's always been nice enough, but a little odd, too."

After phoning the desk clerk and saying he could earn a hundred dollars if he tracked down Gil Martin and told him to get to Mrs. LaMonde's *ASAP*, the clerk informed Candace there was no need to track down Mr. Martin because he was sitting in a rocking chair on the hotel's front porch. He added that he would be glad to pass on the message, no charge.

Candace thanked him with flat sincerity.

The three women went outside and stood in the driveway, waiting. Soon Gil arrived; Candace told him about the note. "So we're headed for the police station, and we need a ride."

"Well, I almost left," he said. "I guess it's lucky that I went back to the hotel."

"I guess," Candace replied, and the women got into the Town Car.

"What happened to the silver Mercedes?" Gil asked.

"Devon's husband figured out how to start it."

"*Ex*-husband," Devon clarified.

"He showed up unannounced," Candace continued. "Then he took off. Emmie went with him. He said he wanted to find out who killed Walter."

"An admirable idea," Gil said.

She looked over at Devon and wondered why she hadn't offered a snarky comment about Josh being connected to anything *admirable*. Devon was far nobler than she would have been. "Let's just go to the police," Candace said brusquely. "And get this over with."

"All of us?" Gil asked.

"It doesn't matter. Devon already figured out who you are. And who cares what Libby is thinking these days?"

Libby was in the back seat of Peter's limo again, doing as she was told. She hated that Candace was always so pushy. But even though Candace had told the driver they were going to the police station, Libby suspected otherwise. Candace and Devon had asked about Cousin Harold, so maybe Libby was in for a surprise. Maybe they were really going to Vineyard Haven to be there when the ferry docked. Maybe Cousin Harold was arriving from Wharton to give her some moral support now that Walter was dead.

That would be nice.

The boat club wasn't crowded. Josh slid into a parking space; Emmie presumed if there hadn't been one, he would have boldly double-parked. Conlan wouldn't have done that; he was too respectful of other people. Peter Cartwright wouldn't have, either. He'd have been too afraid of being chastised. Everything Peter did needed to be perfect. As for Walter, well, Emmie had to admit she'd never really known Walter, God rest his soul. Conlan hadn't been too keen on him, so mostly, whenever they saw Libby and Walter, it was in a group: fundraisers or charity events, the girls' recitals or equestrian competition.

Equestrian!

The word, of course, reminded her of Boyd. But that time, instead of a small rush of warmth, Emmie felt a little sick to her stomach. She grasped the tiny paper bag and tried to divert her thoughts back to Walter.

Josh got out and stuck his head back in the open door. "His car's not in the lot here, either. Come on, let's check out the boat."

She took a deep breath. She'd have to accompany Josh if she were going to be a proper witness. She set the bag on the floor and got out. Then she pattered along behind him, across the lot and the wharf, then down the weathered dock that poked into the harbor. She hoped the man who'd been the maître d' last night at the clubhouse wouldn't recognize her. She still couldn't believe she had curtsied.

Suddenly, Josh stopped. He pointed to a small white boat, bobbing in the water. "This isn't a good sign," he said.

Emmie and Conlan had never been into sailing. Still, she knew the small boat was called a dinghy, and that it was used to transport people to and from their yachts. Along the edge of the bow or stern (she'd never learned the proper term for the back or the front) the words, *LIBAL 2* had been painted. There had been a discussion in the group one night over cocktails: Walter had named his sailboat the *Libal,* which was a combination of Libby and Alana's names. Coming from a world that was resplendent with big shot lawyers, he'd once said that he thought any confusion of *Libal* with *Libel* would be hilarious. Yes, Emmie had not really known Walter very well. But she did know what the small boat was.

"This shouldn't have been tied up here over night," Josh said. "Maybe it's so early in the season that the overseers don't care. It's not as if the harbor is full of other boats."

"If the dinghy's not supposed to be here," Emmie asked, "where should it be?"

"For starters, I remember Walter always took the boat club launch back and forth—not the dinghy. Maybe they don't have the summer schedule yet for the launch. But if that were the case, Walter wouldn't have tied up at the boat club if he weren't going back to the boat. He would have tied up at the dinghy dock."

"Where?"

"The dinghy dock, over by the restaurant. It's where non-club members park. Or where anyone parks if they're going to be on the island all night."

Emmie nearly laughed. The term *dinghy dock* sounded so silly. But the plaster-like look on Josh's face warned her that laughter would not be acceptable. She would have bet that Boyd would have laughed. Boyd . . . and even Conlan.

Cooling her face with a few quick waves of her hand, Emmie composed herself. "Maybe Cousin Harold parked the little boat here because he didn't know it was the wrong place. Maybe Harold, not Walter, had been out on the sailboat."

Josh made no comment. He looked into the dinghy as if it held the answer.

"Help you folks?"

Emmie turned and saw a man walking toward them from the small house marked HARBORMASTER.

"We're Walter LaMonde's friends," Josh said. "Actually, we met a few years ago. Josh Gregory." He extended his hand to the Harbormaster and totally ignored Emmie. The Harbormaster neither introduced himself nor showed recollection of having met Josh.

"What do you want with LaMonde's dinghy?"

"I thought we'd go out to the *Libal* and take care of a few things."

"Can't let you do that."

Josh smiled. "I assure you, we mean no harm. We were out with Walter yesterday, and my wife left her purse on board."

"That so?"

Josh nodded.

The Harbormaster scratched his sun-tanned chin. "Well, you might want to tell that story to the police, then, because this dinghy's been tied up here since Friday. I've only allowed it because I heard about Walter's troubles." He did not elaborate as to whether he was referring to the fact Walter had lost his money or that he was dead. Instead, the man simply stood rock-still. It did not appear he was going to budge in either body or attitude.

Taking a step back, Josh smiled again and said, "We were only trying to help. As I said, Libby and Walter are our friends. We're trying to help Libby sort things out. Walter is dead, you know. Or maybe you didn't."

Full of himself, Emmie thought. That was the term for Josh Gregory. She had a brief desire to tie *him* up at the dinghy dock. With a pompous snicker, Josh began to walk back toward the parking lot.

Emmie wanted to tell the Harbormaster that she wasn't Josh's wife, that her husband never would have been so rude. Nor her lover, for that matter.

"Wait," the Harbormaster called.

Josh took three more steps, then stopped and turned, as if he were doing the man a favor.

"What happened? How'd he die?"

"He was shot," Josh said. "Looks like murder."

"Do they know who did it?"

"Not yet. You have any ideas?"

"Shit, could've been anyone. He tried to get me to buy into one of his investments. I almost did. Rumor has it I was lucky to have had second thoughts. Might be some other islanders didn't."

Oh, great, Emmie thought. *Hundreds of islanders, maybe more, who might have had Conlan's favorite word—motive!*

Josh shrugged. "All I know is I wanted to go out on the boat to look around. The police are overloaded. They're sifting through the evidence at the scene."

Emmie didn't know where Josh had come up with that idea. Still, it was nice he didn't admit that Libby and Walter had lost all their money.

"Where'd it happen?"

"They found his body at the house."

"In the phlox," Emmie contributed, but neither man seemed interested in that.

"What do you expect to find on the boat?"

Josh shrugged. "Don't know. Won't know, until I find it."

The man looked down harbor at the cluster of freshly-painted sailboats that were anchored. "Guess I could go with you. To make sure you don't touch anything."

"No problem," Josh said, then changed direction and went back toward the dinghy.

"We'll take the launch," the Harbormaster said. "It's faster than that old thing."

Emmie followed the men across the wharf again, hoping that her pregnancy test kit wouldn't melt while left alone in the unventilated car.

"Accident up on County Road," the woman behind the desk at the police station told Devon. "The officers will be tied up for a while. But I'm pretty sure the forensics on the LaMonde case is with the Staties now. They've agreed to help out. You know where the barracks are on Beach Road?"

The Staties, of course, must be Vineyard-speak for the barracks that Josh had always laughed about. "Isn't it the lovely Victorian around the curve from the hospital?" Devon asked.

"That's it. Beautiful old place. The Commander and his family live on the second floor. Anyway, I can call them if you want. Tell them you're coming."

"No need. We'll be there soon enough." She went back to the car where Candace, Libby, and Gil waited patiently. Well, Libby and Gil were being patient. Candace was perched as if ready to pounce.

"Do they want to talk to all of us?" Candace asked. She sounded breathless, the way Emmie often did.

Devon shook her head. "They're not here. We have to go to the State Police barracks. They're helping with Walter's case." She could not bring herself to say "Walter's *murder*" in front of Gil. "We should bring them the note."

Though they only had one car, Devon felt as if they were part of a parade, an entourage making their crime-solving debut. She pictured them marching up Fifth Avenue on St. Patrick's Day waving shamrocks and following a kiltie band. But that made her think of Emmie's husband, and then of the girls. She wondered if they were having fun while their mothers were not. A little knot twisted in Devon's heart when she thought about Alana and how hard it was going to be for her to learn that her Dad was gone.

A few minutes later they arrived at the State Police barracks: a beautiful house with a pristine lawn, pale yellow siding, and white, gleaming trim. It looked as if it had once belonged to a wealthy sea captain.

"Do you have the note?" Candace asked, as if somewhere between there and the Edgartown PD, Devon might have managed to lose it.

She nodded, because it was safer than causing friction.

"You're sure you don't want me to come in?" Gil asked.

"No!" Candace barked. "Devon will do it. We'll stay outside unless it's absolutely necessary."

If it weren't for the circumstances, Devon might have found Candace's proclamation amusing. Had she forgotten that her brother had just spent twenty-five years in prison? Of any of them, he would probably know how to navigate the system.

She bit back a smile, then got out of the car and, once again, marched blithely into a law enforcement facility as if she did it every day.

Inside, a young man in gray and blue was seated behind a steel desk.

Devon stepped forward and waited until he looked up. "I'd like to speak with the officer in charge of the Walter LaMonde investigation."

He checked her out as if she were a suspect. "Why?"

She took a step back. She hadn't expected that kind of reception. "I, well, I was friends with the deceased. Well, my husband and I were. For a long time. And I'm really close with Walter's wife, Libby?" She had no idea why her last sentence came out like a question or why she was suddenly nervous. "I was at the house when . . . when the body was found. I didn't get much of a chance to speak with the police, but I thought I might be able to help."

"How?" He stood and placed his hands on top of his thick black belt, just above his hip line. He was shorter than she was, and considerably younger, which might have eased her unexpected discomfort, but did not.

When Devon had returned to college she'd taken a class in public speaking where she'd learned that the best way to warm up your audience was to smile. Show teeth. Act as if you were happy to be there. *Okay,* she thought now. *Start over.* She smiled again. "I understand that you're working with the Edgartown Police on Walter's case. Are you the liaison in charge?"

He fixed his gaze on her, a long, silent look that suggested he might have learned that trick at the academy, the same way she'd learned about smiling. Devon relaxed. She almost felt sorry for him. He was, after all, only trying to do his job. For all he knew, she was the murderer. Or murderess.

He hemmed a little, hawed a little. Then he said, "No. The Commander is working directly with the police. But you just missed him. He's going to the mainland to meet with the D.A. We need to make sure all the bases are covered."

"Is he going on a police boat? Or will he take the ferry?"

The cop glanced at his watch. "He'll be on the five o'clock. But he'll come back tonight."

It was already four-forty. They weren't far from the pier; maybe they could catch him.

"Thank you," Devon said and rushed out the door before he had the chance to ask her more questions.

"To the ferry terminal," she instructed once she was back in the car.

Gil popped the gearshift into *Drive* and headed for the beach road as if he were a native, or at least, a seasoned washashore.

23

No one was on Walter's boat. Emmie didn't know why Josh seemed surprised, what with the dinghy docked at the boat club.

She stayed topside while the two men went below. She figured the Harbormaster would be a more credible witness than she would, if a credible witness were needed. She looked around the harbor at the boats that sat in silence. It was the end of a weekend: their owners were probably home now, wherever "home" might be. Once mid-June arrived, no doubt the place would come alive with the sounds of voices and loud music and with the scents of suntan lotion and barbecue wafting up from the decks. She turned and faced what she knew was the island of Chappaquiddick, a place that remained shrouded in accusations of, well, infidelity. And a curious death.

Reality began to darken her spirits. She wondered if Boyd had tried to call her since she'd left the car, which now was locked up with her phone and that damn test kit inside. If he'd tried but hadn't reached her would he think she didn't care? That she'd changed her mind about him, about them?

Had she?

She thought about Conlan again. If he, not Walter, had been the one who'd died, Emmie would be free to marry Boyd and have her happily-ever-after. The truth was, though, she would be devastated. Conlan was so many things to her, including her loyal, devoted husband.

Her eyes stung with tears. Suddenly she hated everything about this weekend. All these goings-on were ruining her fantasy. And her fun.

"Nothing here." Josh's voice startled her. She hadn't heard the men come up the stairs.

Emmie shrugged and refrained from saying, "What did you expect?" Instead, she asked, "Can we go back to the house now?" She really wanted to take that damn test once and for all. She really wanted to know what kind of decision she would need to make.

⌣⟶

They were stuck in traffic at the drawbridge that spanned the channel that linked Lagoon Pond to Vineyard Haven Harbor. Candace wondered if they were doomed to drive around forever with the *Forgive me, Libby* note.

"Even if we miss this boat," Devon said, "the officer said the commander will be back tonight."

Candace stared out the window. There was no need for anyone to comment; it was apparent they were all too tired now, especially Libby, who was curled across the facing bench seat, in what finally looked to be a peaceful world, nicely framed by pharmaceuticals. "Are we going to get the girls?" Libby suddenly murmured.

It would be a long, damn drive to Conlan's castle, Candace wanted to retort, but Gil said quietly, "Not yet, Libby. The girls are having a good time." He used those smiling eyes of his and Libby smiled back and went to sleep.

Yes, Candace thought, *my kid brother is still a charmer, kind and gentle and completely unpretentious.* It saddened her to think he could never be as proud of her as she was of him. It saddened her to think that her choices had ruined so many things. She tried to stop a tear from welling in her eye; she looked over at Devon. "Gil wants to be a teacher."

"A teacher? That's wonderful."

Devon, of course, was as kind as Gil. Why hadn't Candace ever noticed that?

"What grade do you want to teach?" Devon asked as she leaned a little toward the driver.

Gil kept his eyes on the drawbridge that was arched toward the sky. "I'd thought about junior high. Those years seem like the most challenging." Junior high school was when he'd started hanging out with Bobby Benson. "But I'm not sure any school district will want my illustrious credentials."

"And I say that's nonsense," Candace said. "Times have changed." Then she figured now was as good a time as any to apologize, especially with Devon there. Gil wouldn't brush Candace off in front of someone else. She drew in a small breath, then lowered her voice a notch. "By the way, I'm sorry, Gil. I'm sorry if I ever thought you'd killed Dad. In my heart, I knew you never could have done it. But you didn't come home that night. And when they put me on that witness stand . . . well, I was so scared, I couldn't lie." She didn't know if her admission was enough to warrant his forgiveness.

He didn't answer right away. He could not have known her heart had moved up to her throat.

Then he said, "Don't you know why I didn't tell them my alibi?"

Devon tapped him on the shoulder. "Maybe the two of you should talk about this in private."

"Why?" Candace asked. "You're the one who brought up forgiveness."

Devon sat back on the seat and turned her gaze to the bridge as if she couldn't hear the conversation.

"After I left Dad in the bar," Gil continued, "I bought two quarts of beer and went to the park, just like I told the cops. But I omitted the part about picking up Mindy Gleason. We spent the night together."

Candace laughed. "And you didn't want to ruin Mindy's reputation? Oh, my God, you were more saintly that I thought."

"There was more," he said. The cars in front of them inched forward as the bridge finally began its slow descent. "When Mindy said she'd tell the cops she'd been with me, I told her I'd deny it. After all, the real reason I let them convict me was because . . . Jesus, Candace . . . I thought you were the one who had done it."

"What?" her voice chirped.

"I thought you'd killed the bastard to protect Mom. And me." He inched the car forward. "And to protect you. I thought you'd killed him to protect all of us, Candace. He was such a bastard."

The air inside the car grew weighty with sadness. Devon seemed to notice: she cracked her window and twisted on the seat.

"You went to prison to . . . to save me from going?"

"You were a girl, Candace. You were my sister, and I loved you. I could no more picture you in prison than I could picture Mom. I knew that of the three of us, I could handle it the best. Besides, once he was gone, none of us needed to worry about him coming around again."

"But . . . but I didn't do it." *Not that she hadn't wanted to on more than one occasion.* Like when he'd pushed her down the stairs. Or broken their mother's arm. Or thrown Gil against the kitchen wall. Yes, she had wanted to kill the S.O.B. But she'd never had the courage.

"His latest girlfriend did it. Her DNA confirmed it. Thank God they'd saved his bloody shirt."

"That's why they set you free."

"Yes. They had to. Of course, she claimed 'self-defense.' Who can argue with that? She won't do much time, if any, though. She's over seventy now. And crippled from arthritis."

Silence hung for a moment. Then Candace said, "I know you were angry with me last night. When I told you I thought you did it. But it's okay, Gil. I'm not angry that you thought I did."

"You're wrong," he said. "I wasn't angry about that. I was upset that you never came to visit me. That you never even sent me a damn card."

That's when Candace could not hold back the tears. "I'm so sorry, Gil. I was so sad . . . and so afraid."

"If Louis D. were here, he'd say it's 'water over the dam.' That it's time to forgive and forget."

"Who's Louis D.?"

"A friend. Actually, my best friend. Not counting you."

"I love you," Candace said, and Gil nodded with a smile.

Then the line of traffic opened up. Gil maneuvered the car across the channel just as the five o'clock ferry blew its horn, pulled out of its berth, and headed toward Woods Hole.

"So much for catching up to the commander," Devon said.

"I have a better idea," Candace said. "Let's go somewhere nice for dinner."

"We have lobsters at the house," Devon said.

"We'll throw them in the pot later and make lobster salad to-morrow. The police said we have to stay here, remember?" The prospect of the Art League election paled now compared to letting her feelings settle and spending time with Gil. "But first let's turn around and go get Emmie. I feel as if we've been ignoring her."

Emmie couldn't believe the others were gone when she and Josh got back to Libby and Walter's. All she had wanted was to do the test, but now she felt compelled to entertain Devon's ex.

He went into the library and made himself at home.

"May I fix you a drink?" Emmie asked because Conlan would have wanted her to be polite.

"Scotch would be nice. Glenlivet, if they have it. On the rocks." He picked up a magazine, put his feet on the coffee table, and dismissed her as if she were a servant. She wanted to ask what the heck he was doing, like, was he planning to stay there all night? Devon wouldn't be happy about that, but Emmie decided it wasn't her place to tell him.

"I'll stay here until the others get back," he said, as if reading her mind. "I'd like to be sure Libby's all right. And to see if I can help with funeral arrangements."

Maybe Emmie had been too quick to judge him. Maybe he was trying to be nice and his way just wasn't like Conlan's. She stood in the doorway still staring at him.

"If you'd feel more comfortable," he added, "I can wait out in the guesthouse. Unless Devon is staying there. That might be awkward."

"No. Devon slept here last night. Candace said she stayed in the room right next to Libby's in case Libby needed anything during the night. Devon's a good friend, you know?" Josh didn't disagree. "Anyway, we all have rooms at the Harbor View. We had no idea we'd arrive to such a . . . mess."

He kept his gaze on the magazine, but Emmie didn't think he was reading. She wondered if he was thinking about Devon; maybe he was feeling sad. She actually felt a little sorry for him.

"Wherever they are," he said, "I don't expect they'll be long. They wouldn't make dinner plans without you. Why don't you call them?"

"No, you're right. They'll be back soon."

He turned a page.

"I'll get your drink now."

With her purse in one hand and the small bag in the other, she made her way into the kitchen. Might as well fix that scotch quickly, so she could check her phone messages then finally duck into the bathroom.

But as she tossed her phone and the pharmacy bag onto the counter, she heard a small *ding* that indicated she'd had a call. She grabbed the phone.

Madigan, Boyd.

So. He had called.

In spite of herself, her heart started to skip. He must have called when they were on the boat but her damn phone hadn't gotten around to dinging until then. Unless it had before and she hadn't heard it . . . Then she thought, *Damn! What am I doing? Boyd called!*

She didn't care about Josh or the Glenlivet. Grabbing her cell and the test kit, Emmie dashed to the powder room, slammed the door, and dropped onto the toilet seat without lifting the lid.

Boyd.

She stared at the phone, willing her breath to slow. Until it did, she wouldn't be able to speak clearly; she wouldn't be able to tell Boyd that she loved him and that she might be pregnant.

He'd never known about the abortion. Daddy said it would be better, kinder, to say that she'd miscarried. Perhaps Daddy had been a little ashamed, too.

Setting her phone on the glazed concrete vanity, she pulled the box from the bag. There was no need to read the instructions: She'd done that when she'd made her first attempt.

She unsealed one end, untucked the cardboard flap, unwrapped the plastic covering, and stared at the wand in her hand.

That's when her cell rang.

She grabbed for the phone without checking Caller ID.

"Hello? Hello?" Her words came out in a rush.

"Emmie, dear, are you all right? You sound frenetic. Aren't you having a good time?"

It wasn't Boyd. It was Conlan. Her loyal, devoted husband.

"No," she whispered, "I am *not* all right, Conlan. I'll call you later, okay?"

She clicked off the phone and dropped down onto the toilet seat. There was no way she could do the test now. Not after hearing her husband's sweet voice.

She tucked the unused wand into one of the vanity drawers. Later, there would be time to face her consequences. Later. Not now.

"What are you doing here?" When Devon had seen the Mercedes parked in the driveway at the house, she'd hoped it was a sign that Josh was gone. She'd hoped that Emmie had driven him to the ferry. On second thought, she wasn't sure if Emmie knew how to drive. Probably not.

Not that any of this mattered once Devon entered the library and he was sitting there in all his maddening glory.

He stood up. "I wanted to be sure Libby is all right."

"She's the same."

He set down a magazine he'd apparently been reading. "Have you had dinner?"

Was he asking her to go out with him? Was it a ploy to get her to sign the damn divorce papers? "We're going out soon," she replied coolly. "I'd ask you to join us, but I don't think it would be appropriate."

He flicked his gaze away, over toward the bookcases and the desk where Candace had found the note asking Libby to forgive him . . . or *her*. It occurred to Devon that though they'd assumed the note was from a man, and that the murderer was a man, maybe it had been a woman. But who? And how many more questions were there to answer?

"Has anyone thought about a funeral?" Josh asked, jolting Devon's thoughts wretchedly back to him.

"We can't have a funeral until the police release the body," she said. "They won't do that until the autopsy's complete, until they have what they need. Besides, nothing can be planned until Alana comes home. And, so far, she doesn't know."

"When are you planning to tell her?"

"Soon." She glared at her ex-husband because glaring was so natural now when they were in each other's space. He turned his attention back to the magazine he'd put on the table. If one of those loud, ticking clocks had been in the room, the pendulum could have marked time with the tension. "Josh," she said, "go home. You're not needed here."

He put his hands in the pockets of his gray slacks that looked less out of place now that he'd removed his sports jacket. "You're forgetting that Walter was my friend."

Oh, she wanted to say, *I remember that only too well.*

"I went to the golf club," he added. "I learned that Libby's cousin, Harold, was here during the week. He and Walter played golf."

"Where is he now?"

"Don't know. But I did check the *Libal.* You know, Walter's boat."

God, he could be condescending. Had he done that when they'd been together? "I take it he wasn't there, either."

"No," he replied with a long stare. "And his car wasn't in either lot. But the dinghy was parked at the boat club. I talked to the Harbormaster—he let it slip that he'd almost invested with one of Walter's relatives. He said there might be others on the Vineyard who actually had. So others might have trusted him, then lost a chunk of money the way Walter did."

Josh was giving Devon a headache. "Fine. I'll be sure to tell the police." She could have told him about the note. If he were Candace's husband, she would have. If he were Emmie's husband, she would have. But she wouldn't tell Josh. She did not want him involved. She only wanted him out of her blessed sight. "Go home, Josh," she said again.

He sucked in the corners of his mouth as if stopping himself from saying something nasty. Then he turned and walked out of the house, his footsteps echoing as they crunched on the clamshells. Wherever he was going, he did not take Libby's car.

24

Gil guided Libby to the spot where he'd found Walter's body. Libby focused on the dirt that looked muddled and dank now that dusk was settling in. She did not seem to want to move, and Gil didn't want to rush her. He took a few steps back to where Candace was standing, waiting.

"I often wondered," he said, his voice barely above a whisper, "if you'd gone to Mom's funeral." He hated to bring up the reminder, but he'd always wondered if the service had been nice, if there had been pretty flowers—lots of white and yellow daisies, the that kind she had loved—and if the congregation had sung "Amazing Grace." He'd wanted to know how many people had gone, because she'd deserved a standing-room-only, full house.

Candace, however, was crying quietly again. "I didn't go," she said. "I didn't find out until after she'd been buried."

He put his arm around her and drew her close. "I didn't go, either. I could have gone. But I didn't want to embarrass her by showing up in my orange jumpsuit and shackles."

Candace looked at him and wiped her tears. "We didn't deserve her."

He shrugged. "We did our best. She knew we loved her."

Libby suddenly spun around. "Well, I did not love Walter," she exclaimed. "He was an ass! Now, can we have dinner, please? I'm absolutely famished." That's when the porch door banged open, then closed.

"Speaking of asses," Candace said, "there goes Devon's ex."

Gil watched the man stomp down the driveway as if he had something important to do. It was hard to imagine that someone like Devon had been with someone like him.

Emmie joined them; they piled into the Town Car. Again. Libby said she wanted to go to The Red Cat on State Road in West Tisbury. Gil drove; none of them spoke. Candace supposed they all were weary. After all, none of them had even mentioned changing clothes for dinner.

They found the location of the restaurant, but it had a different name now, which confused Libby, who still didn't seem convinced that so many years had elapsed. Gil suggested they stop anyway because he, too, was hungry. He also said there was a high percentage of BMWs and Mercedes in the lot, so the food must be more than adequate.

Candace smiled at how quickly her brother had sized up her friends.

"Does this mean you'll dine with us?" Emmie asked Gil as they all got out of the car.

"He will," Candace answered for him. "Even drivers need to eat dinner." If Emmie thought that was an odd remark she made no further mention. She was not exactly in a position to question social correctness.

The restaurant was in an understated, shingled house that sat on a pristine emerald lawn. Inside, a fireplace glowed on one end of a warm, cozy room; clusters of low candles were grouped as centerpieces; the décor was refined yet elegant with spindle-back chairs and intimate, well-spaced table placements. However, unlike Peter would have done, Candace hadn't thought to make reservations.

"I'm very sorry," the polite hostess said. "But we have nothing available for five."

Maybe she had recognized Libby and knew about the family's recent woes. Or maybe she had seen Gil in the *New York Times* photo. Candace was about to protest when Gil intervened. "If you have a table for four, I'll grab something later," he said, retreating toward the door. "The ladies are more hungry than I am."

"No," Candace said. "We're five for dinner. We'll go elsewhere."

The hostess nodded, and Libby said, "This isn't the right place, anyway."

Emmie made no comment. She seemed preoccupied, which wasn't surprising. But at least she'd stopped talking about her boyfriend or the chance that she might be pregnant.

Once they were back in the car, Devon said, "Candace? We need to talk about getting Libby to Falmouth tomorrow."

"Right. I guess we can't wait for her husband to come home and take care of her."

"And on top of Walter's death, Alana shouldn't have to deal with her mother, too. This will all be hard enough on her. Once she knows what's going on."

Candace looked out the window, at a foursome of restaurant customers who'd just arrived in a Jaguar: two couples, late thirties, forty maybe. They laughed and chatted as they strolled to the main door, the ladies cloaked in cashmere shawls, the gentlemen in neatly-pressed twills and boating shoes. She wanted to unroll the window and shout, "Hey! I'll bet my net worth is greater than yours!" But then she realized things change, life changes, priorities and values often change, too. Hers certainly had in the past couple of days.

She tapped Gil on the shoulder. "Let's just go to Oak Bluffs and get something there. Burgers would be fine. Or fried clams." She turned back to Devon. "Then we can figure out what to do about contacting Alana." She looked at Libby to see if she reacted to her daughter's name, but Libby's eyes were closed. She must have fallen asleep again.

⌣‿⌐

Devon was glad when they dropped Candace, Emmie, and Libby off at the house. Candace had said Devon had earned a good night's sleep at the hotel without worrying about another unexpected visit from her ex-husband, or another outburst from Libby. Then she'd told Emmie they could take turns listening for Libby, but that they would have to sleep in the East Wing guest rooms. After all, there had been no housekeeping person to put fresh linens on the bed where Devon had slept or to tidy the en suite bath. Devon secretly supposed that Libby had needed to dismiss the cleaning service.

When they arrived at the Harbor View and walked into the lobby, Gil asked Devon if she'd like a nightcap. "I don't know about you," he said, "but I need to unwind after this very strange day."

Devon agreed.

In Henry's Bar, she ordered a wine cooler; he ordered a beer. They settled into a small table tucked in a corner.

"So," Devon said. "You think this was a strange day?"

He laughed. He had a nice, non-judgmental laugh, not a Josh kind of laugh. "My sister always made life interesting. It's nice to know that her legacy continues."

He drank his beer; she sipped her drink. He was easy to be with.

"Tell me about Louis D.," she said. "Was he a man in prison?"

He nodded. "Louis D. was the best. He taught me how to deal with life on the inside. He taught me how to deal with loss. He was a really good man—for a killer."

Devon nearly dropped her glass.

Gil laughed. "I guess that came out wrong. Sorry. But I was lucky to have met him. He protected me. He had a son who was nearly my age."

"Did you meet him? His son?"

He paused a moment, then shook his head. "No, I never had the pleasure. His name is Leonard now. He lives in Pennsylvania."

Then she asked, "Was it hard? Coming back into the world? My gosh, so much has changed . . ."

"No kidding. Twenty-five years ago women had big hair. And men wore gold chains and bracelets." He chuckled. "I never was able to get into that fashion. It's interesting, though, that Candace has a Town Car. I remember they used to be bigger than they are now. Bigger than a Cadillac. Or at least that's how they seemed."

They talked about cell phones and computers and the miracle and challenges of the Internet that Gil said he'd been able to access on a limited basis, but that it still scared the hell out of him. They talked about the fact that the Soviet Union no longer existed and about September 11th. They talked about how lifestyles had changed and how, wherever you looked, it was rare to see anyone light a cigarette now.

They ordered two more drinks, but neither of them seemed interested in what was in their glass. When Henry's announced

"Last Call," Gil suggested they move to the rocking chairs on the front porch.

"You know my life story," he said, once they sat facing the harbor and the lighthouse. The night air was clear; a half moon had risen and haloed the fringe of Chappaquiddick. "Now it's your turn. Tell me about yours."

So she did.

He knew many of the books her father had taught; he knew many of the arias her mother had sung. He had spent a lot time in the prison library; his sister had always stressed the importance of education, he said.

She told him about meeting Josh and having Julie and naming her after Josh's grandmother because she had been nice to Devon. She told him about the separation and about her long stretch of depression.

He listened.

She even told him about the night she had stalked Josh and how she had hauled off and clocked him with her bag.

He laughed. So did she.

She told him how infuriating it had been that Josh had showed up on the Vineyard, and how she was glad that he was gone.

When a chill began to rise up from the water, Gil went inside the hotel and returned with blankets. They wrapped themselves up and talked some more. When they ran out of words, they sat and rocked until the sky started to lighten and the gulls and the pinkletinks began to stir.

"I guess I should get some sleep," Devon finally said.

"Me, too," he replied.

Still, they lingered awhile, watching silhouettes of a few fishing boats as they chugged out of the harbor, heading to the

Elizabeth Islands or over to Menemsha. Devon wanted to stay right there, next to Gil, forever. She never had felt so safe.

⟨───⟩

It had been eons since Candace had driven, but at least it was a manageable Mercedes and not Peter's big boat of a car.

In the morning, after quick coffee and leftover muffins, Candace and Emmie coaxed Libby into the back seat and engaged the childproof lock so she could not escape. Libby had not woken up in good humor.

"Whose car is this?" she snipped as Candace backed out of the driveway. Last night, she'd consumed the last of the sedatives the doctor had provided. Now, instead of sleeping, she was snipping.

"It's mine," Candace said, to shut her up.

"Where are we going?"

"Boston."

"Why?"

"To pick up the girls."

"What are they doing in Boston?"

"Getting ready for their recital." Candace figured if she pretended this was about their daughters, Libby might be less restless. It worked. For about five seconds.

Then Libby spat, "Why are you two wearing the same clothes you had on yesterday?"

Candace side-glanced Emmie. "We like them," Emmie said.

The twelve-minute ride to the hospital seemed to take twenty-four hours.

"Why are we stopping here?" Libby demanded.

"Drugs," Candace replied, and got out of the car, leaving Emmie in charge of Libby.

She didn't know the name of the doctor who had been on duty Saturday, but knew there must be a record.

"Dr. Erickson is not here today," the receptionist in the lobby of the Emergency Department said after she'd perused her computer.

Candace leaned against the counter and tried to look as if she were justifiably pleading. "Please." She spoke softly, though her fingers were tightly curled up in her pockets. "I really need your help. The doctor let Mrs. LaMonde go home with our friend because he thought she might be better by today. She isn't. And we all hoped Mr. LaMonde would show up and take over her care. But his body was found yesterday. He's dead." She lowered her eyes as if she were saddened at having to report the unfortunate news. "Please. Libby still thinks it's 2003. And she's become short-tempered and nasty. Definitely not her personality. I've known her twenty years and have never heard her bitchy until now." She returned her beseeching gaze to the receptionist who was young, twenty-five or thereabouts. She had long, black hair and lightly tanned skin and dark eyes that were fixed on Candace.

"How'd he die?"

"Murdered." As Candace might have predicted, the air in the lobby suddenly grew still.

"Oh," the young woman said. "How awful."

"Yes. So if you can please get me the appointment with the neurologist in Falmouth, I will bring her. Or at least get me a name. If I have to barge into his office and beg, I will. Someone has to help her."

The young woman stood up. Candace noticed then that she wore a small name badge with TRACEE etched on it. She wondered when the younger generation had taken it upon themselves to spell their names in trendy, non-memorable fashion.

"I'll be right back," Tracee said.

Candace stood, tapping one foot, then the other.

"Did you get your drugs?"

Candace whipped around and there stood Libby, hands on both hips. Emmie was off to one side, looking apologetic.

"She said she didn't like being stuck in the car," Emmie said.

Thankfully, Tracee returned quickly. She handed Candace a small square of paper. "Doctor Laura Bingham," she said. "She has an office at Falmouth Hospital and will be expecting you. Do you know where that is?"

"I'll find it." Candace took the paper and stuffed it in her purse. "In the meantime, can I get her any medication? So we can get her there safely?"

Tracee shook her head. "Sorry. The doctor here feels Doctor Bingham should see Mrs. LaMonde in her current state."

"Mrs. *LaMonde*?" Libby nearly stepped on Candace's feet. "*I* am Mrs. LaMonde. Why are you talking about me?"

Candace put a hand on Libby's shoulder and guided her toward the sliding glass doors. "Libby," she said, "shut up. We're going to help you now."

"Then we'll get the girls?"

"No, Libby," Emmie said before Candace could lie again. "Sometimes it's better to accept reality in order to get on with your life."

Libby looked confused, but Candace supposed it really made no difference.

25

"I'm not going to Falmouth with you," Emmie announced once they reached the car. "I know you must think I'm awful, but I need to know whether or not I am pregnant. I can't wait one more day." It felt strange to make a decision that meant putting herself first. Strange, yet satisfying.

Candace visibly grimaced. "Whatever. Frankly, all I want is to get this all over with and go home."

"You'll be okay in Falmouth without me?"

"I'm a big girl. I'll manage." Then she added, "Sorry. I'm simply worn out."

Emmie ignored both Candace's barb and her apology. She looked off toward the harbor. The ferry was rounding the bend, about to pull in. "Go," she said. "If you hurry maybe they'll let you on that boat. Say it's an emergency. I'll take the bus back to Edgartown."

"The *bus*?"

"I'm sure one will come by soon enough. I think I can find the house."

"Have you ever even been on a bus, Emmie? You have to pay, you know. A dollar. Maybe two. Do you have any cash?"

At least she'd remembered to bring her purse with her that time. "Of course I have cash. And it's time I grew up and did things on my own don't you think?"

Without waiting for Candace to reply, Emmie stuffed Libby back into the car.

"When you get to the house," Candace said, "make the salad, okay?"

Emmie said she would. Candace had steamed the lobsters last night: Emmie could certainly figure out how to add mayonnaise and celery. With newfound confidence, she raised her chin, waved, and scanned the lot for a bus stop.

"Reservation?" A man in the small gatehouse at the pier asked.

"No. This is an emergency. My friend is sick. The doctor at the hospital said you always have space for an emergency." Of course, Candace had made that part up. She couldn't very well say that crying "emergency" had been Emmie's suggestion.

He peered at her over half-glasses; his thick, salt-and-pepper eyebrows grazed the frames, no doubt hooding his vision. She wondered if he were questioning how pressing an emergency would be when it involved a woman in a Mercedes that bore New York license plates.

"My friend's husband was murdered," Candace added. "Yesterday. Here on the island. Perhaps you've heard about it?"

His brows shot up. "We don't have many murders here."

"Well, now you have one more. And I have to get his wife to Falmouth Hospital. She's in a state of shock. If you don't believe me, call Doctor Laura Brigham. That's who we're going to see."

He looked into the backseat where Libby sat, belted-in, thankfully silent. "Okay," he said at last. "Pull into Lane 5. Then you'll have to go inside and get a ticket."

She thanked him and followed the white-painted lines to the proper lane. Then she turned off the engine, cracked the window, and locked Libby in the car as if she were one of those black dogs like the bronze one perched atop the red clapboard building next door where they sold t-shirts and God only knew what else.

Hustling toward the terminal, she dodged a few cars and people that had spilled from the gaping mouth of the ferry that had just docked. She steered clear of making eye contact with anyone whose path she hurriedly crossed. If anyone gave her the finger there was no telling how she'd react.

"Two adults and one car," she said quickly when she reached the ticket window. She showed her driver's license that she renewed regularly (though, until now, she'd never known why). She pulled out her credit card then bounced on her heels, not understanding why she was so nervous.

"Only two adults?" came a voice from behind her. "Who are you leaving behind?"

She knew the voice, but turned around anyway. "Josh. I thought you left last night."

He shrugged. "By the time Devon ordered me away, it was too late to make arrangements on the other side. I stayed at the Harbor View. I'm surprised you didn't see me."

There was no point in telling him she hadn't stayed there last night, but that his ex-wife had.

"Anyway," he continued, "I have a car meeting me in Woods Hole this morning. I'll catch the Acela out of Providence. Three hours from there to Penn Station."

Candace really didn't care what direction Josh Gregory was going in, or how he planned to get there. But she supposed if she said, "Well, bully for you," that would not be polite. "That's nice," she said instead.

"So," he said, following her back out to the parking lot, "is everything under control?"

"Everything is fine. I'm taking Libby to see a neurologist in Falmouth."

"Has anyone called Alana yet?"

"We're going to do that today. After we find out what's going on with Libby. We don't want to upset the girl more than necessary."

They reached the car. "Well," he said, "I'd like to come back for the funeral. But I don't expect Devon will let me know when it will be."

Candace shrugged. "We don't know anything right now." Then she pointed to the boat. "I think walk-on passengers have to go up that ramp on the side." He gave her a half-assed grin, then walked away. She got in the car and reminded herself to stay there once they were on board. The last thing she wanted was to go topside and be trapped into idle conversation with Josh.

Devon looked at the clock, surprised that it read nine-fifteen, even more surprised that she felt as if she'd slept all night instead of only a few hours. She had slept well, and dreamed about . . . what? *Oh!* She laughed. She'd dreamed that Josh's prickish attorney had been run over by a yellow taxi. Perfect.

Then she thought about Gil. How could she not? How long had it been since she'd enjoyed being in the company of a man? She'd had many moments of pleasure when she'd been with Josh. But, looking back, she had to admit that many had been forced. She'd always tried so hard to act as if she fit in with his life. With Gil, she'd simply been herself.

Stop it, she cried, pushing back the covers, pulling herself from the bed, and marching toward the bathroom. Why on earth was she thinking about him? There was no future there, could be no future there. Devon wasn't ready for a future of any kind that involved a man, certainly not one she'd met only forty-eight hours ago. Certainly not Candace's brother. And an ex-convict to boot.

Still, she thought, as she slipped out of her robe and stepped into the shower, she had never told anyone some of the things she'd told him, including that she'd named Julie after Josh's grandmother because she'd been the only one in his family who'd been nice to her.

Julie.

Oh, God, she thought, someone was going to have to call the girls today and tell them about Walter. Would it be best to say there had been an accident and save the truth until Alana was safely home?

Then Devon thought about Gil again. Maybe he could offer a sensible opinion, one that wouldn't be clouded from being too close to the people or the situation. Maybe he could contribute an objective perspective.

Gil.

She smiled again. She wondered if he'd been with a woman since he'd been eighteen, since he'd spent that night with Mindy Gleason at Chautauqua Park.

Turning on the faucet, she let out a small cry of exasperation. *Stop it,* she warned herself again. There were more pressing issues than the flutter in her stomach when she thought about Gil Martin. She let the hot water stream over her, hoping it would wash away her childish notions and emotions.

She was vulnerable, she knew.

Chances were, he was vulnerable, too.

And though it had been years since Devon had been with any man other than her husband, she knew that vulnerability could be a curse. She knew she would need to be cautious, for both their sakes. No matter what, Gil was a nice man. She did not want to lead him on. After all, she had her new life that she was still settling into. He had one that had yet to begin.

No, she thought, *I won't let this happen. He is nice, and he is kind, but I don't need a man right now.*

If only her heart would work as smartly as her brain.

The bus driver had been terrific. He asked where Emmie was from and if she was having a good time on the Vineyard. She didn't tell him about Walter. There were only two other passengers, and they'd gotten off the bus in Oak Bluffs, so he practically brought Emmie right up to Libby's front door. She was glad she hadn't told him that she and Conlan preferred Nantucket for summer jaunts and had only visited Libby and Walter when they'd felt compelled.

As she walked up the driveway, she felt—for the first time ever—almost in control of her life. But when she went onto the porch, then inside the house, her mood shifted. She walked down the hallway, past the kitchen, toward the powder room, aware that an eerie chill was crawling over her. She realized she was alone. Alone in a place where a man had been murdered.

Her pulse started to hammer. Her breathing grew shallow.

Why hadn't she realized that sooner, before she'd let Candace drive off with Libby? Why hadn't she considered that she'd be alone with Walter's killer still—what was the term?—on the loose? At large?

"How about *not caught?*" she whispered into the formidable air.

Then a single thought popped into her mind: *Would the killer come back and shoot her, too?*

She quickly ducked into the powder room. She leaned against the counter that held the stone vessel sink. She told herself she was being ridiculous. Why would anyone want to shoot her? It wasn't as if Conlan knew about Boyd yet. Neither did Boyd's wife, as far as Emmie knew. No. No one would have cause to shoot Emmie Malloy. Certainly not the same person who'd done away with Walter LaMonde.

Still, to be safe, Emmie retraced her footsteps down the hall and, that time, she locked the back door. Then she forced herself to turn to more pressing matters.

Padding back toward the powder, she wondered if she should return Conlan's call before she took the pregnancy test. She was sorry she'd practically hung up on him last night. But how could she think straight when she'd held her future—his, too, she supposed—in her hand? Yes, maybe she should call him now before she got sidetracked. He was still her husband, after all. And he always knew what to say to calm her down.

Back at the sink, she took the test wand out of the drawer, set it on the counter, pulled her cell phone from her purse, and hit the "1" on speed dial. Conlan was *number one* because, until only a few weeks ago, he had been. Another wave of guilt rippled through her.

The phone rang once, twice, then Conlan's voicemail came on.

"Your Highness," she said, attempting to sound nonchalant. "It's me. I am sorry I wasn't nice last night. It had been such a dreadful day." She stopped herself from blurting out that Walter was dead, that she'd seen part of his body sticking out of the phlox. It wouldn't be nice to leave all that on voicemail. She let out a small whimper. "Call me back, okay? But wait a few minutes. I need to do something right now, so I won't be able to answer the phone. Love you." She'd added the "love you" part because, well, she did. Just because she loved Boyd in a different way, did not mean she didn't love Conlan. She was confused about some things but not about that.

Shoving the phone back into her purse, Emmie picked up the wand. She lifted the toilet seat, sat down, and positioned herself. This time, no matter what, she would get her answer. Nothing would distract her. Nothing. No one.

She peed on the wand.

And then she heard loud, insistent banging. And shouts. Lots of shouts.

She froze. *No!*

She held tightly to the wet wand, determined not to flinch. But then came another shout, that time earsplittingly clear: "POLICE! WE'RE COMING IN!"

She jumped up from the bowl and set the wand carefully onto the counter, which was some kind of feat because her hand was trembling.

"Stop shouting!" she shouted back. "I'm here! I'm here! I'll let you in!"

She quickly washed her hands, pulled up her panties, fluffed her skirt, and darted from the bathroom just as she heard the cracking of wood and saw the back door burst open.

"Wait! she cried. "Wait!"

242

It was too late. The doorframe was in splinters and three uniformed officers—two State Police and the female cop who'd been there yesterday—had already crashed their way into the hall. They looked like the same ones who had been there yesterday.

"What are you doing?" she cried again. "Why did you break down the door? I told you to stop shouting! I told you I was here!"

"We didn't hear you," the female officer said.

"Well, how could you hear me over all that shouting?" At least she had stopped trembling.

"Are you alone?" one of the state cops asked.

Emmie wanted to ask why, but decided that might not be a good idea. "Yes. My friend, Candace, has taken Mrs. LaMonde to see a doctor. She isn't well, you know. Mrs. LaMonde, that is." They didn't say they already knew that, but she figured they did.

Then the female officer pushed a piece of paper toward her. "We have a warrant to search the premises."

Of course, the first thing Emmie thought about was the pregnancy test wand sitting innocently—or not so innocently—next to the sink in the powder room. "*No!*" she shrieked, more loudly than she supposed she should have. "I mean, why do you need to search the house? Walter was found in the garden." Of course, they knew that, too.

"Sorry, ma'am," the female officer said as if Emmie were old enough to be her mother. "But please, you'll have to wait outside."

God help her, she raised an eyebrow and stared at the woman.

Then one of the males placed his hand on his hip, which was where, Emmie noted, his gun was visibly holstered. Her heart rushed to her throat.

She shrank. "May I . . ." she asked meekly, "may I go get my purse? I'd like to call my husband." Maybe Conlan was done with whatever he'd been doing. Maybe he would realize how badly she'd been trying to reach him. And maybe she could retrieve the test wand before she was embarrassed to death.

"Sorry, ma'am," the female said again. "There will be plenty of time for phone calls after. Right now, we need you to leave the house."

Emmie started to tremble again. She moved off the porch and out to the yard. She rubbed her arms with rapid, staccato motions and then edged down the driveway toward the main road. Maybe the nice bus driver would come around again. Maybe he had a phone she could use.

26

Devon stepped out of the shower and dried her body with a thick, white towel. She wondered what a man—a new man—might think of the way she looked. And what about Gil? Were his visions of a woman's body still stuck in teenage mode? Did he know that a naked woman—her legs, her breasts, her butt, her belly—weren't as tight and taut after forty as they'd been at eighteen? She wrapped the towel around her and dried her hair with another. She brushed her teeth, then stood back from the mirror, looking for any telltale damage that the virtually sleepless night had left on her face.

There was none that she could see.

Still, she was definitely not eighteen. Not in face or body. Not in mind. She was a mature woman. She was not going to behave like a girl with a teenage crush.

That's what Devon was thinking when she heard a soft swish-across-carpet. She cocked her head; there was no other sound. She went back into the bedroom: An envelope rested there, on the floor, just inside the door.

A copy of the bill, she thought, remembering they had planned to check out today. She picked it up; the upper left corner bore the Harbor View logo. But as she flipped it over to open the seal, she spotted a note scrawled on the back.

The note read: *Are you awake? Gil.*

She smiled.

She went to the door and opened it a sliver, wide enough to see his gentle smile.

"I was trying to decide if I should knock."

Standing in her towel, Devon knew she must tell him she wasn't dressed; she must suggest they meet downstairs for breakfast in fifteen minutes. Or twenty. But he was smiling that lovely smile, and she was feeling an odd stirring in her belly. She knew better, of course. She'd hashed that out only moments ago.

Which was why she was surprised when she said, "Would you like to come in?" and he said, "Yes. Very much."

He stepped inside.

She closed the door.

"You're not dressed," he said.

"I know."

They stood about a foot apart. His eyes were a shade of polished pewter in the new morning light.

"I wanted to see if you were interested in breakfast."

"Not yet."

"Not yet?"

That's when Devon did something she'd never done before. She moved closer toward him, took his chin in her hand, and kissed his mouth, as if it were the most natural, most normal thing to do.

He kissed her back and said, "I didn't expect . . ."

She hushed him and kissed him again. That time her towel fell to the floor.

"Oh, God," he said.

She took his hand and led him to her bed.

When they had finished, Devon looked around the room. His clothes were heaped in a hasty pile; her towel peeked from beneath the rubble. She laughed.

"Laughing can hurt a guy's feelings," Gil said.

"Are you kidding? You were wonderful. You are wonderful. I can't believe I did that, though. I can't believe I seduced you."

He propped himself up on one elbow and studied her. "Actually, that part was really nice. I never would have done it. I'd have been too chicken."

"As I recall, Candace said you were a saint."

"Oh, sure. A saint who's been in prison for twenty-five years."

"You're forty-three, then?"

"I guess. I sort of lost track."

She did not say she'd thought Candace was forty-three. She saw no sense in revealing his sister's secret, if that was what it was. "I'm forty-three, too," she said.

"You are so beautiful." He traced the roundness of her breast with the light touch of one finger. Then he leaned down and kissed her.

"You are amazing," she said. "After all you've been through . . ."

He rolled onto his back and looked up at the ceiling. "After all I've been through? That's kind of a joke, isn't it? I mean, sure, I've been locked up. I gave up my privacy, and I mastered a spork. I've had no one but men to talk to, which was probably the worst part. They're not always agreeable, you know?" He cocked that smile again, and Devon smiled back. "And sure, I missed a lot of good stuff. But I missed the bad stuff, too. I never knew what it was like to be my sister, playing dodge ball, trying to cover up her lies so she could put together a decent life. I never knew what it was like to try and hold a job, even if I hated it. I never knew what it must be like to have my child be a convicted murderer.

247

And I never knew the pain of loving a woman, only to have her dump me."

Devon let out her breath. "My God," she said, "you really are amazing."

He laughed then turned back to her. "So you're not sorry you seduced me?"

She shook her head.

He slid on top of her again. "Then you won't mind if this time I seduce you?"

She laughed again until he covered her mouth with kisses, until he prodded her lips apart with his warm, moist, eager tongue.

Emmie waited what seemed like forever when, at last, the bus grumbled up the street. She waved her arms briskly.

"Stop!" she cried. "Stop!"

It stopped. The door squished open.

"Help!" she pleaded. "Do you have a cell phone I can use?" She scurried up the stairs into the bus. Only one person was seated in the back, a young man who looked about Brandon's age. "Will you excuse us?" she said to the young man. "I only need to bother the driver for a minute."

The young man shrugged and adjusted his headphones.

"What's wrong?" the driver asked. "Do you have an emergency? Are you all right?"

He was the same man who'd brought her to Libby's: *How right she had been to think he was nice!* "Did you hear about the murder? The dead man was my friend's husband. It was awful, simply awful. And now the police are searching the house for clues, and they made me leave, but I have nowhere to go, and I don't have my phone. I need to call my husband. Can you help me? Please?"

Of course, he handed her his phone. Her Daddy had always said Emmie had a way with men that made them melt, not because they wanted sex but because she could seem so needy and they liked feeling like John Wayne who she'd heard about but had never watched one of his cowboy movies.

"Can you ride while you make your call?" the driver asked. "I have to head back to Oak Bluffs, make a swing around the island, then do the run out to the airport." He motioned the route with his hands as he spoke. "I can drop you off on my way back from there, if you have the time. It will take a while."

"Perfect. Maybe the police will be done by then. But I don't have my purse. I have no money for the fare."

"No charge," he said, with a genial wink. "We're trained to help damsels in distress."

She thought John Wayne might have been proud. Then Emmie grinned and took the phone. She sat two rows back from the driver and two up from the young man and the bus drove off toward Oak Bluffs.

That's when she stared at the cell phone and realized she did not know Conlan's number. She always only pressed the number "1." As for Boyd's? Forget it. She didn't know his number either.

So Emmie simply sat there and looked out the window and pretended to smile. But on the inside, she wondered what the results now read on the wand in the powder room and if the police had confiscated it and how it happened that she had landed in such a hopeless mess.

Candace said she was Libby's sister so she'd be allowed in the exam room, a tiny, claustrophobic place with a paper-covered table, two blue plastic chairs, and a stainless, salt-air-weathered steel cabinet. Framed photos of ocean scenes, dunes, and gulls graced the light beige walls. A poster of a full color, cutaway illustration of the human brain was taped to the door. A similar depiction, that one in 3-D resin, had been mounted on a metal base and stood atop the cabinet. Candace leaned against the wall and folded her arms; Libby hopped up on the table. When they'd been on the ferry, Libby had stayed quiet; after turning off the engine, Candace had turned on the stereo and found a station that was playing easy listening music that she prayed would keep Libby quiet. She also prayed the car battery wouldn't quit for the forty-five minute trek. It had not.

But as they waited for the doctor to join them now, Libby became agitated. "You lied to me," she said. "I thought we were going to get the girls."

Candace shook her head. "I didn't exactly lie, Libby. But you need to see a doctor before the girls can come home. We talked about this, remember? About how you're confused?"

Libby lowered her head and checked her manicure. "Walter's dead. I'm not confused about that, am I?"

"I wish you were. But, yes, Walter is dead."

"We have to plan a funeral."

"As soon as Alana comes home."

"They're not at a recital, are they?"

"No, Libby. They're not at a recital."

"And it's not 2003?"

"No."

"And George Bush is not the president?"

"No. He hasn't been for years." She saw no need to bring Libby up to date on presidential politics. The woman had suffered enough lately.

They sat in silence. It was sad to see Libby this way: at least when she was confrontational, she had some life, some spunk. But now it was as if her spirit had withered in tandem with her mind.

A slight young woman entered the room. Her white lab coat ballooned around her tiny frame; her wire-rimmed glasses were a decade out of style. She wore sneakers and held a brown clipboard. She offered her hand to Libby. "I'm Doctor Bingham."

"Libby LaMonde."

"And I am Mrs. Cartwright. Libby's sister."

"She isn't really my sister," Libby said, her nasty edge returning. "She was my friend, but she lied to me to get me here."

The doctor glanced at Candace who smiled and said, "I'm afraid Libby's memory is playing tricks on her, isn't it Libby? Remember, we just talked about President Bush?"

Libby ignored her.

"Would you prefer it if your friend left?" the doctor asked.

Chewing on her lower lip, Libby said, "I guess she can stay. She'll only drive me crazy later if she doesn't."

Doctor Bingham checked her clipboard, then fielded a few generic medical questions. Surprisingly, Libby responded. Candace wondered how much stock a neurologist could take in answers provided by a brain in disarray.

"I'll need you to take off your clothes and get into a johnnie," the doctor said. "Mrs. Cartwright and I will wait outside." She opened the cabinet, removed a folded square of blue cloth, and handed it to Libby. Then she motioned to Candace.

Outside in the hall, the doctor spoke softly. "Has Mrs. LaMonde had a recent shock? Has she witnessed anything traumatic?"

"We found her husband murdered. Is that traumatic enough?"

The doctor remained unflustered. "Was that when she became dissociative?"

"No. My friends and I arrived Saturday. We found her this way. We didn't find Walter until yesterday. He was dead in a flowerbed. Out on the back lawn. He'd been shot. I don't know how many times." No sense holding anything back.

The doctor eyed her clipboard again. "Do the police know who shot him?"

"Not yet. But we've wondered if Libby might have seen it happen. Could that have created this . . . what do you call it . . . dissociative disorder?"

"Dissociative fugue. And, yes, it's possible she witnessed the killing. Or, do you think it's possible that she shot him?"

Candace blinked. Her lower jaw dropped; she could not seem to stop it. She'd always been put off by mouths that dangled open, as if they belonged to a species of low intelligence among the primate set. And now she'd been reduced to one of them.

"Is it possible, Mrs. Cartwright? Would she have had any reason to kill her husband?"

"Well, no. I mean, I highly doubt . . . they had a good marriage, I think . . . we've known them for years . . ." Candace supposed that half the world would have been quite amused to see her so tongue-tied.

"There were no recent problems that you know of?"

"Well . . ." How much to tell? How much to tell? "Actually, they had some investments that went bad."

"A lot? It may sound like I'm prying, but these things might help us sort out her situation."

Candace nodded but closed her eyes so she wouldn't see the doctor's reaction when she said, "They lost millions. Everything they had. Except the house on the Vineyard, we think, which had been in Walter's family for generations. Walter is her husband. The one who's dead." She opened her eyes, but saw no shock on Doctor Bingham's face.

"Thank you," the doctor said and made another note. "Now, if you don't mind, I'd like to examine Mrs. LaMonde in private. I'll speak with you again when I'm finished." She disappeared back into the room that held the 3-D model and the poster of the brain, and Candace was left standing in the empty hall, wondering why it had never occurred to her that Libby might be the one who'd killed Walter.

Gil left Devon's room feeling . . . he couldn't describe how he was feeling. What were the words for having one's body, mind, and spirit merge together into a single, blissful form? *Euphoria,* he supposed. Or *nirvana.*

He returned to his room and quickly showered. He wanted to hurry so he could see her again, so he could watch her move, catch her scent, surrender to her smile.

Stepping into the shower—the big, clean shower with a bounty of soaps, gels, and shampoos like he'd never imagined in the cold, tile caverns at Attica—he suddenly realized he could cross number three off his list of things he'd been cheated out of: he'd now slept with more than two women, and this one was definitely old enough to vote.

Then he wondered what Louis D. would think if he knew Gil had found a terrific lady.

He'd probably grin. And nod. Then he might tell him to be careful. After all, it was because of Louis D.'s woman that his bad seed had surfaced and he'd been relocated to prison.

As Gil lathered now, he thought about Louis D.'s son, Leonard. He wondered if the boy had found happiness despite having lost both his mother and father. Then he wondered if the boy had ever known how much Louis D. had loved him. Still loved him. Which was why, Gil knew, the man had taken such good care of Gil. In his own way, Louis D. had pretended that Gil had been his. And Gil had wound up the lucky one.

27

Devon showered again. She'd wanted Gil to join her, but she knew if that happened, they would never leave the room, never have breakfast, never go back to Libby's where Candace and Emmie had hopefully returned from Falmouth with good news about Libby's prognosis.

Of course, she would have much rather spent the whole day with Gil, doing everything together, in bed or out, making love or strolling through the village, sitting by the water or sipping iced tea at a sidewalk café.

She savored her glee a few minutes longer, then stepped out of the shower, dried off, and quickly dressed so she could get on with the day. Gil had said he'd meet her downstairs in the dining room, which might be serving lunch now because it was nearly noon.

She felt rejuvenated: light and cleansed, tingling with good health. She did not recall that sex had ever made her feel that . . . whole. Perhaps it was more than just the physical act. Perhaps it had a lot to do with Gil, the most amazing man she'd ever known. Gil. Candace's brother! She winced a little, but decided there was no way she was going to let that interfere with her great mood. They would deal with Candace when they needed to. And they would deal with her together.

Not that it would come to that. Devon frowned. A small ache formed in her heart. As glorious as last night and this morning had been, she needed to remember they had both been vulnerable. They had both been hungry to be touched. But love? It was far too soon to know that.

Wasn't it?

She dismissed the thought: She needed to focus on how great she felt right now. And on the fact she was starving.

Tossing her phone into her purse, she decided to leave it in the room so her arms would be unencumbered—free to hug the new man in her life without the *JW* leather satchel getting in the way. She reminded herself, again, to keep her emotions in check. Then she changed her mind. These opportunities, after all, did not come every day. Or, at least, not to her.

As she left the room, she wore a slightly mischievous smile. She glided down the stairs as if they were blanketed by a red carpet and she was a well-loved star. Happiness had become unknown turf for Devon, and it felt wonderful. But when she had almost reached the bottom, she sensed a subtle shifting in the air, a kind of bleakness that seemed to drift up from the lobby. An awkward, unsettled silence.

She regained her bearings and stepped gingerly down the last few stairs. She saw the welcoming fireplace and the large glass aquarium that showcased an intricate model of a wooden fishing boat. She noticed the cushy chairs clustered cozily together. A few people sat there, holding old fashioned, printed newspapers. Instead of reading, though, they peered over the tops, toward the reception desk. And then, they looked at her. Her gaze traveled to the desk. She saw Gil right away: he stood near a bookcase. He was speaking with two policemen.

Her mouth went dry. She wished she'd brought her pocketbook so she'd have something to grip, some way to deflect the sudden knot that now squeezed her chest. "Leave him alone!"

she wanted to shout. "He's out of prison! His conviction was overturned!"

Then Gil and the policemen stopped talking and turned their eyes to her. Had he used her as an alibi? Would he have needed to? Surely they didn't think he had anything to do with the murder just because . . . just because his name and his picture had been plastered all over the *Times*.

"Gil?" she asked, as she slowly approached them. "Is everything okay?" But the numbness that now flooded her hands and her feet provided an ample reply.

"Devon Gregory?" one of the officers asked.

She recognized him from yesterday. "Yes."

Handcuffs flashed.

"Please turn around. And put your hands behind your back."

She flinched. Then she did as she was told because Devon always did. Always had.

"It's okay," Gil said quietly. He reached out to her. He touched her cheek. "I'll make this okay."

The ice of cold metal clamped over her wrists.

The other officer stepped forward. "Devon Gregory, we are arresting you for the murder of Walter LaMonde. You have the right to remain silent . . ."

Doctor Bingham said Libby's case was fascinating, and that she wanted to keep her overnight for observation.

"Why?" Candace asked.

The doctor said she felt the fugue was temporary. "She knows who she is, and she seems to know you: she knows you're not her sister. And she has grasped the fact that her husband has died. Those things help us rule out a more serious amnesia."

"Is there something you can do to bring her out of it?"

"No. Not really."

"No medication, no psychological intervention?"

"No. I'm afraid not."

"Then you want to keep her simply so you and your people can observe her? To watch how she behaves? To see how she reacts? And to hope you get to witness her return to normalcy?" Candace knew she sounded testy, but she didn't feel right leaving Libby there. Not when the poor woman was so vulnerable.

"Yes. We don't like someone in her state to be unsupervised. Recovery can be sudden. It can be frightening for the patient. And terribly confusing."

"Excuse me, but don't you think it would be just as frightening for her to be in a kind of sideshow? To be stared at by total strangers who think her case is 'fascinating?'"

The doctor's shoulders stiffened. "I assure you, my primary concern is for the patient."

Though it was probably true, Candace couldn't agree to it. Libby had been through enough in the past few days. "I'm sorry, doctor. Please understand I'm concerned for my friend. Who, if I understand you correctly, is medically all right?"

"She appears to be."

"Then I think I'll take her back to the Vineyard. There are people there she knows. People that care about her. Besides, she'll be in her own home, in her own environment with her lovely things. That should help her be less afraid, shouldn't it?" Now that Libby had been given a medical green light from the right kind of doctor, Candace wanted to get back to the island. There was so much to decide before they could go back to New

York: when to call Alana and what to say, what to do about funeral arrangements, when to notify the *Times* about Walter, how
to help Libby. They certainly couldn't leave her on the Vineyard
in her current state.

Yes, Candace thought, there was so much to decide, so much
to do. Maybe today they'd get lucky and the police would figure
out who had killed Walter. And Candace could return to the city
in time for the Art League election. Despite murder and mental
illness, she couldn't lose sight that the outcome of the voting still
mattered. After all, it was the best way for her to have Peter gift
her with a chunk of cash and the safest way for her to then get rid
of Gil. Once and for all.

The public transportation bus—Emmie now knew it was called
the *VTA* for *Vineyard Transit Authority*—had taken her past marvelous places she'd never seen: Colorful, gingerbread-trimmed
houses lined up as if they were in a doll museum; secret-looking,
still-water ponds where snowy white swans regally ruled; miles and
miles of gray stone walls that the driver—she now knew his name
was Fred—told her had been built by hand at least two hundred
years ago, sometimes even earlier.

Imagine!

She got to see real sheep grazing on velvet-looking grass on a
rolling farm in Chilmark; she saw tiny arts and crafts and souve-
nir shops and a restaurant with a panoramic view in Aquinnah—
Fred said they were *up island*, where much of the land and the
shops were owned by the Wampanoags who were real Indians
like he was.

Him?

Oh, my, Emmie thought, she was being chauffeured by a real Indian.

"Native American?" She felt a need to correct him.

He smiled, his big, white teeth gleaming against his rusty-colored skin. "Indian. Or Wampanoag. Whichever you prefer. My people have been here forever. Like most Vineyarders, we've stuck together."

He stopped so she could see the reds and golds of the clay cliffs; she wished she'd brought some cash so she could buy a handmade beaded purse or a lobster roll to show her support.

They picked up two passengers then continued on their way. Emmie got to see a sandy beach that seemed to stretch forever; then, later, an authentic general store that sat close to the road. Fred said the store was more than a hundred and fifty years old and housed, among other things, the post office. He also said that generations of islanders talked of life and death and politics and nothing special while sitting in the rockers aligned on the old porch.

The sky was so sparkly and the breeze was so clear as it quietly waltzed through the open windows of the bus that Emmie nearly forgot why she was there and what she'd left behind.

After what must have been an hour, maybe more, Fred announced, "Next stop, Martha's Vineyard Airport." Then the bus dipped down a hill and turned right.

Everything was so beautiful, Emmie was embarrassed. She knew she was spoiled, but this was something more . . . important. She was spoiled for all the wrong reasons. Like the way islanders "stuck together," Conlan had stuck by Emmie for many years. Maybe not a hundred and fifty, but a long time. He'd never retreated, never let her think he regretted marrying her. She loved him for that. She loved him for a lot of reasons, she supposed. Oh, sure, there was no grand passion, not like she had with Boyd. But wasn't what she had with Conlan more important? Hadn't he worked hard to build one of those safe, protective stone walls around their family—okay, not a *real* stone wall, but a boundary that had kept them together, kept them out of harm's way?

She thought about Libby. Libby had lost her money, lost her husband, lost her mind. Compared to Libby, Emmie had it all. How dare she jeopardize it for a selfish fling? Just because Boyd made her feel giddy and carefree? Is that what she really wanted? Besides, could she really take a man away from his wife and family without guilt . . . or, later, remorse?

And what about the horses? Spectacular thoroughbreds that cost enormous amounts of money.

She swallowed. Hard. Was Boyd's attraction to her partly because of the dreams he would realize thanks to the life her trust fund could provide? She didn't really believe that was why he was attracted to her, but would it trouble her someday?

She'd never had to worry about that kind of thing with Conlan. She did love him. Yes, she did. He was the man with whom she could be content to sit next to in a rocking chair on a front porch and talk about everything, and nothing special, for a hundred and fifty years. They never would have hot sex in a horse stall, but, gee, they would have the rest.

As the bus rumbled along, Emmie now knew what she had to do. It didn't matter if she were pregnant. She was going to do the one thing she knew she could live with. She was going to put away her girlish fantasies and act like an adult. She would tell Conlan what she had done. She would tell him she might be pregnant by Boyd—again. If Conlan left her, she would face the consequences. It was a risk she had to take. But, no matter what, she would not marry Boyd. It would not be fair to any of them.

And if she were pregnant—well, she'd worry about that later. Deep inside in her tummy, she felt a big surge of relief.

A few minutes later, Emmie saw a sign for the airport. Fred steered the bus down the side road, past a strip of business buildings until they reached the terminal. Emmie was surprised the place was so small—she avoided airports whenever possible, and certainly not without a stash of Ativan. But she was even more surprised when Fred moved the lever that made the door squish open and Conlan—her loyal, protective husband—boarded the little bus.

She blinked three times, then blinked again. Conlan stood in the small aisle; he was no mirage. If he was as surprised to see her as she was to see him, he didn't say.

"You said you weren't all right," he told her. "You said you'd call me back. That was yesterday. I was worried about you."

Emmie stood up and threw her arms around him and gave him a giant hug. "I don't deserve you," she cried. "I really, really don't deserve you." Later, there would be time to tell him what she'd done.

Then she introduced Conlan to Fred and Fred to Conlan and the men chatted a bit. Then Emmie and Conlan sat down and he took her hand and the bus rumbled from the airport down another wonderful road.

They sat in the ferry queue, waiting to board. Libby was in the back seat, so it looked as if Candace was her driver. That struck her as funny so she laughed.

"You find this amusing?" Candace snapped, her eyes darting to the rearview mirror. Candace had already argued with the attendant in the booth: her cry that they'd had an "emergency" earlier, did not guarantee that they could get back. "Unless there's room on the freight boat," the attendant had said, and Candace had growled. There was nothing wrong with crossing on a freight boat, but Libby supposed the term felt degrading to Candace.

"I'm sorry," she said. "The pill makes me feel strange." Before they'd left Falmouth Hospital, Candace had insisted that the doctor give Libby something to keep her relaxed until her "temporary" state had passed. She was, indeed, relaxed, but realized it would be best if she did not laugh again.

Candace drummed her fingers on the steering wheel.

Finally a small, flatbed freight boat backed into the berth. A few minutes later they were directed to board. Candace bumped the car over the entrance ramp, then pulled behind a box truck that advertised Cape Cod Potato Chips.

"Let's get out," Libby said. "I hate sitting in the car while we're crossing." She supposed it might be a good sign that she knew that.

Candace got out and unlocked Libby's door. "No jumping overboard," she said and sounded as if she really meant it.

They climbed an iron staircase to the upper deck that could not have held more than a dozen people. Libby closed her eyes and thought about how Walter preferred to take the freight boat to the Vineyard because he said it was more like "the real thing," not something that catered to tourists. He'd never understood that, technically, as "seasonal" residents, they weren't much more than tourists.

She opened her eyes and looked toward the Elizabeth Islands. She realized that was the first time she'd really thought about Walter since she'd been told that he was dead. She swallowed new-forming tears.

"Does this boat take longer than the big one?" Candace asked.

Libby shook her head. She was afraid if she tried to speak she would start to cry and never stop. Maybe it wouldn't hurt so much if only she could remember . . .

And then, right next to her head, the horn blasted. Sharply. Loudly. Piercingly. Her hands flew to her ears. She'd forgotten about the damn ferry horn! They never should have climbed up here until they were out of the harbor . . .

She looked at Candace. Candace Cartwright. Her friend. Her friend who suddenly didn't look older than her age, which was forty-three. Forty-three! A year older than Libby!

Images suddenly flashed through her brain like miniature film frames: Alana, now eighteen, a beautiful young woman; Walter, who had turned fifty last year; her parents, now retired and holding court in Scottsdale. Then a montage of the past decade and a half rushed through her mind: iPhones, laptops, an African-American president who definitely was not George W. Bush!

She pressed her palms against her temples, trying to ease the flood of memories, until she recalled sitting on the back porch . . . a nine-millimeter Glock in her lap . . .

Quickly, Libby covered her face. A Glock? A *Glock*? What did it mean? *What did it mean?* And, *oh God,* should she tell Candace?

28

Devon was freezing. She sat on the lower bunk in the female holding cell at Dukes County Jail, staring at the dull brown floor. The corrections officer explained that it used to have nice linoleum tiles but a drunken prisoner had ripped them up one night. He'd been making small talk, Devon knew, no doubt trying to help her relax. How in God's name she was supposed to do that in the six-by-eight foot, concrete-walled, fluorescent-lit room was beyond her.

She kept her gaze fixed on the floor so she wouldn't have to see the single-unit stainless sink and toilet that was tucked behind a half-wall that feigned privacy. She kept her hands in her lap so she didn't touch the plastic covered thin mattress that had been tossed onto the steel slab where she sat.

She was almost too scared to breathe. And too damn cold to care.

From the Harbor View, Devon had been driven to the Edgartown Police Department, where she'd been given the chance to tell her story. She didn't know much about the legal system, but she suspected she shouldn't take a murder charge lightly. So she'd refused to be interrogated and had said she'd wait for an attorney even though she didn't know one on the island. Libby might, if she were in her right senses, but Devon didn't have the patience to wait for that to change. Her only hope was for Candace to take charge once she'd come back from Falmouth. No one seemed to know how often, or how hard,

Candace's husband worked these days, but his law firm was prestigious and he had connections.

Because Devon would not "cooperate," she'd been picked up by a white van and transported down the street to the nearly one-hundred-and-fifty year old jail. She tried not to think about the prisoners who'd been there before her.

Paperwork was exchanged, and a dark-haired, dark-eyed, pokerfaced young man led her into the building. He was tall and lean yet muscular, dressed in brown pants and a short-sleeved white shirt, a Duke's County emblem on one sleeve. Intricate tattoos snaked up each arm and crawled out from his collar and up one side of his neck. For a moment Devon wasn't sure which side of the law he favored.

"I'm Officer Parker," he said. "Welcome to the Intake Room."

He told her to stand against the wall with her feet inside a rectangle outlined in blue tape on the floor. He snapped a photo: full face, right side, left. Then he brought her behind a counter and pressed her fingertips in ink and rolled them onto a white card because he said the digital system wasn't working. She had to remove her shoes, her watch, and the pretty silver bracelet she'd put on that morning. She was glad she'd left her *JW* bag and her phone in the room: She wouldn't have wanted the corrections people rummaging through her personal things, the way she and Candace had rummaged through Libby and Walter's.

"It's one o'clock," the officer said. "You could be arraigned this afternoon without an attorney. Or the court can provide you with one. If the judge posts bail you could be out of here."

She shook her head.

He asked if she wanted to call someone.

She dialed her cell phone, hoping one of her friends had thought to retrieve her purse from the hotel room. Off the top of her head, the only other phone number she knew was Julie's. And she certainly wasn't going to call her. But the phone rang six times and went into voice mail.

"You can try again later," the officer said.

She was given cotton slippers and told to sit at a desk in the corner until a female officer arrived to pat her down. According to the clock above the fingerprint machine, she waited half an hour for that humiliation.

She shivered now. She wondered if Gil had already jumped on the next boat off the island. She wondered if his release carried restrictions about him sleeping with another accused murderer. Murderess. Whatever she was being called.

The worst part was, she had no idea why she'd been accused of killing Walter. The officer had said she was entitled to know the *Statement of Facts* that had been compiled, but Devon had said, "No thank you, I'll wait for my lawyer." The truth was, she couldn't think straight. The truth was, she wasn't ready to hear anything without knowing how to defend it.

But how long would it be before her friends found out where she was and that she needed help? *It might take a long time,* she warned herself. *Especially if Gil took off before telling them.*

She rubbed her arms.

Then she heard the jangle of keys. She looked toward the cell door and up to the lone, ten-by-ten inch window that offered a cloudy view into a small hall. One lock unlocked, then another. The cell door opened: Officer Parker stood there, holding what looked like a green blanket and a tan one.

"You want a blanket? It can get cold in here."

She nodded.

"Wool or hypo-allergenic?"

"Wool, please." He handed her the green one; she wrapped it around herself and refused to consider the previous prisoners who had used it.

"Want something to read? We have a pretty good library."

She shook her head.

"Okay, I'll let you know if we hear anything. From anyone." He shut the door. The locks tumbled back into place.

Candace couldn't figure out what the hold-up was. There must have only been ten or twelve vehicles on the lug of a freight boat: why weren't any of them being driven off the ramp, into the parking lot, and off to do whatever it was they had come to the island to do? *What was the freaking hold-up?*

"God, I never did understand how you could live on this island every summer," she said to Libby who was once again belted in the backseat with the door locked. "To always be dependent on the whims of a bunch of misanthropic sailors."

Libby didn't say a word. In fact, Libby had barely spoken since they'd pulled onto this old bathtub, this *bucket of bolts*, Peter would have called it with a chuckle. Maybe she'd decided she was tired of being snippy. Or maybe she was angry with Candace for dragging her to Falmouth. As if the trip had been a huge picnic for her.

Patience, Candace told herself. *None of this is Libby's fault.* Of course, she might feel differently if she later learned that Libby had, indeed, killed Walter. Or if Peter lost the election because

Candace hadn't been there to help. If he lost the election, there would be no money for Gil. How would she deal with that? How, in fact, was she going to deal with him, anyway? Now that Devon knew the real story, how long could it be before the others did, too?

She tapped her foot next to the gas pedal. She wanted so badly to lean on the horn.

Should she . . . could she . . . tell Peter about Gil? Now that he'd been proven innocent, would it make a difference? It would be far better for her to tell her husband than for him to find out from someone else. If only she could get off this damn boat and find out when she could go home.

The noon sun glinted off the back of the potato chip truck that sat, stalled, in front of her.

Candace couldn't take it any longer. Putting down her window, she stuck her head outside and wailed, "Move that piece of shit!" She supposed it was conduct unbecoming of a New York City Cartwright, but what the hell, that status might soon be history for her anyway.

The response came in the form of a middle finger extended out the driver's side of the truck.

She couldn't blame him; she'd always hated that she handled annoyance so badly. He probably wanted to get on dry land as much as she did. Still, she'd never learned how to control her emotions. It was one of several unpleasant traits Candace had sadly passed down to her daughter, Tiffany.

When Tiff learned about Gil, she would probably stop speaking to Candace the way that Peter no doubt would. If only Candace hadn't raised the girl to be so impressed with social rights and wrongs, so tuned into material things, so dependent on an unlimited line of credit. Tiffany would have no clue how to survive in a place like Jamestown with a single mom and a kid brother to help raise.

"Candace?" Libby spoke so suddenly that Candace jumped. She hoped to God Libby wasn't going to scold her for yelling at the truck driver. It would not be surprising. She was, after all, a good friend of Devon's: both of them had always been so maddeningly pleasant and polite.

"Candace?" Libby called again.

"I hear you. I'm waiting for this stupid line to move."

"Candace, I have something to tell you."

She braced herself for another useless comment about their daughters pirouetting in days gone by, then wondered how much longer she'd have to play nursemaid.

"Our girls are in Europe, aren't they?"

Candace spun around in her seat. The cross strap of the seatbelt jerked up and nearly choked her. "What? You know they're in Europe?"

Libby nodded.

"Does this mean you're okay? That your memory is back?" It was an exciting thought, though Libby's complexion still looked similar to the pasty white of the back door of the truck.

"They graduated from Miss Porter's last week, didn't they?"

Candace closed her eyes. "Wow. Thank God." Then she remembered the rest. "What else?" She couldn't bring herself to ask if Libby knew who had killed Walter.

Libby fell silent again. Then she said, "Candace, I didn't go to the graduation, did I?"

She shook her head. "It's okay, Libby. We were there. Devon, Emmie. Me. Our husbands were there, too. Well, except for Devon's."

"Walter's dead," she said suddenly.

"Yes. But you've known that." She fidgeted with the seatbelt, wondering what Libby was going to say next.

"Candace," Libby said, raising her chin and looking squarely at her, "maybe I murdered him."

The air seemed to have been vacuumed from the car. A horn beeped behind them, then another. Candace turned back to the windshield and saw that the truck had left the boat and was moving down the ramp. She put the gearshift into Drive and followed suit. But as she began to wheel through the parking lot, a State Police cruiser was parked, its blue light flashing. A young man in a gray-and-blue uniform motioned for her to stop.

The last thing Candace wanted was to talk to a cop right then. Would she be obligated to tell him Libby's confession, if that's what it had been?

"What is it, officer?" Maybe she was going to be arrested for honking at potato chips.

"Mrs. Cartwright? Candace Cartwright?"

She sighed. They must have found out about Gil and now they'd come for her, too. "Yes." She wanted to lower her head and rest her forehead on the steering wheel. Suddenly she was so weary.

"Mrs. Cartwright, is that Mrs. LaMonde in your back seat?"

She didn't think it was necessary to tell him that technically, it was Mrs. LaMonde's back seat, not hers. "Yes."

"I believe you were instructed not to leave the island in case you were needed to answer more questions about Mr. LaMonde's killing?"

"Killing?" Candace asked. She needed to stall for a few seconds so she could collect her thoughts, so she could decide what her next move should be. She really didn't want Libby to go to jail. It would be so messy on so many levels and for so many people, including her. "Does that mean you've definitely ruled out suicide?"

"Yes, ma'am." He put his hands at his waist, just above his weapon. "We're dealing with a clear-cut homicide. All the more reason you shouldn't have left." He was young and couldn't have had much experience, but he made a good, lawful presence.

"I'm sorry," she said. "But Mrs. LaMonde is ill. I took her to Falmouth to see a doctor. I didn't consider that a misdemeanor. It's not as if I went back to New York."

"You'll need to follow me, ma'am."

"Follow you? Where?"

"To the police barracks. The Commander would like to speak with you. Pull over and let the vehicles behind you off the boat. Wait there until I get the cruiser."

Candace wondered if this day could get any worse. Then she made a decision. "Libby," she said, "whatever you do, don't let them think your memory is back. And, above all, don't tell them you might have shot Walter. Not until we've had time to talk about this amongst ourselves." *Or not until,* she didn't add, *MY brain has had a chance to regroup.*

29

The bus driver drove right to Libby and Walter's house. He said it was okay because he'd dropped off the other passengers at Morning Glory Farm and Emmie and Conlan were the only riders he had left.

When they reached the end of the driveway, Conlan looked out toward the water. "Where did they find Walter?" He'd met Walter through the connection of the ladies and the kids. A practical man, and, of course, much older, Conlan might not have been friendly with Walter if they'd met while playing racquetball or squash. The two men were so very different.

"Over there," Emmie said. "In the phlox. Where the yellow tape is."

Conlan cocked his head. "The flowers are all matted down now. Well, that's too bad."

Emmie had thought the same thing, but hadn't voiced it to the others. She cupped her arm through his. "Let's go inside. Libby's car isn't here, so they must still be in Falmouth."

"Do you have a key?"

"It isn't locked."

Conlan looked horrified. "A killer might be on the loose and the door isn't locked?"

"Oh," she said. "Well, actually I locked it before. But the police broke in, anyway."

Once they were inside, she glanced down the hall toward the powder room. She wondered if the test wand was still there.

"I need the loo," Conlan said.

She let go of his arm and darted in front of him. "Use one upstairs. We were having trouble with this one this morning." She brushed back her wispy hair. "Go ahead. I'll make coffee. Or lunch. Would you like a sandwich? Lobster salad?"

He kissed her cheek. "Sounds wonderful." He headed for the staircase, and she opened her mouth and let out a pent-up rush of nerve-wracked air.

With Conlan safely out of sight, she moved into the kitchen where she clanked dishes and silver and water goblets—Orrefors, not Libby's original Waterford. She found what looked like a loaf of multigrain bread in the freezer and nuked a couple of slices. Then she pulled the bowl of lobster from the refrigerator and began making the salad. No one could say Emmie Malloy was totally helpless without a cook.

Like Conlan, though, she had to pee. And she was anxious to see the verdict of her hormonal state. Her gaze fell to her purse that sat on the kitchen island right where she'd left it before her earlier visit to the powder room when the police had interrupted. Should she check her phone? Had Boyd called again? Did it matter anymore?

And, most of all, was she committed enough in her decision not to be swayed by the *plus* or *minus* results?

Her thoughts drifted to her father. As much as Emmie had missed him since he'd died, at least if Conlan chose to leave her now, her father would be spared the embarrassment that his daughter had screwed up. Again. And the truth was, her mother was so busy with her new life in Palm Beach that she might not even notice. Oddly, Emmie took comfort in those facts. It was as if, for the first time in her life, this decision would be hers and hers alone. No stress, no pressure, no parental guilt, merely Emmie finally doing what Emmie felt was right.

"Need help with the sandwiches?"

She jumped at the sound of Conlan's voice. "No," she said. "Sit down. Lunch is almost ready."

But instead of continuing with her task, she drew in a breath. She was reminded of a smart person who'd once said, *there's no time like the present.*

"Conlan," she said, "I have to tell you something. I've done something naughty." The words had been remarkably easy to say.

"My dear," Conlan said. "Don't be so hard on yourself." His smile was slightly tentative. "Besides if you're talking about your dalliance with that old boyfriend of yours, I already know." He sat down on a stool and put his elbows on the granite slab atop the island.

"But . . ." She didn't know how to finish the sentence.

He held a finger to his lips. "But, nothing. I am only too aware of the disadvantage of years between us. Unless you plan to divorce me, there will be no further talk of this."

"No," she said, and suddenly realized the word had come out in a whimper. "I love you, Conlan. I don't want to leave you. It was just a fling. I was so upset about the children being grown up . . . about them being gone. But it's totally over. I promise, I won't do it again." Tiny tears leaked from her eyes and sprinkled down her cheeks. *Would he feel the same way if . . . if . . .*

He held out his arms. "Come here and give me a hug. Then feed me lunch. I'm starving."

She was right, of course, that Conlan deserved far better than her. With an uneasy smile, she rounded the island, hugged him gingerly, and kissed his cheek. Then she finished making his sandwich and passed it to him. "Excuse me a second," Emmie said as soon as his mouth was full. She left the kitchen and padded toward the powder room with grave anticipation.

The wand sat on the counter, undisturbed. But when Emmie picked it up, the plus or minus and its truth had faded. The result of her test, whatever it had been, was now dried up and invisible.

She still didn't know whether she was pregnant. Or not.

"They found the gun that killed Walter."

The officer had told Devon that she had a phone call, then brought her from the airless cell back to the Intake Room. She was so glad to hear Gil's voice, it took her a few seconds to believe it really was him: He hadn't left the island; he hadn't left *her*. She looked up at the wall now and saw that it was three-thirty.

"It's a nine-millimeter Glock," he added.

She pressed the receiver to her ear. "What?"

"The gun. It's a nine-millimeter Glock."

She rubbed her temple and cleared her throat. She knew this was good news. After all, she'd never owned a gun in her life, let alone a Glock. Surely this would help her get released. "Where did they find it?"

"In your room."

She wrapped the wool blanket more tightly around her. "They found the gun in my room?" She did not understand. Surely there was no gun in her room at the Harbor View, the room where only a couple of hours ago she and Gil . . .

She winced.

"No. They found it at the house. You stayed in the room next to Libby, right?"

"No. I stayed at the hotel last night." Had he forgotten last night? That magical, amazing night?

"I remember it well." She sensed a little smile in his voice. "But you stayed at the house Saturday night," he continued. "The police found the gun in the nightstand next to the bed where you slept."

In the nightstand? Devon didn't remember the nightstand. "But that's ridiculous. Why would I have a gun? And even if I did, why would I shoot Walter then leave the gun there?"

"I asked the cops all that. They said they have to wait for the ballistics report, but they're pretty sure it's the murder weapon. Right now all they have to go by is what's on the Statement of Facts."

Right. That was the paper she'd refused to read. "Did you see it?"

"No. By the time I got to the police station you'd been moved to the jail. They told me the specifics . . . after I said I was your fiancé."

She knew she should feel flattered that Gil thought enough of her to lie, and that she should comment on his sweet choice of words. But she was too numb for those kinds of emotions, too stressed for flattery. She looked down at her hands, at the hint of ink stains on her fingertips. "What about fingerprints? They won't find my fingerprints on the gun. I never saw it, and I didn't shoot Walter." She looked over at the corrections officer who sat opposite her, watching his prisoner with a neutral expression that guarded his opinion.

"There's more, Devon." Gil's voice dropped a few levels, as if he were the one who was incarcerated. She steeled herself for the next accusation.

"Did you have a relationship with Walter LaMonde?"

Her body went rigid. Her eyes widened. She was too shocked to even blink. "What? No! Of course not!"

A few seconds passed in silence. Then Gil said, "The police learned something about a night years ago. Supposedly you were in the outside shower and Walter . . . approached you."

A thick, dank fear crawled through her. She couldn't form her words. All she said was, *"What?"* and then her jaw went slack. Only one person had known about that night. Did Josh hate her so much he wanted her arrested for Walter's murder? Was it some kind of twisted blackmail attempt so she'd sign the damn divorce papers? She couldn't think straight. She started to shake. "I can't believe Josh hates me this much," she managed to say. "Nothing happened with Walter. Josh knows that. Dammit, he *knows* that." Then she told Gil the entire ugly story, including how she'd foolishly acted as if it never happened in order to keep their circle of friends superficially in tact, in order to keep her husband happy.

When she was finished, Gil said, "I wonder if he planted the gun."

"How did he know where I'd slept?"

"Maybe Libby told him."

"Libby? She barely remembers her name."

"Well, somehow he found out and now the cops know, too."

Fresh tears threatened to leak. "I don't understand any of this, Gil. Not just the 'why me?' part, but also, who did it? Libby's cousin Harold must be involved. Who else? The man who delivered the lobsters? The guy who told Josh he'd 'almost' invested with him? Or was it someone who *had* invested and, like Walter, lost it all? But what about the note that asked Libby for forgiveness? Who other than Harold would need to ask for that? The trouble is, none of us knows Harold's last name. Do you think you could look into that? I'd do it myself, but . . ." She was suddenly exhausted.

"Of course I'll check it out. I'll do anything for you. As long as it's moderately legal." He paused. "That part was a joke."

She forced a smile as if he could see it.

"Where is that note, anyway?" he asked.

"Still in my purse. Back in my hotel room."

"Then I have it right here. I'm talking to you on your phone. I picked the lock. I'm still at the Harbor View. On the front porch."

She wondered if what he'd done might be considered tampering with evidence, but she decided not to ask. If anyone could learn the truth, she suspected it would be Gil. "Please," she said. "Find Candace. Tell her I need Peter to get me an attorney. I'd like to get out of here."

"I'll call her as soon as we hang up. And then I'll go back to the police station and deliver the note. In the meantime, are you okay?"

"I'm absolutely wonderful. I'm told they have a great library if I get bored." That's when Devon had a revelation so striking she jumped up. Officer Parker jumped up as well. "Oh, my God!" she shouted, "It's the note! Gil! It's the *Forgive-me note!*"

Parker stepped forward, hands on his hips as if in a warning.

"What about it?" Gil asked.

She pictured the note in her mind.

It wasn't the words that were so striking. What had jolted Devon upright was the paper itself. The crisp, half-sheet of stationery. It was identical to the white linen stationery used by Josh's bespectacled attorney.

⌒

Candace sat in the foyer of the State Police barracks with Libby, awaiting penance for crossing Vineyard Sound without a freaking permission slip. They'd been there several minutes when her phone rang. The small screen spelled out Devon's name.

"Jesus, Candace, where are you?"

It was Gil's voice, not Devon's.

"You won't believe it," she said. "But why are you using Devon's phone?"

He told her Devon had been arrested, and that she was now at Duke's County Jail. "She didn't do it. Her ex-husband might have. Or at least he's involved. But first, I have to find Libby's cousin, Harold. Do you think she can remember his last name?"

She looked over at Libby who sat, hands folded, staring straight ahead, a deer in the headlights of homicide. "Your cousin Harold," Candace asked. "What's his last name and where can we find him?"

A tiny tic had developed on one side of Libby's mouth. "Landers," she said. "He lives in Beaufort now. South Carolina. But I haven't talked with him in a while. Walter handled all of . . . that."

Candace relayed the information to her brother. "Where are you now?"

"At the hotel. I picked the lock to Devon's room. I have her pocketbook and her phone. And I have the anonymous, now infamous, *Forgive-me* note."

"Your skills have come in handy."

"Yup."

"And look at you, teaching yourself how to use an iPhone."

"I found your number on her contact list."

"Little brother, you continue to amaze me."

"We do what we need to do." Then he told her about the stationery on which the note was written. And about a supposed encounter between Devon and Walter.

"I don't believe it," Candace said.

"Good. Because it isn't the real story."

Candace wasn't totally convinced (apparently she'd been right to think Walter was sometimes a little too chummy for the husband of a friend), but she would rather believe Devon and, besides, Walter was dead, so who cared? Still, she supposed she'd need to tell Libby before Libby heard it from the police.

Gil kept talking. "At first Josh seemed eager for everyone to think Libby's cousin killed Walter," he said. "Now he's pointing the finger at Devon. We think maybe he's covering up for himself."

"But why would Josh kill Walter? They were friends."

"Who knows. But I'm going to bring the note to the police. First, though, I'm going to the library. I want to use the Internet to track down 'Cousin Harold.' Maybe he can shed some light on what's been going on. Then I'm going to drop off the note at the police station."

"Better make that the State Police in Oak Bluffs." For a place that was supposedly light on crime, the island seemed to have more than its share of law enforcement locations. She told him how to get there.

Then Gil said, "And Candace? Devon needs a lawyer. She said your husband probably has a good one in his firm. Ask him to come right away, and to bring plenty of cash for bail."

The air rushed from her lungs. Peter would insist on coming to the island now. Candace wouldn't be able to stop him. And she wouldn't be able to stop him from meeting Gil.

"You want lobstahs on Wednesday?"

Emmie hadn't expected to see a man in tall rubber boots, yellow slicker pants, and a faded blue t-shirt that read "Stripers Rule" at the back door. "We just finished lunch. We had lobster salad."

He looked at her and frowned. "What about Wednesday? Will you have guests here Wednesday?"

"I really can't say."

His eyebrows squished together, crowding the rim of his glasses. "Did they find out what happened to LaMonde?"

"I don't know that, either. But my husband just got here, and he'll figure things out." She didn't like the way the lobsterman talked or the way he sized her up as if she might fit into one of his wooden traps. She half-turned toward the doorway and called, "Conlan?"

The man kept his gaze fixed squarely on her until, over her shoulder, he must have seen Conlan approach. Emmie could tell by the way those bushy eyebrows shot toward the sky that Conlan had changed into one of his kilts.

"What can we do for you, sir?" Conlan asked as he reached them.

With a small shake of his head and a quick step back, the lobsterman said, "I'll stop by tomorrah." Then he crossed the lawn and disappeared over the embankment that Emmie knew lead down to the sea.

"I haven't connected with Peter yet," Candace told Devon after the guard escorted Devon into the small reception room where he'd instructed Candace and Libby to wait. He said they typically didn't allow prisoners visitors before they'd been to court, but that he'd make an exception because of the situation with Devon's lawyer being from out of town. "I can't believe they arrested you," she added.

"Gil has been wonderful," Devon said.

"Gil?" Libby asked. "Your driver?"

Candace ignored her. "We gave him Harold's name. He's trying to track him down."

"Like I said, he lives in South Carolina," Libby said. "I remember a few things. Like that our daughters have graduated from Miss Porter's and are in Europe."

"Oh, Libby," Devon said, "that's great."

Libby smiled but seemed a bit skittish.

"Have you eaten anything today?" Candace asked.

Devon shook her head. "They brought me a tray, but I wasn't hungry."

Candace stood up and looked at the guard, who sat behind an ancient steel desk that had been jammed into a corner. He wore earpieces that he'd plugged into something electronic that must have been emitting music because he was lightly tapping his right foot. She raised her voice so he could hear. "Is there a take-out restaurant near here?"

"Gas station," he replied, matching her intonation.

"Excuse me?"

"Next door." He pointed outside. "The gas station. Inside it's a market. They have ready-made sandwiches and stuff."

"The *gas* station?"

The guard shrugged. "Don't know what else is open. It's not high season yet."

Candace felt it was best not to shoot back a barb. She closed her eyes, took a breath, then said, "Mrs. LaMonde will stay here while I get Mrs. Gregory something to eat. You're free to inspect the food when I return, in case I slip a file into a slice of cake." The guard looked at her with mild indifference, and Candace swooshed out the front door as if she were wearing one of Emmie's circular skirts.

"So," Devon said to Libby after Candace left, "you're really okay?"

"Not completely. But I do know what day it is. And the year. But I don't know who killed Walter."

Devon lowered her voice. "I'm sorry, Libby. I'm so sorry that he's . . . gone."

Libby tilted her head. "I don't think you killed him."

"Well, of course I didn't." She supposed she should tell her the story that Josh had told the police before she heard it else-where. "Libby," she said, "aside from the fact they found a gun in the nightstand of the guestroom, Josh told the police something. Something that happened a long time ago."

"About you and Walter? I know. Your driver told Candace. But it didn't matter. I already knew. I saw you from the bedroom window that night."

Devon was stunned. "Nothing happened, Libby. Walter was drunk and he was fooling around. He didn't mean anything by it. I'm sure that he didn't."

"You don't have to cover up for him," Libby said. "I saw it with my own two eyes. But don't think I was shocked: You were neither the first nor the last. Walter tried to screw every skirt that went near him. Sometimes he succeeded. Sometimes he didn't. And, by the way, thanks for shoving him away. I saw that part, too." Her face suddenly brightened. "Wow. I remembered all that!"

Devon did not have the heart to tell her it had happened years before the timeframe for which her memory had been blocked. "What else, Libby? What else can you remember?"

Libby paused and gazed up at the ceiling. "I remember that Walter sold his Mercedes to a man on the Cape. It gave us some cash to live on."

In addition to being something current, it explained why they hadn't found his car.

"And here's a big one," she continued. "I never told any of you, but when you and Josh split, I realized how badly I wanted to be free, too. I told Walter I wanted a divorce. He said 'over his dead body.' Strange, isn't it? Anyway, instead of getting a divorce, I had an affair." She looked back at Devon and nodded twice, then three times. "Yes, I did. I had an affair."

Devon thought about Emmie and her rekindled relationship with the horse trainer. Then she remembered the note on the stationery that she'd linked to Josh.

Josh.

Was it possible he'd been Libby's lover?

Devon's throat started to close. An odd sensation squished inside her chest. Her hands started to sweat. She wanted to know, but didn't dare ask. It had taken her too long to shed the pain of him leaving; she did not want to dredge up those feelings again.

Then another, darker thought formed: *Was Libby the woman with whom Josh now wanted to pursue a legal relationship? And had they . . . oh, God, had they killed Walter together?* Libby said she'd wanted a divorce, but that Walter had said *over his dead body . . .*

The walls of the room seemed to close in. Devon wanted to stand up and to pace, but the space was too small and she feared Libby would notice her anxiety and would . . . would do what? They were in a jail. A correctional officer—a *lieutenant*, no less—sat at the desk, guarding her. Devon was protected. As for Josh, she'd lost him years ago; her life was good now. No, she had nothing to lose.

She needed to ask Libby outright. But when Devon turned to her, she saw that the woman was shriveled and pale against the gray backdrop. She thought about Libby's decorating talents, and how she must hate the blandness, the colorlessness, all around them. Then Devon remembered Josh's comment: "Libby liked to spend Walter's money."

Had he said that to make it appear he was mocking her? To deflect suspicion that he and Libby were sleeping together? That they had killed Walter in order to live happily ever after?

And if all that were true, what, if anything, did the note have to do with it?

She stood up, paced four steps to the left; three to the right. She didn't acknowledge either Libby or the cop, though she sensed that they wordlessly watched her.

The presence of the note was baffling. Had it been Josh's handwriting? Devon hadn't paid attention. At the time, she'd never dreamed he might be involved.

And yet, she didn't know anything. Not really. Not for sure.

30

Outside the market at the gas station, Candace finally gathered the nerve to call Peter. His reaction was predictable:

Libby might have killed Walter?

The police arrested Devon?

"And to think I expected you'd have such a nice weekend!" His angst-barometer ticked up like rickety cars ascending an old wooden rollercoaster.

He said he would borrow his pal Joe Reynolds's pilot and his reliable G-5, that it was too late in the day to try figuring commercial flight times and schedules because his brain was too log-jammed to manage those kinds of details. He said he would try to be there by five o'clock.

Candace told him to bring one of the criminal experts from the office and plenty of cash for Devon's bail. She tried not to feel guilty that if she'd called Peter sooner, the attorney might have been able to make it to the island that afternoon and Devon wouldn't have had to spend the whole night in jail. She hoped Gil wouldn't be angry about that. Then her guilt snowballed as she thought about him. "And, Peter?" she asked. "You'd better be braced for a few more surprises." She focused on the pavement in the parking lot and was grateful that Peter's mind must have been racing so quickly he didn't ask for details. They said good-bye, then she called Emmie and briefed her on all that had happened.

Emmie seemed uncharacteristically calm. After listening without interruption, she said pleasantly, "Conlan is here."

Conlan?

Before the last few days, Candace would have wanted to know more. She would have asked about the pregnancy dilemma, the resurrected old lover from Miss Porter's, and what Emmie planned to do. From the early days of sharing those *special stories* with Gil, Candace had loved embracing other peoples' secrets in order to avoid facing her own.

Instead of prying that time, Candace simply said, "Good. Then you and Conlan can walk to the jail over on Main Street, pick up Libby's Mercedes, then go to the airport to get Peter. He should be in before five." After some childlike banter, it was determined that, yes, Conlan knew how to drive.

Candace hung up, went into the market, and was directed to a refrigerated case. She scanned the collection of clear plastic containers then plucked two chicken salads on wheat bread, two tunas on marble rye, and four surprisingly tasty-looking pieces of cake. She wondered what Mrs. Derberfield or any of the Art League ladies would say about her less-than-gourmet menu choices.

After paying the clerk, she went back outside and tried once again to call Gil. No answer. He might have figured out how to use the cell phone, but apparently he didn't yet know that persistently checking the device was now the American way.

Back at the jail, she went in the front door and doled out the food to Devon and Libby. The officer politely declined. Then Candace asked if it was all right for them to stay a little while longer until their other friends arrived to get the keys so they could pick up Devon's attorney.

"This is way against protocol, but, lucky for you, no one else is being processed today."

Candace had no idea what that meant, but she thanked him, settled in a chair next to Devon and took a bite of chicken salad, which turned out to be fresh, not the cheap food service kind.

Libby started in on a tuna; Devon claimed no appetite. Who could blame her?

An hour later, Emmie and Conlan appeared in the doorway; Conlan was wearing a skirt. The officer didn't flinch: He'd no doubt seen worse. He did, however stand up and say, "You're only here for the keys, right?"

"Unless they'd like something to eat," Candace said. She meant it to be humorous, but the officer glared at her.

"Thanks," Conlan said, "but we just gorged ourselves on lobster salad."

Emmie had her arm tucked happily through his: the gesture looked sincere. "Speaking of which, the lobsterman came by again," she said. "He asked if we wanted to place an order for Wednesday; I told him we don't know how many people will be there by then."

"He's a strange old guy," Devon said. "Don't let him tell you Libby owes him money; I paid him yesterday."

Libby lifted her eyes from the cake. "Really, Devon, he's hardly an old guy. His name is Linc Weston and he's just out of high school. He works with his older brother, Charlie."

Devon frowned. "The man I saw hasn't been in high school for decades."

"No kidding," Emmie said.

Libby set down her fork and frowned. "I don't understand. We've bought lobsters from Linc and Charlie for a few years. What did the guy look like?"

"Like a fisherman," Devon said.

"He wore those tall boots—what do you call them?" Emmie added.

"Waders," Devon said. "And he wore glasses."

Just then Candace's phone rang.

"Can you talk?" Gil asked. "Somewhere where no one will hear you?"

As Libby watched Devon and Emmie and Conlan converse, snippets of her memory began to eke back: she recalled sitting on the three-season porch on the pale yellow cushion atop the white wicker loveseat; holding the gun on her lap; trying to decide what to do.

Then she remembered the man who rose up from the embankment that lead down to the harbor. She remembered his waders. She remembered his wig. And his glasses. But even with his disguise, she had known who it was, the same way she now knew that Walter had come out of the house onto the porch, that the men had exchanged angry words about her—about *her!*—and that Walter had grabbed the gun from her lap.

"No," Libby had pleaded. "Don't!"

Her hand flew to her mouth now as she tried to stop herself from screaming out loud.

Candace had extricated herself from the small group and gone outside. She'd walked down the steps, stepped onto the sidewalk again, and crossed Main Street. Wandering into a small, triangle-shaped park now, she noticed a cannon and a pyramid of cannon-balls that were held in place with cement. She sat on a bench and took a breath. "Tell me," she said into the phone.

"Libby was right," Gil said. "Her cousin, Harold, is an investment manager in South Carolina. But she was wrong about one thing: He no longer handles their portfolio."

"No kidding. Because, thanks to him, there is no longer a portfolio to manage."

"That's where it gets interesting. It seems that Walter liquidated everything Harold had managed for them . . . *all* of their money . . . over a year ago. He told Harold he had a chance to invest with a friend in a surefire company that was practically guaranteed to turn their assets into a real fortune."

It always amazed Candace that so many rich people wanted to be richer, how they often determined their standing in the world by how their net worth measured up to that of their friends. Thank God Peter had always been too preoccupied with his internal dramas to get stuck in a mindset like that. "Did he say what kind of investment it was?"

"It went to a company that planned to harvest liquid gas fields on an island in the South Pacific. But Walter called Harold a couple of weeks ago, begging for money. He told Harold the whole project had tanked, taking the investors down with it. Including him."

"Did Harold know the name of Walter's so-called friend who did the investing?"

"Brace yourself."

Candace closed her eyes. "Okay, little brother, don't tease me."

"The guy's name was Josh Gregory."

God help her, she whistled. It was as if she were a girl again back in Jamestown, as if Gil had just told her a juiced-up piece of gossip that she could fit into one of their stories. Then she said, "I saw Josh on the ferry. He's headed back to New York on the train."

"Well, my gut tells me he's in this way up to his eyeballs."

As Candace walked back to the jail, Libby, Emmie, and Conlan were walking out.

"The guard threw us out," Libby said. "We'll head out to the airport. I'm driving. Conlan claims he knows how, but my car is one of the few possessions I have left. I don't want to put that pressure on him. It's nice enough that he's here."

Candace was glad to know Libby's brain was functioning again, though with the three of them, robust Peter, and the re-quired attorney, the Mercedes might be a bit cramped. There was no point in mentioning it; she was done trying to run the whole world. She stepped aside to let them pass.

Back inside, she begged the officer to let Devon stay another couple of minutes before he returned her to the holding cell. "I just received some important information about her case," she said.

She must have looked honest because the officer relented. "Five minutes," he said.

Candace quickly relayed Gil's new information to Devon. "What do you think? Would you have ever suspected Josh of pedaling an investment scheme?"

The prisoner shook her head. "He was never a risk taker. Not for himself; not for his clients. I would have thought he was always too afraid of losing. Josh hates to lose at anything."

Candace refrained from adding that Devon might also never have thought he'd have an affair. And certainly not with one of her friends.

Devon lowered her eyes. "Do you think he killed Walter?"

"I don't know. But it sure seems like he was the 'friend' who lost their money—not Libby's cousin Harold."

Then Devon said, "I think Josh and Libby were having an affair. That stupid *Forgive-me* note was on a half-sheet. The masthead had been cut off, but I'd swear it was the same paper his divorce lawyer uses. I got a letter from the slime-ball the other day. It was printed on the same damn white linen. Not many people still use that kind of snotty corporate-image paper. Anyway, among all the rhetoric, the letter he sent me said Josh wanted to 'pursue legalization of another relationship.'" She raised her hands to simulate air quotes.

"Josh and Libby? Seriously, Devon? If Josh did write the note, maybe he was just asking for Libby's forgiveness because he'd lost their money."

"Who knows? I only know Libby admitted she'd been having an affair and had wanted a divorce."

"Did she want it before or after she knew she was broke?"

"Before, I think. Otherwise, I doubt that she would have taken the chance. Libby would not have wanted to wind up without both a husband and money."

The way you'd wound up, Candace thought. "I wonder if Josh lost his money, too," she said.

Devon dropped her face into her hands. "Oh, God, I don't know. This is so confusing; I don't even know if that stupid note was in Josh's handwriting. And you could be right—maybe it has nothing to do with Walter's murder. Maybe I'm only hoping Josh did it so he'll go to prison, and I'll feel vindicated for everything he put me through."

They were silent a moment; the lieutenant looked at his watch, then back at them.

"If it wasn't Josh," Candace said, "Who did it? The little, bespectacled lobster guy?" She laughed; Devon did not.

It might have been the word "little" or, more likely, "bespectacled." Whichever it was, the light bulb snapped on—*ding*—and Devon suddenly knew what had happened.

That time, she stood up so quickly that Lieutenant Parker bolted upright and reached for his gun. She started to pace. Back. Forth. Back again. "Oh my God, that man was no lobsterman . . . it was Davis Bachman, *Esquire.* It was Josh's attorney!" She whipped around and faced Candace. "He had on a wig! And he must have glued on those ridiculous eyebrows. With the foolish waders, the grungy t-shirt, and a layer of makeup, he must have known I wouldn't recognize him. I've only seen the man once."

Candace frowned. "I don't get the connection. What would Josh's attorney have to do with Libby and Walter?"

Devon tried to slow down her thoughts, tried to assemble the pieces. "He's a *divorce* lawyer, Candace. Don't you see? Libby must have found him through Josh."

"And?"

"And . . . and . . ." She flopped back on the chair. "And I have no idea. But it's too much of a coincidence to not be connected. You heard Libby say the guy who delivers the lobster is a high school kid. The man in the waders was definitely not him. It was Davis Bachman. I'd swear to it. He and Josh must have been in on it together. Maybe Josh paid him to kill Walter. It would be just like my husband to have someone else do his dirty work."

"But why would Josh want him dead?"

"Maybe . . ." Josh's voice came from the doorway that lead into the Intake Room, where Josh now stood with another correctional officer beside him, "Maybe he never forgave the bastard for what he'd tried to do to his wife."

31

Devon had been so deep in thought she hadn't seen Josh standing there, shaded by the late day's light. "What are you doing here?" she growled.

The lieutenant stepped forward and blocked his path. "And this is . . .?"

"Josh Gregory," the other officer said. "Your prisoner's husband."

The lieutenant sighed and stepped back. "It's getting crowded in here. I'll be on the front steps. But I'll leave the door open." He wagged a long finger. "Don't any of you do anything stupid."

"No problem," Josh said, and of course he was no doubt believed because, if given the chance, Josh could convince a vegan to chow down on a burger.

He turned back to Devon. "Davis Bachman, my attorney, called me. By the way, you were right: He posed as the lobsterman. He was also sitting in the lobby at the Harbor View, reading the newspaper, when you were arrested. I was in Boston, waiting for the train to New York. When he called and told me what happened, I had to come back. I couldn't let our daughter think you'd killed anyone. Or that I hadn't done anything to stop you from being convicted."

Devon bit her lip and gritted her teeth. "Did you do it, Josh? Did you kill Walter?"

He held up his hand in the arrogant way he had of telling her to be quiet because he had taken center stage. "After you and

I split up, Libby asked me the name of my lawyer. She said she wanted a divorce, too. She'd tried calling you a few times, but she said you must have busy. You never called back."

Devon remembered Libby's calls: they'd come when she'd been on the couch.

"I gave her Bachman's name," Josh continued. "It turned out they fell in love. Or some such nonsense."

Libby, in love with Davis Bachman? The short, bespectacled attorney? She might be a terrific decorator, but she sure had bad taste in men. "Did Bachman kill Walter?"

Josh held up a hand. "Please, Devon, hear me out. I owe it to you to tell the whole story."

Devon's mother had often said that listening was the finest gift one could give. Still, it was hard to be patient and listen to Josh when what she really wanted was to slug him again with her purse. "Shouldn't someone to record this?" she asked the new officer.

Josh rolled his eyes. "Can you hear us, officers?"

"I hear you fine," came the response from the front stairs. "And I'm writing it down."

"And I'm recording it," the other officer said, as he positioned his phone toward the group.

"And I'm a witness!" Candace shouted. "Did you get my name, officers? Candace Cartwright? Mrs. Peter Cartwright?"

"Got it," one muffled voice replied, then both Devon and Candace looked back at Josh.

"The night Walter . . . approached you," he said, "it's true I didn't want to believe it. But I never forgot. When Libby told me she wanted a divorce, she said he'd been screwing around for years. I told her about what he'd tried with you; she already knew. She said she'd seen the whole thing." He flinched a little, as if he, in fact, cared. Then he cleared his throat. "That's when I could no longer deny that you'd told me the truth. But by then we were separated, and you'd clearly moved on with your life. When Walter wouldn't agree to the divorce, Bachman was pissed. He said he would bring the man down. He knew that the most vulnerable place to hit any man was in his wallet. Or, in this case, his portfolio. Once it was gone, Bachman hoped Walter would kill himself. Then Libby would be free to be with him." He emitted a low *tsk*. "Of course, Bachman is only an attorney. He needed my investment help. And I saw a chance for revenge. For God's sake, Devon, Walter had been my friend. And you'd been my wife."

Yes, Devon remembered that. "So you stole his money."

"No. Walter never understood his finances; he preferred to pay someone to do it. Libby's cousin, Harold, had done a decent job. It took a few months, but ultimately I convinced Walter he could increase their net worth by eight or ten times if he turned everything over to me. I told him that an energy company's liquid gas field was being explored, and that the stock was going to soar."

"Was there such a company?"

Josh shook his head. "It was bogus. I sent him a fake prospectus. I knew he'd never read it. After he pulled everything away from Harold and given it to me, I sent him email updates every day. I sent him fake dividends. I did that for almost a year. I even faked articles on how well the business was going."

"He never suspected?"

"He was too busy dreaming about profits. And when he tried to bring others in on the scheme, I said they were too late."

"What about Libby?" Candace interjected. "Did she know what you were doing?"

"No. Bachman said he would tell her once it was over. He was afraid if she knew ahead of time, she'd act differently around Walter, and he would catch on."

"What did you do with their money?" Devon asked.

Josh laughed. "I put it in Treasury Bills. The yield isn't great right now, but I knew it would be safe. The plan was that after he either shot himself or was so humiliated by the losses that he let Libby divorce him, I was going to make up a story that the venture had come back to life. I was going to give him back half the money. Or all of it, if Libby wanted us to."

"Wait a minute," Candace said. "Are you saying you still have their money? That Libby and Walter have never been broke?"

"Bingo."

Devon picked up a plastic fork and stabbed at a piece of cake instead of stabbing Josh in the head, which she would have preferred. "But Libby still doesn't know?"

"No."

"She said Walter sold his car so they could have cash."

"That must have killed him. He loved that car." Josh snickered, of course he did.

Suddenly, Devon was hungry. It was as if her body had decided everything would be all right now; she was safe to return to the land of the living. She took a bite of the sweet chocolate and slowly chewed.

"No offense," Candace said to Josh, "but I think you know more than you're saying."

"You're right. But I also know Walter's death was an accident."

"Did you kill him, Josh?"

Devon swallowed. She wasn't sure if she was ready to hear what was coming next.

"No."

She relaxed. God help her, she believed him.

"Bachman brought the divorce papers to the Vineyard," he continued. "He said he didn't want Libby to suffer any longer, thinking that the money was gone. He also said he wanted the satisfaction of being the one to serve Walter. 'Let him try to dodge me,' he said, as if he were a tough guy from the hood. Anyway, he claims he went onto the porch, just as Walter was coming out. He confronted Walter, who went into a rage. Libby sat there, not saying a word. For some reason, she was holding a gun on her lap. Walter grabbed it and chased Bachman outside. They fought. The gun went off. Bachman survived; Walter didn't."

"And Libby saw her lover kill her husband."

"Yes."

Candace folded her arms across her linen knit sweater. "I'd say that could trigger a dissociative fugue."

Devon nodded, then asked, "But who told the police there was a gun in the room where I slept? Who put it there? Who told them about Walter and . . . me?"

"Bachman. Emmie told me you'd stayed at the house in the room next to Libby. Last night, I stupidly told him. It turns out he already knew what Walter had tried to do to you: Your name was one of several that Libby had included in her lawsuit."

She supposed it would take time for her to accept that Libby had known about Walter's behavior all along and had never let on to Devon. Not once in fifteen years. "But why did Bachman want me arrested?"

"Libby was the only one who could corroborate his story. He was tossing red herrings all over the island, hoping to buy time until Libby's amnesia abated. If it's any consolation, he didn't think they'd actually arrest you. By the way, no matter what you might have heard, Libby's cousin, Harold, was not on the island in the past few days. Bachman showed up at Walter's yacht and the golf club, pretending to be him. That's where he learned about the kids who delivered the lobsters. He tracked them down and paid them a few hundred dollars to let him go to the house in their place."

And Devon presumed that he no doubt made up a story about Libby and Walter expecting a "guest" so they would think Harold had been there.

"But you acted like Harold had taken their money," Devon said, "and that he must have killed Walter. And yet you knew none of it was true?"

"I was giving Bachman time to figure out what to do. Like I said, he was pretty upset when Libby suddenly didn't know who he was. Don't forget, all this had started so they could be together."

"So Bachman wrote the *Forgive-me* note," Devon said. "On his law firm's stationary." She turned to Candace and asked, "Where's Gil?"

"He was going to bring the note to the State Police. They're helping out with the evidence. He said he'd be in touch later."

"Maybe he can stop Libby. It's possible that the real reason she went to the airport was so she could hop on a plane. Now that her memory is back, she might want to go to Europe and be with Alana. Before that happens, she needs to know the whole truth. Including the fact that she isn't a pauper."

"Should the police get her?"

Devon shook her head. "Call Gil. I think the cops have enough on their hands."

"No kidding," came the voice from the front steps.

Josh looked at Devon. "Gil?" he asked. "Is that the ex-convict who's been your driver? The guy Bachman saw with you in the hotel lobby?"

Devon saw no reason to answer.

Epilogue

The plane landed at Logan International at one o'clock the next afternoon. Gil steered Peter's limo into the passenger pick-up area; the girls squeezed into the back where their mothers waited; their fathers had stayed on the Vineyard. Candace delivered the news about Walter. Devon was pleased to see she did it with grace and compassion. Alana blanched, then cried. Libby held her close; Julie, Tiffany, and Bree poured out genuine sympathy. Devon knew that, in time, Alana would be fine: after all, she had her best friends for girlfriend support. She hoped that no matter what changes came into their lives, that bond would never be broken. True friendships were too hard to come by.

Back on the island, Peter had arranged a small memorial service for Walter. Devon was surprised that many Vineyarders came to show their respect: the Edgartown Harbormaster, several people from the golf club, the two brothers who delivered lobsters. Thankfully, if any of Walter's lovers had heard he had died, they'd had the good sense not to show up. Nor did Davis Bachman, Esquire, attend: he was out on bail, staying at the Harbor View, waiting to be cleared of the murder charge. He did, however, expect he would be penalized for obstructing justice and for leaving the scene and for not reporting the "incident." He claimed he'd "freaked out" when he realized Libby's mind had snapped when the gun had gone off. Peter's associate, Joe Reynolds, had agreed to represent him.

Devon had wound up spending the night in jail until the morning when Reynolds was able to get the paperwork untangled, the judge appeased, and the arraignment of the real killer. She was released in time for breakfast that she shared with Gil at *Among the Flowers*.

Josh was reprimanded for his conduct over the fake liquid gas field, and he said he expected a "suitable" fine to be levied. Libby did not want to press charges; she said she was sure her husband had merely been playing a prank, and that no real financial harm had been done. "Besides, the way the market has been careening, we might have lost more if we'd kept our money with Harold," she'd added. Then she vowed to be more on top of her portfolio than Walter had ever been.

The service was held in St. Andrew's Episcopal Church on Winter Street in the center of Edgartown. It was a cozy, earthy-brown, brick, little church: Devon remembered the church and how the doors were nearly always open, always standing in welcome, unlike in the city where one now needed a password or an appointment to enter a house of worship. She thought it was most appropriate that the pulpit had been crafted from the bow of a ship and that two of the stained glass windows had been produced by Tiffany Studios. The setting seemed to represent the merging of Walter's worlds: life on the water and New York society. No matter how misguided he had become, he still was entitled to a proper, God-fearing good-bye.

Peter gave the eulogy, which was positive and kind, even when he told the congregation that Walter had mailed in his ballot for the Art League election, and though he'd voted against Peter, Peter didn't hold it against him. Word had arrived that he'd won, anyway.

Of course, Candace had seen no reason to bore her husband with the tawdry details of Walter's besmirched life. Peter had been shell-shocked enough when she'd introduced Gil: "He's my brother," she'd said. So far, Peter had handled it well. He'd even hinted that he'd once heard a rumor about Candace having a mother upstate. He'd kept it to himself so he wouldn't upset her—she'd been pregnant with Tiffany at the time. He refused to let Gil return the cash Candace had given him. "Whatever you need, my boy," he said. "You're part of the family, after all."

As for Tiffany, well, she said it was cool to have an ex-con for an uncle, that it might give her some sort of cult status when she got to law school.

Obviously, their daughters were no longer little girls.

Libby and Alana sat in the front pew. The others sat behind them, off to the left; their daughters, off to the right. Devon knew that Julie would be instrumental in helping Alana heal. She was glad she'd passed on that "caring" gene to Julie; she'd been foolish to think that it got you nowhere in the end.

The men sat across the aisle: Peter, Conlan, Josh, and Gil. Conlan even wore pants.

After the service the church members hosted a reception in the cozy Parish Hall with coffee, finger sandwiches, and desserts. It was solemn, yet comforting. Devon noticed that Peter stood in one corner, deep in conversation with Gil. She wondered if Candace knew how much she had underestimated her husband, and if she noticed that Peter and Gil now appeared to be bonding over Mrs. Fenn's chocolate chip cookies.

When the reception ended, Gil made his way over to Devon.

"Candace's husband offered me a job," he said. "He said I could work in his office. He also said there would be a position for me if I want to get a law degree."

"What about teaching?"

He smiled that wonderful smile. "I don't know. Honestly, until now, I didn't think I'd have many choices."

Devon laughed. "So what did you tell him?"

His eyes locked onto hers. "I told him that before I do anything, I need to find a man named Leonard, who lives somewhere in western Pennsylvania. I owe his father a lot, Devon. I want Louis D.'s son to know that in spite of his crimes, his father is a good man. I also told Peter I wanted to wait until I knew where you might go. Then I thanked him and said I'd stay in touch."

At first, Devon didn't know what to say. Then she said, "That's a nice idea, to find Louis D.'s son."

"And the part about you?"

"The part about me is nice, too. Actually, it's even nicer." She moved closer to him, ready to kiss him, when Emmie rushed past them.

"Which way to the ladies' room?" she cried.

Devon laughed and pointed the way. Then Candace and Libby appeared. Candace asked Gil to excuse Devon; she said the ladies needed to talk.

The three women stepped outside, into the warm Vineyard day.

"Do you have any plans?" Devon asked Libby.

"Well," Libby said, "Alana wants to resume her European trip with the girls. I think she wants to go back to Ireland. I'm not going to stop her. Brandon's a nice boy. Emmie has raised her kids well."

They all smiled. None of them said, "Yes, what an unexpected surprise."

"I'm going to turn the house back to Walter's family," Libby continued. "I don't want to stay on the Vineyard. I'll go back to New York; I'll find a new place. When enough time has passed, I might marry Davis. But first, I want to follow your lead, Devon. I want to be able to take care of myself."

Tears welled in Devon's eyes.

"I've never told you how much I admire you," Libby said. She gave her a gentle hug, in Southern Belle style.

"I think we all do," Candace added. "You're not afraid to be honest. Not with others. Not with yourself."

Devon was stunned. These were the women she had once tried so hard to emulate, even after she'd grown to detest New York and all the *JW* handbags that represented its world.

Then Emmie flew out of the building and danced toward them, her skirts catching the light breeze. "I'm not!" she cried. "I'm not! It must be menopause!"

Devon's eyes met Candace's. Of course, they both knew what she meant. "Are you happy?" Devon asked.

Emmie nodded briskly. "You have no idea. But I'll still go and cuddle the babies. I will always cuddle the babies."

Devon started to ask what that meant, but decided it wasn't her business. Then Josh was at her side.

"Can we talk?" he asked.

And so, because he had been her husband, still technically was, and because he was Julie's father, and always would be,

Devon stepped away from her friends and began to walk down the sidewalk. He caught up with her pace.

"Are you going back to New York today?" he asked.

"Why?"

"I thought we might go together."

"Why?"

"I thought we could have dinner . . . or something."

"Don't worry, Josh, I'm ready to sign the divorce papers. I'll meet your thirty-day deadline."

"You don't have to."

They turned the corner. She looked back to the church. Gil stood by the front door. He watched her watching him.

"Yes," she said. "Yes. I'm ready now."

"But . . ."

"But nothing. You will be free to marry your other 'relationship.' I have to be honest: for a while, I thought it was Libby."

He shook his head. "It was no one. There is no one. I didn't know Bachman had written that until he told me last night. He said he thought it would help hurry things up."

"He made it up?"

"Not completely. I'd once told him there was another woman, even though there wasn't. I was embarrassed by the real reason I'd left you."

They walked past one gleaming-white, black-shuttered Edgartown house, then another. "Why, Josh?" Devon asked. "Why did you leave me? Why did you leave . . . us?"

He took a few more steps. He smoothed his hair back from his temples where it was no longer gray. Devon was reminded that he'd never really liked being on the Vineyard: He'd said the ocean breeze always made him look tousled. He had never seen the magic of that. "I was having a midlife crisis," he finally said.

"Call it crazy, but when I turned forty-five, all I could think of was that my life was more than half over. I figured that, at best, I only had about sixteen thousand days left. Give or take. Anyway, it made me claustrophobic. I was choking; I needed to be free."

Another woman might have doubted his explanation. But another woman might not have known that Josh had always counted the days that led toward milestones. In this case, it had been sixteen thousand. Give or take. He'd escaped while he'd thought there was still time to start over.

They continued walking. Devon breathed in the clear island air, wondering why she had never returned to this place that had been her mother's heart home and that, she realized now, was hers, too. She wondered if it was too late for her, or if . . .

Then she said, "Josh, if you're trying to offer amends, thank you. If you're looking for anything more, it's not going to happen." She was grateful that he didn't argue.

Then Devon veered off the sidewalk, turned around, and headed back toward St. Andrew's Church where Gil silently waited, his future, and maybe hers, beckoning in the salt air and the sunshine.

About the Author

J ean Stone has been writing stories that take place on Martha's Vineyard for many years. She is the author of 17 novels, most of which have been translated into numerous languages around the world. A graduate of Skidmore College, Saratoga Springs, New York, she previously owned an advertising agency in western Massachusetts.

Made in the USA
Monee, IL
26 August 2022

12637442R00194